The Drama Room

A Collection in
Three Acts

Elizabeth Searle

A surprising, edgy, and original writer.

Jayne Anne Phillips
Winner of the 2024 *Pulitzer Prize*

Time to stop scrolling and start reading, because whatever is in your phone is better addressed in the pages of Elizabeth Searle's THE DRAMA ROOM: A COLLECTION IN THREE ACTS. Searle's edgy, yet compassionate stories often pull from the day's news but their touchstones go deeper into American culture. She anchors narratives atop American classics as varied Edgar Alan Poe's "The Masque of the Red Death" and the musical The Fantasticks. Across her celebrated career, her ongoing genius is in forefronting the culture's present sickness. What is out there—pandemic contagion, predatory men, mass shooters, politically retrograde thinkers—might be ... in here, inside the family, the school building, the work place, the bedroom. Fast-paced and entertaining, Searle's stories offer high drama, but also a clear sense of what it is like to have an anxious brain and an aware body in a world heaving with turmoil.

Debra Spark
author *Discipline,*
and *Unknown Caller*

In THE DRAMA ROOM: A COLLECTION IN THREE ACTS, Elizabeth Searle, novelist (WE GOT HIM) and scriptwriter (I'LL SHOW YOU MINE), offers 12 high-stakes stories that probe contemporary maladies from the physical (the Covid epidemic), to cultural (reality hunger, infidelity, school shootings, loneliness, and hi-tech mass communications), to spiritual (materialism, celebrity, identity), and focuses primarily, but not entirely, on vulnerable teenagers, male and female. Searle is more compassionate than censorious, more Salingeresque than scathing (think of Nathaniel West or Flannery O'-Conner). She is adventurous in exploring points of view, voices, and streams of consciousness; suggestive with symbolism; deft in managing perspectives in time, And her endings are genuine, visionary break-throughs.

DeWitt Henry
founding editor of ***Ploughshares***
author of ***Top Cop Kills,***
and ***Trim Reckonings***

Elizabeth Searle's THE DRAMA ROOM: A COLLECTION IN THREE ACTS holds a deadly serious fun house mirror up to American society, magnifying its political distortions, skewed mores, sexual anxieties and the haunting effects of aging, medical diagnoses and hapless, ill-timed personal decisions. Searle's dramatic instincts are fearless, scathing and often comedic; her dialogue is a master class in brilliance.

In her libretto, 'Tonya & Nancy: the Opera,' based on public quotes, Elizabeth Searle has taken a bizarre, notorious incident in American women's figure skating history, and made of it a lethally funny commentary on the graceless maneuvers of fear and ambition, on the media as Greek chorus, on how to demonstrate, with the rapier slice of a skater's blade, Simone Weil's conviction that the only question worth asking is "Why am I being harmed?"

Melissa Pritchard
author *The Odditorium*,
and *Flight of the Wild Swan*

The accomplishment of Elizabeth Searle's work is that it feels contemporary and timely and relevant but never merely topical or trendy; her formal experimentation in story after story is a powerful reflection of our disequlibirum.

David Shields
author of **Reality Hunger**

Lust, violence, love and grief—if there is an edge, Elizabeth Searle will push it and if there is a pulse, she will put her finger right on it. The stories in her latest collection, THE DRAMA ROOM: A COLLECTION IN THREE ACTS, showcase an enormous range in awareness and understanding of the human condition and the author's skillful gift to surprise and deliver.

Jill McCorkle
author *Life After Life,*
and ***Old Crimes***

First printing, October 2025
Library of Congress Control Number: *pending*
ISBN 978-1-965784-30-3 Hardback
ISBN 978-1-965784-31-0 Paperback

Cover Art, Design & Typography by **Kurt Lovelace**
Cover *Bauhaus Dessau* **Alfarn** by Céline Hurka, Elia Preuss,
Flavia Zimbardi, Hidetaka Yamasaki, and Luca Pellegrini.
Body in **Nimbus**, Chapter Titles in **Jenson** by Robert Slimbach
Flourishes set in Emigre Foundry **Dalliance**, by Frank Heine
Emigre Foundry **ZeitGuys**, by Bob Aufuldish, Eric Donelan
Typefaces licensed Adobe, Linotype, & URW GmbH

PierianSpringsPress.Com
PIERIAN SPRINGS PRESS, INC
30 N GOULD ST, STE 25398
SHERIDAN, WYOMING 82801-6317

To
WILL
With love & pride
For my son & fellow scribe

CONTENTS

The
Drama
Room

Act One

Openings

THE MASK OF
THE RED DEATH

The Masque Of The Red Death is a story by Edgar Allan Poe, the dude with super-sad eyes. But I spell 'mask' plain, like the M-A-S-K that I wore on my last bike ride. Plain black. My story, like E.A. Poe's, is set in Plague Times. Set, you know, now. *Write a Story inspired by one of the classic stories we discussed in class.* Only we didn't discuss them 'in class.' Our classes since April were all Zoom, like everything now. But whatever. Here is my story, inspired by *The Masque of the Red Death*.

(BTW, I guess I should delete this part leading into the story. But maybe I won't. Maybe I just don't care if you pass me or not in this last Incomplete; if I ever officially graduate Arlington High School. No matter what, I'm still a member of the doomed Covid-19 Class of 2020.)

My story starts in Grandad's garden, behind what he called his "twilight-blue bungalow." In pre-twilight, which he called The Golden Hour. The time that everyone looks their best. In sunny September of 2019 Grandad cut peach-colored roses to give 17-year-old me in a prickly bouquet. Peace Roses, he said. Then Grandad told me, matter-of-fact, *You'll be a beauty one day*.

You—I mean 'me' but I like saying 'you,' because it makes this story about someone not-me—you always felt pretty in that garden in the sunset-y light. You and Grandad, both bathed in gold. You held the peachy Peace Roses; Grandad brought out his serious camera. The one he'd used in his Boston Portrait Studio. He took your picture, over and over. One came out so cool with your long hair lit up all tawny gold, you used it as your first/maybe-last Tinder photo—

(Boy, I'm getting off track from the assignment here, but I want to show why E.A.P.'s 'The Masque of the Red Death' made me cry. Which almost nothing does anymore, since I got all cried-out back in April. I wish to God, like Grandad used to say, I was not writing this story.)

FWIW: You never really used Tinder, but you did put your Golden Hour photo up there and scrolled the faces sometimes with your then-BFFs, ha. Ex-BFFs, since Break. To be fair, you all made the Spring Break plan together, the way you did everything, like working together last summer at Chilly Cow Ice Cream on Mass. Ave in Arlington, Massachusetts: 100 flavors, ice cream in every color. Grandad said you'd be artistic like him because of your love of colors. You often dressed in peachy golds, like Peach-E Keen ice cream. Which you gorged on, gaining five pounds by August. Losing that weight by Fall counted as a crisis to you. The ex-you.

FWIW2: After that summer, at the start of your Senior year in September 2019, you came back to school with your best-ever tan and your sun-highlighted hair from weekend days at Singing Sands Beach. You knew you looked good, girl. Knew it when you sashayed down the school halls in one Girl Herd; knew it when

Grandad took that golden-lit honey-haired garden photo in late September. Way better than your official Senior Portrait. *You'll be a beauty one day.*

Only: one day will never come. Not for Grandad- who is never seen in our family's best photos because he's taking them. Not for you—because you'll never look at your face after April 8th, 2020, and see beauty. Yeah, maybe you'll see a pretty, made-up face, but it's a mask. As Grandad used to say, Beauty is more than skin-deep. Peel back your skin, you'd find blank black.

Like the cloth facemask you pulled on, slipping out of the house on the first Sunday of June, 2020, for what you told your zoned-out Mom was just one more bike ride. *One dumb decision* is how Mom and your school counselor said you should look at the whole Spring Break thing. You didn't mean to hurt anyone, especially not Grandad. Not that 'hurt' is the word.

b. March 10, 1948-d. April 8, 2020

They carved that in stone, only it took extra-long to get the stone. With all the new deaths and all. But the finished stone was put in place last week, end of May. You and your mom visited the stone in the graveyard near the Mystic Lakes. She watched you study the stone, like she was waiting for something. For the stone to crack. For you to crack too, snap out of it, maybe, though your mom didn't say anything like that. She almost never mentions your weeks-long depressive daze or your trip to fucking Florida.

After which you Ex'd your Friends from your life because they didn't want you mentioning Grandad dying of Covid anywhere online. Anywhere anyone they knew might see and connect the Covid-dots back to them. Not that the deadly 'dot' was any of them.

They all tested Negative. Lucky them. They'd all get to graduate, move on. It was up to you to remember that fateful Florida trip: over and over. Especially on Graduation Day, June 7th, 2020—as you biked off toward the non-ceremony in which you were a non-graduate. Under ugly muggy clouds, in the bike lane, you whizzed up Mass Ave, past Spy Pond, furiously fast.

Spring Break; late February 2020. You can't say you all weren't warned. But—hard as this is to believe now—it was kind of a joke, back then. Students from China wearing weird medical masks in airports and on campuses, on TV. You never saw those masks for real till you were on the plane to Florida. Till it was too late to turn back. You'd already—this was one of your arguments to your Mom, echoing what your girlfriends said to you—*bought the tickets*.

Yes, you were only Seniors, but all of us were 18. And Ana, the oldest and prettiest of us, had a boyfriend at Full Sail University. She'd met him while visiting her Cuban grandparents in Miami. And Ana's ex-Dad—always trying to buy back her love, like my no-show Dad and all the divorced Dads—he had a condo in Orlando, Spring Break Central. You'd all stay with him.

What did you get in Florida besides asymptomatic Covid19? You got your second-best tan ever: you, who prior to April of 2020 was most famous within your circle for your tans. You got to feel the special silky Floridian sand under your feet; you got to see the goddamn Gulf. The waters lapped the beaches more languidly than the chill crashing blue-grey Atlantic you'd grown up swimming and bodysurfing. First wading into, on tiptoe, freezing. Then you'd be the one of your frozen friends to dive right in. One whole-body heart-stopping shock.

In Florida, the air felt humid yet lighter than here. Everything felt lighter in Orlando; you girls out on what

Grandad called a *weekend tear*. Spending both days on the beach and both nights bopping in too-crowded too-sweaty group dance-parties. Crashing in Ana's ex-Dad's airy under furnished condo. The Dad was supposed to be there, but he wasn't. You all were on your own. But you all washed all the dishes, like good girls. And you only slept with one guy. Well, gave him head. A UMass guy you already knew. You didn't run wild, like Mom worried.

You flew home feeling A-OK compared to your girl-friends, throwing up their Bloody Marys in the closet-sized airplane bathroom while you guarded the flimsy vibrating door. A bubble of fear expanded inside your chest as you led your then-BFF's, pale under their tans, back down the narrow plane aisle, noting those paper medical masks on a surprising number of faces.

What was up with that? And with those scary head-lines scrolling across the airport's giant TV screens? Travel Bans, Lockdowns. We lucked out, you told each other sleepily as you dragged your wheeled bags across the Logan terminal and hopped in your separate Lyfts.

You knew there was a virus, sure, everyone did by the start of March. But Mom thought it was a hoax, and we didn't believe we'd all be 'locked down' within a week. You wore white, showing off your tan at that birthday party at Grandad's twilight-blue bungalow. *I should bring out my good camera,* was maybe the last normal thing Grandad said to you, hugging you or maybe you hugged him.

Then suddenly you were following Mom past the spookily emptied shelves of the Arlington Center CVS, over-buying toilet paper and tampons. *Really it was my fault,* Mom told you, sobbing, when the doctors deter-mined that Grandad didn't have the flu or pneumonia but Covid.

My fault, Mom insisted, using her no-arguments

tone. Because she'd let you go on the stupid Spring Break weekend; because she'd urged you to go to the family birthday bash, which meant after Grandad got diagnosed, we all (April Fools!) had to take the test. I was the one who came out Positive. *But asymptomatic,* the doctor told me like I'd won some prize.

It's no one's goddamn fault, Grandad shouted later. You and Mom pressed your heads together to see him in his hospital bed, on Mom's phone, on FaceTime: Grandad fuzzy like he was already a ghost, but his voice deep and sure as ever, cutting off your choked-up attempt to apologize again.

Nothing and no one could have stopped it. Except, ghostly Grandad added as a final jibe at Mom, his Damn Republican daughter, *your damn President.*

But wasn't it really *Your damn daughter?* Namely: *you?*

FLASHFORWARD to June. Graduation Day, so-called. You panted behind your mask as you cycled up toward Arlington Center and Arlington High School, keeping that black mask on despite its smothering stale-tasting cloth. You liked being hidden, your strawberry blonde hair—once your pride—unwashed and ponytailed under the helmet you'd promised Grandad you'd always wear, back when he bought you the bright yellow bike for your 16th birthday.

You're glad now—ages later—that the helmet plus mask hide you. The masqued-up dudes at Prince Prospero's end-of-the-world bash, they each died frozen in some final posture of fear and despair, or however Poe put it. Basically, they all dropped dead in their tracks, trying to run away. Only there's no fleeing some shit. That's the point of the story, right? Prince Prospero and his big-ass castle, each room a different funky color;

Prince P. thinking he and his BFFs are safe in there, partying hard at their Masqued Ball. Their own what-the-hell Plague Party.

Which must've been as crazy-crowded as the Spring Break parties—really only two—you all crashed that weekend, your then-BFFs and you. Uninvited, like the rude red-hooded dude who crashes Prince P's party. Red because in the Red Death, the victims cough up 'scarlet' blood. Scarlet blotches bloom all over their faces like a mask that never comes off. Unlike creepy sneaky Covid, which can hide, unseen: your skin glowing and tan, after Orlando.

Mom crashed a party or two in her wild days, which was one reason why she let you go to Florida. She'd wanted you to follow her high-heeled footsteps and go to UMass Amherst, aka Zoo Mass, which your then-golden-girl mom rocked her way through back when Animal House was a big joke and people got to party their brains out and nothing bad happened. Because that was before Party Girls like you turned out to be—surprise!—Death.

Then, in April and May of 2020, everyone tries to hide in their homes and Shelter in Place, all that crap. But in the end, in Poe's story, no one—not even Prince Prospero—escapes. You really like how fast Poe made everyone die at his The End.

Could you do that too? you wondered as you biked into Arlington Center and saw them up ahead. Gathered on the street corners along Mass Ave leading up to Arlington High, where in a normal year the graduates would gather on the Football Field. Instead, clusters of 'friends and family' stood on each corner, some dressed up, some not; some masked, most not. Some holding goofy oversized CONGRATS GRADUATE!! balloons.

Many held cellphones at the ready, poised to shoot. All faced the street. No one turned as you glided your bike to a stop in the Bike Lane. Then wheeled your bike to the back of a smallish crowd bunched together by Not Your Average Joe's, where you used to gather after games.

"Not your average graduation," a Dad said loudly to scattered laughs. "Drive-by diplomas!"

"They're coming," a Mom-voice (luckily none you recognized) called out.

You froze, keeping well behind the crowd, bowing your heavy helmeted head. Actually freaking praying no one saw you, recognized you. You kept one hand on your bike handlebar. Because you can touch a bike lightly and it obeys. Balanced beside you, ready to whiz you off.

Distant cheers arose: like a parade without live music. Or no: faintly, different rock songs played from different cars, so it sounded all mixed up, jangly. Your stomach churned. Shit, what if you threw up? You swallowed hard, remembering throwing up your pink Cosmos into the toilet of the Condo bathroom of your ex-friend's ex-father—who never did show up. *Blame my Dad,* Ana (let's call her Friend A) insisted to you when she pulled you aside at the funeral she had no business even attending. But at least she did, unlike Friends B-D.

They all stopped talking to you after you blew up at them, the last time you ZOOMed together, when they asked you not to mention Grandad dying of Covid on, like, Twitter and shit. Which you (coward that you are) didn't wind up doing anyways, not wanting to get known as Arlington's Typhoid-Whoever. So you quit Twitter-and kind of quit school, too.

Grownups kept sending you messages all April and May, the Counselor ZOOMing you and your mom when you stopped 'attending' the lame Zoom classes. Now—unless you finish this story, finish your final Incomplete for your English Lit teacher—you may not graduate at all. Not that anyone in your Covid-19 Class got a real graduation ceremony, got to 'walk.'

Instead, the Arlington High Class of 2020 formed a Car Parade: decorated cars and SUVs rolling up Mass. Ave. Closing in on you: everyone blowing horns; yelling at Friends and Family on the curbs; strains of Cardi B. and BTS mixing with Billie Eilish from the green-headed girls.

"Go SPY POND-ERS," not-green-haired cheerleaders chanted from their own corner.

Guys you used to like waved in the Arlington High Spy Ponder hockey shirts they'd been so proud to earn, that wouldn't mean much after today. The Drama Geeks in sparkles swung Rainbow flags and the shy kids smiled stiffly from back seats; Student Government kids hoisted Black Lives Matter signs. A hailstorm of car horns, dueling soundtracks, noisemakers, shouts.

Everyone cheering but you. In your old helmet and new mask, you stood watching like the masked Death Dude who'd get them all in the end. Stalking the Prince through the trippy rooms of his own Palace. Each room a different bizzarro color. In Orlando the linked hotel suites at the Saturday night party flashed with strings of colored lights, multi-colored. Not a different color for each different room which would have been cool. Cool, too, if you'd all dropped dead amidst dancing and hooking up. Instead of an End worse than Poe's.

Death lives! Lives on and on, like car after car of kids you barely knew. A whole lifetime of days ahead, knowing if you hadn't gone to the goddamn Break, Death in the form of You might not have seized your grandad, who would be here at your un-Graduation. Your dad was going to come but when he found out you weren't even graduating, he cancelled his trip. You almost phoned Friend A to bitch to her about that, him. Her dad even worse. If her dad hadn't invited you all to his bachelor condo, would Grandad be here, towering above the other picture-takers? Would you be graduating? you wondered just as—like Black Magic—you saw them.

Holy shit. Ex-Friends A through D, rolling toward you. Bopping their heads to Taylor Swift. Crammed atop the back seat of Friend D's convertible, waving like they're all Miss America. Ex-Friend D. at the wheel, eyes fixed straight ahead.

At least D-for-Driver hadn't spotted you yet. You turned in panic, guiding your bike off the curb, stupidly stepping onto the side-street leading to Not Your Average Joe's parking lot. Meaning to jump your bike and speed away. But you froze as the girls' car passed. You stood there exposed beside your bright yellow bike.

So of course—you dummy!—your waving ex-friends saw you. First, shit: Friend B. slowed her wave then nudged Friend A, Ana, the closest to you. Both in life and in the car passing you directly. So you had to meet Friend A's shocked made-up stare. Her full dark hair blown-out extra-big like yours would've been today; her rounded black-lined eyes locking your own bared blue eyes, the one part of your face not hidden by your helmet-plus-mask. Friend B had already turned her blonde hair-extensioned head away to wave to the other side of the street (B-for-Bitch!) but Friend A burst into a scared smile. She waved at, not toward, you.

She even (you couldn't be sure, it happened so fast) waved you over, gestured you to follow—to bike into the parade somehow and climb onto the car? Like nothing happened? Like they'd even let you in: Friends B through D, rolling on by. A boat-sized Cadillac of jocks followed, blowing obnoxiously loud airhorns. The guys who you girls used to deem Too Dumb to Live.

"Con-GRATS," folks shouted gamely from your curb.

"Good LUCK, dudes!"

"They're gonna NEED it," sarcastic-Dad voice called

out above the rest.

The Parade was winding down, the cheers more muted for the straggling final cars. Soon the Moms and Dads and restless siblings would turn from parade's end and see you. Though no one knew you were Death except your Ex-Besties; the lucky ones who had tested Negative, who had rolled on, graduating without you. Friend B. turning away like you weren't even there! You re-mounted your bike, mad at that. You could be a Bitch on Wheels too, today.

Helmeted head low, you pedaled into the Bike Lane, the rear cars of the parade still visible a block up ahead. Two Police cars rode right behind with their blue lights flashing in muzzy sun. Like the multi-colored hotel-suite lights in Florida, hypnotic. You biked toward those lights.

A parked car pulled out, almost clipping you, the Mass. Ave. traffic matter-of-factly resuming. Screw that! You were the tail-end of the Graduation Parade, only no one knew it. Just like no one at Prince Prospero's party knows at first that Death is coming for them all.

Do you ever think of hurting yourself? the usually smiley Guidance Counselor asked you via Zoom and you shook your head no, lying. *Yep, every time I bike,* you could've said. But they'd have tried to stop your biking. You never did cross the bike-lane line till Graduation Day.

You kept zipping down that Bike Lane, getting closer. Catching up to the retreating tail end of the parade. You pumped so hard your legs ached and the ache felt good. Chasing the whole Class of 2020 like Death finally does chase down Prince P. But no one cared that the Prince died—not the way your mom would care if you did. Even though lately, you felt she could hardly stand to look at you. Would it be a relief to her, not to have to see you?

The blue lights of the police cars kept flashing, urging you on. But you didn't want to be trailing alongside the parade, in the damn Bike Lane. You wanted to be *in* the parade.

Zig-zaggedy fast—like you'd pictured doing all Spring—you veered out of the Bike Lane, into the lane of cars that had resumed rumbling down Mass Ave.

"HEY," A mad-mom voice yelled behind you, brakes screeching like a scream. Her horn blared: a big *No!* Your bike wobbled in its sound waves. What a dumb idea, to chase the parade; to veer onto Mass Ave, trapped now in the traffic. Too Dumb to Live!

"YOU'RE OUTA LANE," the mad-mom hollered. No shit, Sherlock. She pounded her horn again, this time staccato style. *Out, out, out—* Like your pulse when you lay awake at night lately, wishing for sleep that would never end.

Your head dizzy, you tightened your sweaty hold on your handlebars. Did the dumb deserve to die? Did *you?* Your heart pumped in your chest like it wanted *out out out.* Should you just veer over that final line, the solid yellow one, smashing straight into oncoming cars?

You braced your body, daring yourself to do it—wrench the handlebars, cross the line—when you felt a ping. A tiny silent explosion. Your iPhone, vibrating? Mom? Or — somehow you sensed this—not Mom. Someone else? *Grandad?* you thought as you slowed your bike, slowed it too fast. But you had to check your texts! Your last clear thought before the Mom car behind you rammed your rear tire, jarring your bike and body. The mom and her brakes screamed. You screamed too through your mask: jolting forward, losing hold.

You pitched over your handlebars: your bike falling away behind you, your body swept off on a wave without water. Headfirst, you catapulted into an SUV bumper:

curved like a giant pillow. Your helmeted head thunked its metal. A blast of pain like light; a dark inner tornado sucking you under. *Crack*—black.

Then a man carrying you. You stared up at a man crouched beside you on the sidewalk where he'd laid you down. Grandad with a weird beard and a policeman's hat? His face going freaky-fuzzy like Grandad's did that final FaceTime time. Then you blacked out again.

Maybe you should end your story there, like you'd died. That way, you could skip the hospital part. Lying for days in a jail-railed hospital bed, trapped in itchy stitches and bandages. It sucked. And everyone kept saying how lucky you were, are. Your femur fractured, which hurt the worst. But, Mom kept repeating, it could've been *way* worse. You managed a nod, the lower half of your face bandaged so you could barely talk. Or you pretended you could barely talk. Severe abrasions, the doctor explained, ordering you not to scratch under your bandages.

But it itched like Hell. Sometimes you wondered if really you had *died*, had landed in some kind of Hospital Hell like poor Grandad at the end, only without the ventilator. But no: your mom sat at your bedside the way she couldn't sit at his, chattering on about her drinking-buddy fellow-divorcee dermatologist. How she would use silicon sheets to 'flatten' your scar. The real doctor told you and your mom that scraped-off skin can heal but cannot 'regenerate—'

Your mom nodded but she wasn't listening. But then, your mom still believed her 'damn President' that Covid would disappear soon. Mom told you so as she drove you home, driving you crazy as she settled you into your bed, saying again how your scarred face could be made smooth again. You pretended to agree just to make her stop talking. She beamed her best Mom smile at you and shut your bedroom door softly. Shit, you felt so much older than your mom.

And older than Ana—who it turned out had been the one who'd texted you, just before the crash. Her text either almost-killing you or saving you, who can say. She must have sent it from her perch on Friend D's convertible in the Graduation parade. Short and sweet and clueless: *saw u- u ok?* It wasn't till days later when Mom finally left you alone in your room that you thumb-texted Ana back: *'n (duh).'*

By then she'd heard about your crash, heard rumors from our fast-scattering former classmates. Some of them had sent emails and e-cards. Ana at least did text back, hoping you'd feel better soon; hoping we'd *get 2gether* once she got back from the Cape. Her usual June trip to her family's summer home there. Where you might be now, soaking in the sun beside Ana, in your former life. Instead of lying here pale-faced in your peach-painted room as if you did die.

But no. Alas, as my new BFF Edgar A.P. might say. I'm still here. The girl with the scraped-off face.

(I might as well switch back to 'I'—to end this story. My story. Might as well just, like Twitter trolls say, *own it).* My damn dumb story: the story that will forever frame my life-to-be.

Lucky me. Still breathing and still so-called recovering here at home, mid-June, 2020. My bike helmet so-called 'saved' me. The goddamn helmet I kept on because Grandad made me promise. And I couldn't break that promise. I couldn't stop dreaming it was Grandad carrying me to the sidewalk; those dreams more vivid and real than real life, my silent sunny bedroom.

Where I feel here, but not here. Only less not-here than at the hospital. At least here at home, these last couple cooped-in weeks, I get to be alone. Like everyone's been telling me I don't want to be. I keep my window open, gently humid June air drifting in. Any fresh air tastes better than disinfected-piss hospital air. Mostly, being alone feels good, in a sad way. Just me and Edgar Allan P, his black-and-white face blurred on the Xeroxed stapled story on my nightstand. Sad old (actually, sad young) Prince Prospero didn't have anyone watching over him like Mom, or like I feel/imagine Grandad still doing. Prince P. just had his Frat Boy friends who didn't give a damn if he dropped dead. Friends who turn out to be only skin-deep.

I sit propped by floppy normal-smelling pillows as I type, trying not to scratch under my new lighter bandages. Not to feel the pill-numbed ache in my thigh. Instead, I keep typing away on this way-overdue final assignment. Which will finish my high school degree and 'graduate' me—into what? And what *will* my scraped-off face look like, once the bandages come off?

At least the damn face masks we'll all be wearing forever will cover it up: whatever scars I might wear, forever. What passes as a hopeful thought, for me. The new older me. Typing slower, dusk falling outside. Beside THE MASQUE OF THE RED DEATH on my nightstand sits a vase of brown-tinged roses rescued by Mom from Grandad's now-overgrown garden. Not Peace Roses, which bloom later in summer. Another kind of rose, with a name Grandad would know.

Gazing at those dead but-still-pretty roses, I consider again ending my story like Poe's, everyone dying. Me dying, anyways. What I'd wondered, all Spring, if I want. But no: I've typed my whole story true, so far. And that, in a sad way, feels good too. So I'll just keep going.

Once I finish this thing, any-which-way, I'll be an

official member of the Covid-19 Class of 2020. Doomed yet not dead. Not yet. All of us rolling forward into an End Yet a Beginning. Lucky us. I pause to sniff the funky Not-Peace Roses. At least my nose isn't broken; at least I'm still breathing. I hold in that last breath. Last, I mean, in this story.

The (I thought I wanted to type this last word, but now that I'm doing it, I don't) *End*

THE DRAMA ROOM

1. Former Fantasticks

At silent 6AM, by the dawn's early laptop light, I find them again: our stars. Onscreen, online—two fellow Thespians; two former Fantasticks. Blasts from my past. A boy and girl, then. And see, I'd loved, in my tortured teen way, both of them. I feel my fingers shake. Even now, in listless locked-down May of 2020, the morning air is suddenly charged with that old expectant backstage hush. As if flipping a switch for the first Light Cue in a show, I finger-tap the link that leads me back.

To the Corona High Drama Room. Hey, it was the '80s. Photos from PEOPLE plastered the Drama Room walls, overlapping: Meryl Streep and Molly Ringwald and Tom Cruise and Jodie Foster and Madonna. Plus, a giant-sized Patrick Swayze (RIP) and Jennifer Grey; the *Dirty Dancing* stars that our own two stars pretended to be at our infamous Fantasticks cast party.

More on that later—the real-life drama. I usually wasn't part of it, or not in any way that showed. Because I was backstage, wearing all black. My broad-for-a-girl shoulders carried the shows; my prematurely maternal boobs hid the youngest dumbest heart of all. So I saw the most. Because I was invisibly in the background, smoking Ms. L's Virginia Slims with Ricardo in the Prop Closet; because I was the least wild of the late-80's Corona High Thespians, I'm the one left to tell the tales.

Not that I'd do that now, online. Not that our stories amounted to a #MeToo—at least, not with me as the 'Me.' I always kept quiet, confiding only in Ricardo. The one that our two stars hurt the most. What if I contacted them, now? What if, in memory of Ricardo, I typed the truth?

I hug myself in the chill of my Paradise Valley condo. The home I used to share with Mom, the central-air these days always too high for one person. But I need the ice-cube office-cubicle chill to keep me awake as I numbly crunch sales numbers. I face down my screen, neither of us in work-mode yet. I lick my sticky sweet lips. I'd almost choked on my Diet Mocha, seeing it onscreen, his name.

Freddy Tyler. It shines before me now, tiny and bright. I jam on my new reading glasses and re-focus, processing the pixilated name listed among others on a defiantly upbeat Summer 2020 TheaterBuff page. Still 'Freddy'—though he's supposedly grown older, like all of us.

Try to Remember. Annie Samson, ingenue eyes wide, watching Freddy sing. Me in the wings beside Annie, facing her dirty-blonde curls. Breathing her sweet teenage-girl sweat as she waited, trembling, to go on. Ricardo lying crammed into his silver-painted coffin-sized box onstage, awaiting his cue. *Try to Remember.* All of us listening to Freddy belt out the chorus. *And follow, follow, follow.*

2. Corona High

It all began in the Drama Room. Our haven at sports-crazed sun-dazed Corona High in Paradise Valley, Arizona. Back when 'Corona' didn't mean a virus and 'Corona High' referred to post-game parties where tan football jocks supposedly did lines of cocaine. At school they definitely did numbers on us Thespians. A joking jock once announced over the loudspeaker that all 'Lesbians' should gather for their Yearbook Photo in front of the school by the 'fag pole.' Amidst our lowliest Snack Bar humiliations, we'd tell each other to tap our heels together like Dorothy in Oz so we could be transported back—if only inside our heads—to the Drama Room.

My freshman year, I first viewed the Thespians from the audience, beside my Mom. I saw YOU'RE A GOOD MAN, CHARLIE BROWN both times. Well, one and a half times, since Opening Night I'd left at intermission to get sleepy Mom home. Walking her to our rusty Vega; driving super-carefully since I only had a Permit and wasn't supposed to drive at night; slipping the emptied Wine Cooler bottle from Mom's purse; helping her to our couch; turning on Late Nite Cinema Classics.

"Why do you have to see it a-*gain?*" Mom quavered the next evening when I left to watch, alone, the second night of CHARLIE BROWN. As the Techies stomped out for their sheepish shared bow, I made my decision. Those kids in black were the ones who made the whole show run. And I was already used to that. Being the hidden one really in charge.

September 1986. I made my Drama Room entrance in my sophomore year, keeping my head down, THE FANTASTICKS cast list about to be posted. The anxious wanna-be stars clustered around a central stage platform. Unnoticed, I slipped into Ms. Laydon's empty patchouli-scented office to apply for TECH CREW. Through the open office door, I caught my first glimpse of Annie.

In her corner, posing with her permed hair and pert dancer's body and wide lipglossed mouth and stage-sized whisper, she held court. But Freddy Tyler had out-cooled Annie by not even showing up for the posting. He was busy with one of his 'semi-professional' theater gigs.

"Freddy's SO gonna be the Try to Remember dude—"

"And if Annie doesn't get The Girl—"

As the actor and actress types angsted their way around the oversized Drama Room, I sunk onto Ms. L's couch and filled out my Techie form, signed my plain name. *Peg Jarrett.* Then I lifted the newest PEOPLE from a sloppy stack. My lank 'wings' of hair hid my face. Someone entered the office. I felt that someone bend close, skimming my same page.

And I gazed up into the dark-lashed eyes of Ricardo Lopez.

"Of course, people have told you," he breathed, "you look *just* like Jodie Foster."

Of course, no one had told me any such thing. But Ricardo fixed on the part of me no one else usually noticed. My clear-skinned clear-eyed face.

"Yeah, I've thought that too—about me and Jodie," I agreed. "But not Jodie in TAXI DRIVER. More like Jodie in ALICE DOESN'T LIVE HERE ANYMORE—saying in her weirdo voice, 'Weird.' You know, she really should've said it about Phoenix..."

Ricardo nodded big, as if already onstage. Then this skinny dude with the movie star eyes and acne-ridden skin fell on his knees before me. Simultaneously, we recited: "'Weird. That's weird for Phoenix—and *Phoenix* is the Weird Capital of America.'"

We collapsed onto the beige carpet in shared snorting laughter. We sat out the cast-list wait on the squeaky couch, his lean and my not-so-lean thigh pressed together through our jeans. My dirty-blonde and his black hair brushed as we bent over a vintage photo spread. Ricardo's finger quivered, pointing to a black-and-white Montgomery Clift, circa A PLACE IN THE SUN.

"Not that I'm anything like—" he whispered to me. "But that's who I'd *want* to look like..."

"You look way more like him than I do like Jodie," I whispered back as he suddenly stood.

A flurry outside the office: Cyndie Laydon had finally sauntered into the Drama Room. From her own office, we watched her post the Cast List, her messy hennaed hair twisted in a bun. Her dusky pink pants seemed sewn onto her muscular ex-dancer legs.

"OK Chickies, this is it!" Ms. L. spun dramatically. "Make way, children!" She shouldered through the students gathered round her like fans. The first squeals rose like sparkler rockets.

Smelling of cigarettes she never smoked in front of us, Ms. L. padded into her office. She nodded at frozen Ricardo and me like we were already familiar fixtures. She collapsed heavily yet gracefully into her swivel seat, facing her script-stacked desk, a single photo on her desktop, shoved to the edge.

A mustached man with a squinty dead-on gaze. Older than thirty-ish Ms. L. The man that Ms. L. (like a famous and evasive star) would call 'my friend;' the man who ran the downtown Phoenix cowboy bar where the best of 'our boys' would later go to work. And, well, to play.

"Wish me luck," Ricardo muttered and he rushed out the office door. Then Ms. L. glanced at me wryly, her mascaraed eyes glinting like she and I were the only sensible ones, watching from afar.

"You did it! You got it," I heard Annie's satellite gals shriek.

"I *did?*" she shrieked back with almost convincing shock. "Wow I'm so stoked!"

From across the Drama Room, Ricardo flashed a braces-revealing grin as he signaled me—me!—with his jaunty thumbs-up. Oh Ricardo: if only you could've been mine.

3. Follow, Follow, Follow

Freddy Tyler, I read again onscreen, on this May morning in 2020, three decades later, bleary-eyed. How can I tell if it's really him? I press another key, following a link into the Tweet woods. Freddy's personal page vibrates. I scan it, noting links to Midwest theater companies in St. Paul, Minneapolis. One with a 'Like' from an '*AnnieSam-G*'

My eyelid twitches. My old 'Sergeant Carter' eye twitch. Or so I'd dubbed the tic in high school, in honor of the stressed-out Sergeant character on GOMER PYLE. The kind of TV-trivia reference that Ricardo always 'got'. Surely *AnnieSam-G* is Annie Samson? So Freddy *is* Freddy.

If only I could phone Ricardo. I fold my arms over my pillowy breasts and my solid stomach. Pre-pandemic, I'd kept my weight under control. Now I've slid into Taco Bell/KFC take-out. I peer through my glasses, my right eye still twitching as I face Freddy's page. Hundreds, not thousands, of followers. Fantastick Freddy. His Twitter photo is a set of red theater curtains, closed.

Maybe he's known in the small world of Midwest regional theaters. Those theaters at risk for closing, like the Little Theater where I've been volunteering, doing Lights. Keeping the Thespian spark in me alive. But with their 2020 Season all on Zoom, they don't need Lights. Don't need me.

Nothing I might post about Freddy or his past would get noticed, much less go viral. Years ago, when he'd just moved to LA, before he'd gotten his HIV diagnosis, Ricardo confided to me that he'd tracked down Ms. Laydon teaching at a Community College in Flagstaff, Arizona. From just that fact, she'd be findable. I glance at the headlines atop my screen: a hotly disputed #MeToo accusation.

I remember an infamous 2018 'selfie' that did go viral: an actress and #MeToo activist in bed with a 17-year-old actor, his boyish gaze distant and stagey. Like Freddy's. Maybe the last time I really thought about Freddy, till today. I reach for my lowest desk drawer, my once-secret stash of cigarettes. I fumble with the pack. I've been putting off a masked drugstore run. One cigarette left.

The one time I saw Ricardo cry was when Freddy left town before graduation. Without a word to Ricardo, as if nothing had happened. I finger my last cigarette, as yet unlit. On my inner soundtrack, the catchiest Fantasticks melody warms up, unstoppable once it starts. Like this itch in my fingers to smoke. Or to break a silence that no one alive knows I am holding.

Try to remember and—Before I can stop my finger, I press FOLLOW.

4. The Kind of September

Suddenly that September, my sophomore year, I switched from being tomboyish Peg Jarrett (in grade school, Piggy Peg) to being the cheery jean-jacketed Head Techie, 'PJ'. For the FANTASTICKS cast and crew, the standard sunny Arizona autumn was suffused by the new glow of belonging. To each other; to 'our show.' Together, we strode the Corona halls with new purpose. Bursting after school into our auditorium to rehearse. Gathering for laugh-fest lunches inside our Drama Room.

In my former Freshman life, I'd hid behind dark blond hair that looked 'dirty' no matter how often I washed it, shadows under my eyes from watching late movies with Mom. I wore oversized tee shirts, hiding my big breasts and stomach. I'd dropped out of Girls' Basketball, which I only looked like I'd be good at. What I was really good at was carrying a whole show (more fun than a whole crappy condo household) on my broad Sophomore shoulders. Suddenly that September, I was 'running lines' with almost-famous Freddy. Suddenly, even skillfully, I was aiming spotlights at petite Annie Samson, aglow in the peach-pink leotard that set off her swimming pool tan. She sang 'Soon It's Gonna Rain' with a longing that made me want to stop and listen. But I kept moving. Hauling folded scrims and providing the packets of 'sparkle' that Ricardo tossed in the air, bursting from his glittery box. I kept special track of Ricardo's—aka The Mute's—every prop. Not that I shot Ricardo any Annie Samson Stares.

Onstage, Annie aimed those intent ingenue gazes at the jock cast as the 'Boy.' Offstage, she aimed them at the elusive Freddy, aka El Gallo. Freddy came to rehearsals late and left early. Because, as he often 'let slip,' he was 'doing' another show that fall, at a semi-pro. theater in Tempe. Freddy was tall and bony, his lean beaky face a blank. Until my spotlight lit his suddenly expressive features.

He raised his head high, his hawk nosed profile dramatic. Sometimes Freddy sang softly so as to, he explained, 'save his voice.' In later rehearsals, when he'd let it rip, I worked to hold my hands and the light steady, especially when Freddy launched into the big song's killer climax.

5. Love Was an Ember

Was it? An ember about to billow, even for me? The week before Opening Night, Ricardo and I huddled in our usual gossip-and-smoke session in the Drama Room's prop closet. The two of us compared notes on how many times Annie gazed with real offstage longing at Freddy.

"Like Ms. L.; she's got her eye on Freddy too—and on you," I informed Ricardo.

"Me? Oh c'mon," he protested, unconvincingly casual, burying his cigarette stub in the trash. "You think ol' 'Cyndie Just Wants to Have Fun' might ask me to audition? For her boyfriend's Dance Hall thingy? To 'cowboy up-'" Ricardo struck a mock-cowboy pose, thumbs hooked in his perfectly fitted jeans. One long leg extended for a balletic leap. To where?

"No way," I told him. "It's Freddy she's got in mind for going pro..."

"And going—'dot dot dot'..." Ricardo added archly, opening the Prop Closet door. *Hot hot hot,* I chanted to myself as I followed Ricardo's black-jeaned ass into the deserted school parking lot. Had I fallen in love—or was this mere friendship? Whatever it was, it hurt.

My teenage heart ached, once the day's hubbub lay behind us. Heavenly scent of orange trees mixed with car fumes as I trudged up to our stucco-walled Cholla Vista condo. The desert evening sky stretched above me: peachy clouds decked with antic streaks of magenta. I tried to picture kissing Ricardo. But I couldn't make the picture fit, gazing into the pollution-enhanced techni-color sunset.

Mom was asleep on the couch, lit by *Singin' in the Rain*. She lay curled in a lump in her tent dress, hugging her heavy arms in the air-co chill. Trying not to wake

Mom—who'd ask me wistfully why I'd come home late again—I settled close to her and lifted her Rocky Road.

In the jumpy TV light, I spooned melted ice cream soup, watching dapper Gene Kelly; picturing Ricardo and his quick sly grin. The boy who got my jokes; the boy who looked at me when I talked. Though not the way I looked at him. What was the line from the Bette Davis flick Mom liked? Why wish for the moon when we've got the stars? Didn't I have Ricardo, my star, as a friend? Wasn't that enough, for now? I slowed my spoonfuls of Rocky Road, making it last.

6. You Must Be

The next evening, sultry at 100-plus degrees, Ricardo and I headed back to the Drama Room to share our post-rehearsal smoke. As we eased open the main door, we heard music. A radio playing Madonna from Ms. L's lair. *You must be my lucky star,* Madonna in her Minnie Mouse voice sang loud enough to cover Ricardo's and my steps. We padded across the carpeted Drama Room floor. To the light under the door. The low voices under the loud music.

"Lower, lower..."

The raspy sprung springs of Ms. L's couch. Then—we inched closer to each other—Freddy's unmistakable stage-trained voice.

Freddy: *Um, you sure?*

Ms. L.: *I'm kinda sure you are—ready, Freddy?*

Silence, then springs. Ricardo and I exchanged gazes like two kids outside their parents' bedroom. I took hold of Ricardo's hand. He squeezed mine.

Ms. L (softer this time, more urgently): *Lemme just help you with that—*

Freddy (softer too): *Um—do you—hear something?*

We spun round. We shot over to the main door, let it

swing shut behind us. Then we raced into the parking lot, leaped into Ricardo's Dad's El Dorado.

"'Lower, Lower'!" Ricardo backwards-steered in screeching Reverse. Off we whizzed, warm wind in our faces. Both laughing. But I felt my stomach churn at the thought of Ms. L. stripping off her skin-tight slacks and unzipping Freddy's jeans. What did Freddy feel, lying there?

"Think she's sucking him off right now? Sucking Freddy's cock?"

I shook my head at Ricardo's wind-muffled question. And his barking laugh.

"M-maybe we oughta go back and—like, rescue him?"

"Betcha Freddy don't wanna be rescued," Ricardo shouted, an edge to his voice.

He veered down Goldust, his convertible weaving like he was drunk. We both chanted, "Ready Freddy, Ready Freddy!"

Till Ricardo's car—with a jolt, overshooting my condo—halted at the next beige brick building. Ricardo didn't notice. He seemed not to see me, even as he twisted towards me, his eyes wildly bright.

He leaned into me and we kissed. My first, our first. A quick smacking stagey kiss.

We both pulled back. Playfully, Ricardo nudged me away. I backed out of the El Dorado, slammed its door. My face all hot; my heart thump-thumping. Ricardo peeled off in a dramatic screech of tires. His taillights zig-zagged, then vanished. Leaving me standing in desert-night chill at the foot of the walk to the wrong damn door.

7. The Rape Ballet

Neither of us acted much differently with each other in the days that followed. Busy days of rehearsing, posting posters round the school, re-spraying silver paint on Ricardo's battered stage 'sword.' Our kiss seemed to have taken place in a dream. Maybe Ricardo had meant it as a joke?

Ms. L. and Freddy seemed the same too, onstage. Ricardo wondered aloud if we'd really heard what we'd heard. If it was a faked performance somehow. The way in the show the kidnapping isn't real, is mislabeled as—a joke I didn't get, even when Ms. L. explained it was a daring 'play on words'—a Rape. A song many schools chose to cut from *The Fantasticks,* but not us: The Rape Ballet.

"Bet you *want* it not to be true—what we both know we heard," I finally told Ricardo. Not even sure what I was implying. I coughed, waving away our shared smoke.

Ricardo shrugged, his face shadowed in the Prop Closet. "Maybe I just want a chance too, like Freddy. Heard he's getting offered a pay-job singing at Josh's cowboy club-thing. Getting 'higher, higher' by going 'lower, lower'..."

I laughed, though I knew Freddy was plenty good enough to rise on his own. Freddy's mom was divorced like mine. Freddy had won some special 'scholarship' for the voice lessons he took at ASU. Ricardo's family lived in cushy Scottsdale; he had two parents and two cars. What did he know?

"You saying you want to go 'lower lower' with Cyndie Lay-down?" I stood up, letting the glittery skirt I held in my lap drop. Annie Samson's stage skirt. It was late, dark outside.

"Lay down with Ms. Lay-down? *Moi?*" Ricardo gave a comic whole-body shudder. I laughed gamely, taking his cue. And I chased mock-horrified Ricardo out of our smoky closet.

We almost ran into the Principal of Corona High. "Whoa there, cowboys," he told us, then awkwardly corrected himself, looking at me. "And cowgirls."

Big bluff Mr. Shaft, a whale out of water. He stood by the Drama Room door fanning his ruddy face with a sheaf of papers. Distantly, the band was practicing our High Corona fight song, a game about to begin. Maybe that was why Mr. Shaft ignored the whiff of smoke.

"You two know where Miss Laydon might be?" he asked us, eying the PEOPLE'd wall.

We exchanged glances. She and Freddy were still down at the theater together, too late. Up to we-knew-what. I drew an uncertain breath. What if they got caught? Would the show not go on? Ricardo beat me to the punch, cutting in smoothly.

"Um, I can take those papers to them, to her." Ricardo lifted the sheaf from Mr. Shaft. Then he shot me a look and shot out the Drama Room door.

"Light on his feet, isn't he?" Mr. Shaft murmured absently to me.

"He sure is." I forced a smile. From the Drama Room doorway, I watched Mr. Shaft amble back out into the balmy dark toward the lights of the football field. Peering in the opposite direction, toward the unlit auditorium, I saw two figures emerge on the path: two slim boys, side by side.

Ricardo called over to me as he and Freddy Tyler sauntered by. "I gave Ms. L. the stuff—My Dad's picking me up and we're gonna drop Freddy off—"

"Great," I said stupidly as the two walked toward the parking lot. Ricardo had never offered to have his stern, black-bearded Dad drop me off. Can I come too? I didn't want to call after the boys.

As they disappeared, Ms L. followed at a distance on the same path: pale and disheveled with her lipstick worn off and her bun of hair mussed. She raised Mr. Shaft's sheaf toward me, a salute.

"Thanks," she called to me as she passed. Like I had—

Ricardo and I had—saved the day.

8. Get Smart

"Wasn't it GREAT?" Ricardo pulled me into a breathtakingly hard hug, in the rush after curtain calls. Everyone hugging and high fiving.

"SO great," I agreed as Ricardo tugged me into the darkest reaches of the wings. The cast was surging back onto stage to receive the shouted acclaim of their families. My mom, I knew, would take longer than most moms to reach that stage.

"So so proud of her!" Annie's mother: her voice always a notch above the other moms. Annie told everyone her Mom 'like totally' hated her.

From the rope-hung wings, we heard Cyndi L. let loose her hooting laugh amidst the onslaught of *Congrats!* and *What a show!* And (directed at Freddy): *THIS young man—HE'S destined for big things!*

"He wants to talk to me." Ricardo's whisper thundered in my ear.

"*Freddy*-he?" I cut in, playing dumb. Ricardo bobbed his head in his big stagey nod, like he'd done onstage, playing the Mute.

Up in my Light Booth, all through the show, I'd kept remembering what Ricardo told me he'd seen after he'd run to the auditorium with Shaft's papers. Ricardo had called out into the empty auditorium. Sheepishly, Ms. L. had climbed down from the Light Booth. Then Freddy had poked his tousled head from that same booth—*my* Light Booth—as Ricardo handed over the papers. Freddy climbed down slowly, meeting Ricardo's gaze (or so I pictured; Ricardo left out that part) while Ms. L. ignored both boys and bustled about the auditorium, locking up.

"Shush—I'll tell you in the car—" Ricardo spun on his

heel. He strutted on stage to receive his due. Belatedly, I slipped onstage myself amidst the fallen glitter. Families were scattering.

"It was lovely, lovey!" Mom filled my light-dazed sight. "And I know it was you, keeping it all running!" She patted my shoulder. I smiled back at Mom. Was it possible, at this hour of the evening, usually a time I'd expect no clear-headed words from her, that she'd had no drink?

I let her pull me into her flowery powdery hug, feeling her lean on me. That was when I smelled it. Only a bit fainter than usual, in her quicker breaths. I pulled back fast enough to make her wobble. "Hey, you know I'm going to the after-party, right? With Ricardo?"

"Yes, yes," Mom assured me in a tipsy stage whisper. She tottered beside me on her unaccustomed high heels as I helped her off the stage. "With your young man, yes!"

I hustled Mom down the aisles of emptied seats to the lobby. "He's not my Young Man," I hissed to her. "And you, are you—OK to drive yourself?" This last came out almost pleading.

"*P*-Jay," Ricardo called out as his mini-entourage of parents and aunts and black-haired cousins swept him through the front doors.

"Meet you at your car," I hollered back. Then I hustled my mom through those same giant glass doors. *Was she OK to drive?* I hugged her again, hurriedly. Watched her wobble off into the night.

I worried about Mom all through the windy convertible ride beside Ricardo. His El Dorado smelled of the yellow roses my Mom had splurged on, for me.

"I can just feel it," Ricardo was babbling at the wheel, "He, Freddy, when he said he wants to 'talk'- maybe he *does* want to tell me all—"

"About Ms. L?" I demanded into the wind. "So you

did ask—?"

"Shit NO!" Ricardo sped through a yellow-turning-red light. "But Freddy knows I saw the two of them up in the Light Booth thingy—"

"My Light Booth," I muttered though Ricardo barely paused.

"And Freddy practically *admitted* it in the Dressing Room before the show. He told a bunch of us he felt like Ms. L. was giving him one big 'audition' with El Gallo—an Audition for Josh's cowboy club. Freddy says he wants that *pay*-gig so he can move right to New York—"

"What—and leave you behind?" I dared to inject. Ricardo burst into peals of laughter, which melded with his screeching tires as he veered into the Samson's high-walled 'development.'

"Now don't tell any-one *any*-thing," Ricardo admonished as he parked. He made a 'Cone of Silence' sign like Maxwell Smart in Get Smart. Then Ricardo re-arranged his blow-dried hair in the rearview. "I look OK?" He faced me: his face shadowed so no acne showed.

"You know you do."

"You too," Ricardo answered, distracted. Meaning I too knew he knew he looked good? I stopped to gather my rose bouquet. So I wound up behind Ricardo as he strode the curved flagstone walk to Annie's Mission-style ranch house. Was he speeding his steps so as not to seem to 'be with' me?

But Ricardo re-smoothed his hair, waiting for me to alight the stoop beside him. "Ready?"

I nodded, hugging the lushly scented flowers. With a stage-worthy flourish, Ricardo rang the Samson's door-bell. As if she'd been waiting just for us, Annie Samson flung open the heavy carved-wood door. She smiled wide, more lovely and vibrant than she'd been onstage.

"Great show, Annie." Impulsively, I shoved my yellow-rose bouquet into Annie's arms.

9. (I've Had) The Time of My Life

What I remember best about the Cast Party is its end. In a night of firsts, I had my first drink-drink from the spiked punch bowl. A syrupy sweet taste of why Mom drank. The Samson's 'shades-of-beige' living room turned blurry bright. 'Girls Just Wanna Have Fun' blared like an anthem, in honor of Cyndie L., nowhere in sight. No grown-ups anywhere in sight.

I danced, making minimal choppy moves with a couple giggly chorus girls. Then when the truly cool actors—the Fantasticks—took to the living room dance floor, I refilled my cup. I collapsed in my backstage black onto a puffy couch, to watch.

"Welcome to my cloud," I slurred to Annie Samson as she settled lightly beside me. Leftover glitter sparkled in her hair. Her sweat smelled of rum. She gave me a sizing-up sideglance.

"My cloud," she corrected, her close-set green eyes still smokily shaded. "My Cloud Couch."

I ran my hand over the puffy fabric, silken and taut like a parachute. "We're floating together."

"And they're out there together," rum-breathed Annie confided to me. Suddenly serious, and sullen. No one nearby. "You know—Freddy and, and him..."

"Freddy and him," I repeated, my rum-slowed mind processing her words.

"Your 'him.' Ricard-o Lo-pezz." Annie nodded at the sliding doors. Doors that led to the backyard 'pool area,' deserted on this chill October night.

The pool was walled-in; the yard beyond that wall was hidden. Our couch faced the shiny glass doors like a big blank movie screen. Other Thespians traipsed about behind us, fleeting bright reflections. Annie leaned close. Her whiny confiding whisper burned my ear.

"They're out there to-*geth*-er—Like, way-close together. They didn't even see me see them..." She pulled back enough to meet my gaze, daring me to deny what she whispered next. "Freddy's not like that, y'know. But do you think Ricardo's gonna, you know, *try* something out there with him?"

I sealed my rum-sticky lips, my head aspin as I held Annie's green-eyed stare. Annie Fantastick, sharing a secret with me. One I hadn't known I knew. I'd gone mute: like Ricardo in the play, all his nods exaggerated. I felt myself nod that way, one big nod I immediately wished I could take back.

10. Happy Ending

ENTER: Ricardo and Freddy, through the sliding doors, separately. FREDDY first, as always. Freddy with a deadpan nod strolling past our couch; RICARDO following, eyes lowered, hair mussed; trailing Freddy. Who makes a point of snubbing RICARDO. Who hovers like a scrawny bodyguard behind Freddy as Freddy slurps his punch then too-loudly toasts his 'FELLOW PLAYERS.'

PJ ON THE COUCH (that's me, amidst my out-of-body experience) rolls her eyes. Yet she raises her emptied punch cup with the others. Including a suddenly wide-awake ANNIE. Gazing with those widened made-up eyes as FREDDY strides grandly over to her.

RICARDO gapes at Freddy who bows before ANNIE and takes her hand.

Somehow (has Freddy gotten control of the piped-in music?) the swelling climactic song from *Dirty Dancing* begins to play. *I've had—the time of my life—*

Freddy and ANNIE rise as one. They begin their own stiffer version of a Dirty Dance. RICARDO, by default, settles beside me on the deflated-seeming cloud couch.

He winks at me (our tell-you-later signal) and shuts his long-lashed eyes. Like it really is all a dream. Freddy and Annie gracefully exit to the kitchen, where the loudest laughers are gathered.

I lurched to a Spanish-tiled bathroom to wretch. Without asking permission, I used Annie Samson's phone to call my mom. Who didn't answer, back at our condo.

Had she had an accident going home? I wondered, wandering back to the couch. It was past midnight. I told glaze-eyed Ricardo that Mom hadn't answered.

He wasn't so out-of-it not to hear my panic. "We're motoring," he announced, rattling his car keys. On the way out, we passed the darkened living room corner where Annie and Freddy lingered, standing face to face, posing as a couple. Passing them, Ricardo tried to catch Freddy's eye. No dice.

"Hap-py end-ing," Ricardo half-sang to me under his rummy breath. Wistfully, mockingly; the way Annie should've sung those lyrics in the show.

Ricardo and I slipped through the front archway unnoticed. How could we have thought, I wondered as we stumbled off the stoop, that we'd become true 'Fantasticks' too? And how could I have nodded at Annie, betraying that secret about Ricardo I'd known without knowing?

We drove to my condo in tense silence. Only the cool night wind in our faces kept us from throwing up on Ricardo's Dad's red-leather seats. As Ricardo pulled the El Dorado to a shaky 1AM halt at my condo, we sobered up, abruptly. Because we saw it—her.

My mom: fallen over, lying on the front stoop in a shadowy curled-up heap. My heartbeat halted, the car still rocking. But Mom not moving. I screamed. Somehow, we stumbled from the car. Ricardo and I ran as one up the walk to the stoop. I imagined in those drawn-out seconds the starless dark of life without Mom. I knelt on the chilled concrete where she'd fallen, curled up, one high heeled shoe off. Ricardo kneeling right behind me, both of us holding our breaths.

I touched Mom's soft shoulder, Ricardo's hand steadying my shoulder. Groggily, Mom blinked. And stared up at me, scared. "Mom," I whispered, scared too, "It's only me."

11. Flash Forward

In our next years as Corona High Thespian 'insiders,' Ricardo and I were to share many a cast-party hangover and Prop Closet confession. Freddy nabbed his prized pay-gig as a star Singing Waiter at J. Hartley's Cowboy Club, where parents had to sign release-forms to let their kids work and where Ricardo later worked too. Seduced in short order by dashing Josh Heart-less himself, who kept up his own supposed romance with Ms. L. Meanwhile, Freddy kept secretly meeting Ricardo, who told only me, whilst Freddy officially dated Annie. And Annie quietly spread gay-boy rumors about Ricardo amongst the bully-boy jocks. Rumors that I told myself Annie surely would have spread anyway— with or without that mute nod I never did confess to Ricardo and never could take back.

So much to discuss, or not discuss, smoking Cyndie L's Virginia Slims. Cyndie surely knew—we intuited by glances and remarks—that we knew what she'd been up to. But she kept us busy, show after show. And I guess we (Ricardo pointed out in his final long-distance phone call) kept her out of trouble.

"I kinda wish I could, I don't know, re-do that part," Ricardo told me years later, from LA, weak-voiced yet firm too. "Maybe I shouldn't have—kept her secrets, y'know?"

"Maybe we shouldn't," I corrected him gently. "Remember," I added, since his memory had gotten spotty, "we *both* stopped Mr. Shaft that night..."

"I guess," Ricardo went on dreamily. "You played a role, sure, in a minor way..." I forced a half-laugh, Ricardo's words stinging. "Back then, I felt like we were both these—minor characters," Ricardo went on, rambling the way he did on his meds, "The ones who show up in a scene *because* we are gonna, y'know, witness something big involving the big characters. Like remember when I said to Cyndie L as La Director, Why am I there? Me being the 'Mute,' me wanting some motivation or shit." Ricardo paused to cough. "And she says: You're there to see them. Them being, you know, the stars..."

"Hey," I cut in, trying to think of an un-corny way to say: *Hey Ricardo, you were always a star to me.* "Hey Ricardo, you want me to fly out there? To LA?"

No, Ricardo answered softly from his hospital room, his loyal LA boyfriend by his side. No, Ricardo decreed: I needed to stay with my Mom. She was starting to slip beyond confusion around that time. Like she was drunk when she wasn't. Sometimes, I confessed to Ricardo in that phone call I didn't know was our last, Mom snapped at me, warning me against getting 'fat' like her.

"I kinda miss her seeing me like, y'know, her star..."

Ricardo sighed hard from LA. "My parents are more disappointed I'm not some big star than they are that I'm—sick." He hacked, harder and louder. "Your mom," he went on in his new 'slower but wiser' tone, "She's always loved you like you are."

I tried a joke, almost the last thing I said to him ever. "You're saying *you* think I'm 'fat'?"

At his Memorial Service in LA two weeks later, I snuck up on Ricardo's elegantly black-clad mother. She'd chosen to display by his closed coffin a framed professional photo of young frozenly smiling Ricardo, his acne air-brushed away. His mother was gazing at the photo more tenderly than I'd ever seen her gaze at the real Ricardo.

12. Back-Space and Start Again

I savor for breakfast my last cigarette. A decade ago, the first time I quit smoking, I gained back all the weight I'd gradually shed. Which was when my final wanna-be-actor boyfriend 'shed' me. A memory that hardly hurts, anymore. I don't miss any of them as much as I miss Ricardo. Or even my fellow theater-nerd pals from more recent years. Some of them emailing lately to organize a Little Theater Zoom chat. Which sounds as lame as Zoom Theater itself. But, I think today as I shower, it might be better than nothing. I barely look at my new naked girth as I pull on the loose comfy clothes I'm glad to wear all day, working from home. Still a half hour left before my workday begins.

Settling back in my well-worn desk chair, I scroll past stories on Black Lives Matter marches. I Google the 2018 bedroom 'selfie' of the 37-year-old activist/actress, her face plain without make-up, pressed cheek to cheek with the 17-year-old actor smirking into his own cell-phone. Was his sated post-sex smirk an act, too? Like Freddy's seeming cool amidst his affair-or-whatever with Ms. Lay-down? I swivel my chair back and forth. This pandemic gives me too much time to think, to backspace and replay old drama. Too vivid to me, these days. Irresistibly, I lean into my screen and click Twitter.

Freddy Tyler, 'erstwhile actor,' sent @ my 'TechyPJ' a mass-message, addressed to #FansOfFreddy, alerting us to a Virtual Reading at a Minneapolis theater. A skip hits my heartbeat as I notice, too, a 'private message' from him. To me! Tremulously, I access Freddy's lowercased words.

You're not Peg J. the PJ from corona-not-the-virus high, r u?

I stare into the screen light: hearing Freddy's resonant voice, stagey even offstage. I lean closer. But I remind myself how, post-Cast Party, Freddy had averted his gaze from Ricardo's in the halls. How much that hurt tender-hearted Ricardo, how Freddy outside of their top-secret make-out sessions ignored him. How Freddy ran off to New York without even a phone call to Ricardo.

Like, Ricardo kept saying dazedly to me, none of it happened at all. But it did happen, I tell myself now. And it did matter. To Ricardo, to me; to Freddy, even if he'd deny it. Why do I feel in the magnified silence of my morning—start of yet another lost day in lockdown— that I can make what I type into this tiny Twitter square matter? My hands, again, shake as I start.

> *yes Freddy, it's me, BFF to Ricardo. i may have seemed clueless back then, but i knew all about you and Ms. L. You and Ricardo. Back when you'd act like, in public, Ricardo didn't even exist. Which he doesn't, anymore, BTW.*

I blink at the blunt words I'd speed-typed. My eyelid twitches like a warning. Ricardo never held a grudge against Freddy, even after being dumped. Shakily, I put on my glasses again. I stare down my tiny-lettered 'private message,' daring myself to press SEND.

Wishing I could, first, phone Ricardo, even longer-distance than LA, and ask his advice. Sensing if I read aloud my message, Ricardo would give a phone pause where I could practically hear him roll his eyes. I squint through my drugstore reading glasses at my petty message.

God, how is it that Freddy Fantastick still makes me feel- and act- so small?

This thought comes to me in post-shower early-AM

clarity. I consider simply not replying, picturing Annie on the cloud couch. Her narrowed green-eyed gaze locking mine: a girl who always got what she wanted, back then. I never should have given it to her, my own mute mean-girl nod.

I scroll again to @anniesamson-g. I don't move to 'Follow' Annie, though, as she might expect me to do. Instead, I turn in my squeaky desk chair from the flat brightness of my laptop. A warmer, more alive light shimmers around my drawn living room shades. The swarming gold of today's hidden sunrise. Wish I could tell Ricardo—in Heaven or wherever—that he was no minor character to me. That of all the men I've loved, he is the only one I miss. I turn back to my screen, its light gone dead.

I tap a key; the laptop re-floods with light, its lifeless tone chiming. An elevator going nowhere, the way each day feels, these days. Except, just now, for the sharp pain in my middle-aged heart. What lingering ache does Freddy feel? Isn't the story of him and Ms. L. his to tell or not? Even if there's no audience? I gaze into my re-lit screen. Trying to channel Ricardo—the older and kinder Ricardo I imagine watching—I backspace away my hastily typed lines. What I type instead, slowly, feels right.

Hi Freddy and yes, it's me; BFF to Ricardo. Glad u r still onstage. Hey Freddy, did u know Ms L was last spotted teaching in AZ at Flagstaff Community College? One more fact u ought to know. Ricardo. He moved to LA, found love there, then he lost his life.

I type the last lines the slowest, my heart thumping as if I'm awaiting a stage cue.

Ricardo loved you. & he loved me too. Try to remember him.

Bloody Show

Sarah is four, maybe younger; she is whatever age memory begins, because this is her first. She is trying to tell a lady that her doll is going to have a baby. Her tongue is almost too young to shape the sentence. Her never-cut hair hangs around her face.

Her baby doll is—

That word. Magic, maybe bad word; P- word that Sarah's big cousins know.

Your dollie is—? the lady friend of Mom's prompts, fixing upon Sarah the intent coaxing gaze Sarah longs for from her mother, who is inside making clinky-ice drinks. Barefoot sunlit Sarah and the shaded high heeled lady stand outside on the patio that smells of damp brick and moss. Sarah rubs her foot on a secret patch of moss and squeezes her soft-bodied hard-headed doll.

"She—she's p- p- p-" Sarah stutters, the lady's gaze urging her toward the word Sarah feels she knows, yet it won't come. Won't let her speak it and free herself from its spell.

"The baby becomes you."

In bed, in her 7th month, her husband's words woke her—setting Sarah, setting everything, in motion. If he hadn't said that, would they have made love that afternoon, that way, that late in her long-awaited pregnancy? Would she and the baby have stayed safe? For years, decades, she would wonder.

"What—?" Sarah rolled over, their Birds of Happiness blanket sliding off her bare shoulders. Her belly jutted up. She blinked in winter afternoon light. Her tall deadpan husband stood above her. Home early, coat off, snow still sparkling in his beard. "Baby," she muttered, "'becomes'—?"

"You. Is 'becoming' to you. I was just looking at you..." Like he hadn't done in months. Dark glints in his eyes matched the sparkles in his grayblack beard.

"At me and him," Sarah reminded Paul, caressing her belly. Her son inside stayed motionless. When pregnant women are nervous, she'd read, fetuses fall into anxious stillness.

"Hey Sare," Paul asked. "You OK? You overdosing on CNN?" He set a SweetNGreek bakery bag on his nightstand, a waxy crackle. Then he turned to the mini TV she kept muted. He switched it off.

Bomb flashes vanished into eternally dark Afghanistan sky. Paul settled on their bed. He stretched his big body beside hers the way she'd lately longed for him to do. She rallied her widest grin, shaking back her ripply unbraided hair.

"Hey..." She picked a last ice crystal from Paul's beard. "First snow."

The year's first snow meant for her and Paul, always, first sex. Her first, ever: thirteen years before, when she was 22 and he 39. On the night of a November blizzard as fierce as the one outside. *Tick tick* against their bedroom window. Rain that had shifted to snow was shifting to pure furious ice. Paul was half-smiling at her.

"We'll have to do something to celebrate," she dared to murmur, tugging their wedding blanket around her. Its once-white wool showed stains of wine and chocolate and semen. How long had it been since they'd made love? "C'mere..."

"You sure?" Paul stretched out, resting his heavy arm on Sarah's shoulders, the worn Birds of Happiness blanket. "If my Grandma had knitted that, it would've been the Birds of Unhappiness..."

Sarah rolled her eyes. Paul and his pessimism; his family's supposedly doomed genes. "C'mon. We've got a plan, right? Our bad genes will clobber each other." She switched to her Headline voice. "Manic and Depressive Have a Baby."

"Manic had that plan," Paul grumbled as Sarah mimicked her own manic smile. At least she, unlike Paul, had never reached what he'd call a 'clinical level.' The past months, since his Dad's death, he'd seemed close to that lowest of lows.

"Manic Versus Depressive. And guess what?" Sarah hauled herself to her knees. Her belly hung over her sweatpants waistband. "Manic won." Stifling her unromantic grunt, Sarah straddled her husband's bear-sized body. Her breasts strained her stretchy maternity bra. "Admit it. This is why you're here so early." She breathed the chill bracing taste of winter on his skin. "I mean, if you want."

Their iron heater clanked and hissed. "I want," Paul breathed back, "But—"

"It's about time," Sarah cut in, surprised by her oversized overheated body, suddenly sexed-up the way it had been in her second trimester. When the distance between them had begun building up: when she'd been so sulky and breasty and needy. And he'd been, in the wake of his Dad's death, so distanced and depressed.

Paul shifted his legs; Sarah heard his feet bump her book at the foot of their bed. WHAT TO EXPECT WHEN YOU'RE EXPECTING. The book had explained it all in a passage she'd practically memorized last summer. Some pregnant women experience increased sexual appetite, their vulvas engorged and ultrasensitive.

I'll say, Sarah thought. She rubbed Paul's zipped crotch through her damp-crotched sweatpants. Her belly curved out full and white, marked by her linea nigra.

Paul fingered the darkened line lightly. "Your racing stripe."

"Damn straight."

He traced the line, his fingertip steady. "You sure earned it."

"You too." Sarah pressed his strong hand, flattening it on her belly.

His hands were what she'd first noticed about Supervisor Paul Stratidakis. A tall tense man with big calm hands.

"The baby does become you..." Paul eased his hand from under hers, studying her. Determinedly, Sarah nodded down at him. Because there was nothing like sex to set things right between them. And she needed things to feel right again before their baby was born.

Tick, tick. Ice tapped their window like it might crack the pane, break in. Paul was giving his sure Supervisor nod. So Sarah began rocking on top of him. Their wood sleigh bedframe creaked a slower version of its sex song. Sarah took hold of Paul's shoulders as if he lay on a real sleigh. Paul rocked with her, under her. She held onto him like she was holding on for the ride of her life.

"But is it safe?" Paul made himself ask. Sarah's pregnant weight, plus the cigarette he'd snuck this morning, made Paul breathless. The belly he'd rarely looked at so close loomed before his eyes.

He cleared his smoke-roughened throat. He kept rocking beneath his flushed fierce-eyed wife. Even in the dim room, Sarah's rich brown hair showed the subtle reddish glints he'd always seen, once he'd first noticed them, and her. What was she up to now?

Quiet Sarah McCall, her pale oval face almost plain, until you looked. He planted his hands on Sarah's new curvy hips, holding her steady. For all its weight, her belly seemed a giant bubble. His cock was stiffening. If he thrust up inside her, would the bubble burst?

"Sure it's safe," Sarah insisted, breathless like him. Her face too pink, her olive eyes too bright. "Couples do it all the *time* this late. Besides, the snow; it's a sign." Her and her signs. She fingered Paul's shirt buttons, tickling his chest. "D-don't you think our lives lately have been missing a, the—" She worked the top button free. "—'point'?"

"Think I know what point you mean..." Now she was talking. Paul shifted his legs, his cock getting (it used to be easy for her to get it) hopelessly hard.

How he'd missed this hot anticipatory ache. Sex with Sarah was his sweetest form of oblivion. He half shut his eyes, half surrendering. But as Sarah unbuttoned her way down his chest, the folded paper in his shirt pocket crackled. The memo from his boss that he'd received earlier. His near-failing Performance Review.

Seeming not to notice the crackle, Sarah smoothed open Paul's shirt. She curled her fingers into his chest hair. "Hey," Paul mumbled, "anything inappropriate will do."

'Inappropriate' was their joke word, with all the new rules and Sensitivity Training at the Center. This past pregnant year, they had both grown cautious about vigorous sex. So they'd given each other head and hand jobs: nothing that rose to the level of an Impeachable Offense.

Sarah's warm fingers grazed his nipples. "How's this for 'inappropriate,' Mister?" Clumsily, her belly bumping him, she wriggled out of her sweatpants, releasing her scent.

"Care-ful," Paul warned. She resettled her breathtaking weight on top of him. Sarah was wearing only what she called, with shy pride, her Maternity Bra. She rocked; her belly's lower curve rubbed, through cloth, Paul's balls. Wasn't this—yes—what he'd come home early for?

As she pulled his shirt further open, the stiff paper in his pocket crackled again.

"What's that?" Sarah asked. He pushed her hands gently back.

"Just a note. From—the front office. My—review."

"Oh?" Sarah's voice and body subtly tensed.

The sternly worded memo had greeted him when he got to his office. He'd read and re-read it while smoking a forbidden cigarette for breakfast and listening to Anton Bruckner. His favorite since his Dad's death in June. Nothing like Bruckner's 8th to take you beyond your own puny brooding. Those unearthly French Horns. Listening with eyes shut was like being dead, only conscious. Black bliss.

As Paul made his afternoon Rounds, tromping from the Severely's residence hall to Moderately's, the year's first snow chilled his bald spot. At least he hadn't been fired outright. Maybe the near-failing review was good, was a way out. To some other job, something more like what he'd done before his promotion. But could they afford a baby on that salary?

On impulse, Paul locked up his Center Director office illicitly early. One thing he'd learned in years of managing on-and-off depressions: when a hopeful mood hit, as one did with the snowflakes, he damn well had to act on it.

So he'd stopped at SweetNGreek. They would find, as Sarah used to say, something SweetNDirty to do—like old times. Then he'd show her the memo.

"We can talk about it later," Paul told Sarah now. "It's nothing so bad..."

Sarah was nodding slowly as if she already guessed it was something so bad. But, Paul told himself, they'd talk it all out after sex. She'd see, Paul vowed as he unbuttoned his own last buttons, why he had to do it, consider something new. Or maybe something old. Even if it meant less money.

And if she said no way? Paul wondered as Sarah opened his shirt all the way. She was balanced on top of him, waiting. His hard-on waited too.

"Hey." Sarah bent low so her loose hair brushed his bared chest. "I got something to show you..." Reaching up with both hands, matter-of-fact as a stripper, Sarah stretched her bra, its nursing slits. Her breasts burst out, swollen in their mesh of blue veins.

She breathed in as if modeling the lingerie she used to order by mail. "Is it 'too much', this bra, or does it 'work'?"

Her breasts bounced with her words, her nipples milky wet.

Below her, Paul answered emphatically, like a husky-voiced boy: *"Both."*

Sarah dared a belly-quaking laugh, her bobbing breasts leaky. What had WHAT TO EXPECT promised in that sole sexy passage? Some pregnant women experience or-gasms or multiple orgasms accompanied by streams of milk spurting from their breasts?

"Christ, Sare." He was stiffening his long body under her, still hesitating. "You're not gonna faint or anything are you? Maybe we shouldn't, if you're too, too..."

"Big?" she filled in, scooting back, reaching down. "Beyond Big?"

"Stu-pen-dous," Paul said, drawing the word out as she unzipped him. Sarah smiled. That word seemed to her the final sign. Back on the May night when she'd woken Paul to tell him the EPT Home Pregnancy test she'd taken had come out a big red Yes, groggy ambiva-lent Paul had somehow found the perfect word. *If that's true, that's stupendous.*

"You said it." Sarah resettled over his unzipped crotch. "I'm fine, really. I *am* stupendous..."

She hunched lower. He pressed the small of her back, easing her to him. His bristly beard scratched her freed breasts. She gasped and squeezed shut her eyes.

The deeply familiar yet startling feel of Paul's tongue. He licked one nipple, milky fluid the book called colostrum. Flavorless when she'd snuck a taste herself.

Paul smacked his lips behind his beard. Sarah met Paul's black glinting gaze. Like they were Supervisor and worker again, beginning an illicit-feeling affair.

"As long as it's—really OK." Paul's hard-on prodded, through cotton, her wet vagina. "Christ, I don't know anything. What's that damn book say?"

"Fuck the book." She stretched back her leg and kicked. WHAT TO EXPECT thudded the floor. Paul gazed up at Sarah as if he had, in fact, no idea what to expect from her next.

Sarah freed Paul's hard-on and straightened with it, her breasts and belly jutting out regally above him. She murmured under the *tick tick* of snow turned to ice. "It's

OK, Saint Paul! Let's just, y'know, go..."

"Go," Paul echoed, rocking harder beneath her, slip-sliding his way in. Her whole warm weight rocked hard too, like she was about to topple.

"Go," Sarah crooned, lost in her own rhythm, her face above him heedlessly happy. Her pale skin glowed in the room's chill half dark. Paul's mouth held the milky oyster taste from her breasts, still alive on his tongue.

He was thrusting up: careful, careful. How long had it been, what with the baby and his own dark moods? Paul moaned with Sarah. He was re-gripping her smooth curvy hips, struggling to hold her steady, his glowing bubble of a wife.

Everything silenced now, in the deepest silence and flesh folds of her. In the beautiful hidden room, where his new son was cocooned. My son, Paul reminded himself as he eased deeper. *Mine, mine.*

Sarah's soft mouth half-opened and her muddy green eyes half-closed. Up and down, but gently. Paul slid his hands to the roundness of Sarah's ass.

"Go, go," Sarah was urging again. So Paul thrust harder again, hardest yet, the sleigh bed shaking. Sarah's belly swelled in his sight, huge with his son.

"Go, yes," Sarah keened, rocking along with his next sure thrusts. Her skin shifting to its deepest pink. Beautiful pink balloon, carrying him away, crying out.

Paul's cock swelled; he burst. When he blinked open his eyes, gasping from his thumping come, Sarah's own gasps were fading. Her face above him shone with a feverish flush. She was blinking too: not down at him but at her bulging brown-striped belly.

Aftershock, Paul thought, gazing at Sarah's stilled dazed face. Like she'd just been through an earthquake only she was the earth.

"GodPaul," she mumbled, one word. "Something's happening..."

Movement, Paul was startled to see. He kept his hands on Sarah's hips, holding on. A protrusion—a heel, a hip?—moved like a shark's fin under the pale stretched skin of her belly. Sarah was holding her belly with both hands. She locked her gaze with his.

What the fuck have we done?

Something was tightening inside Sarah's belly, her groin. Like menstrual cramps only bigger. Plus her crotch was still pulsing from her come. Plus the baby was stirring in there, waking, doing the Watusi.

"What's wrong, what is it, Sare?"

"It's OK; I'll be OK—"

Sarah braced her hands on her belly, straining to contain it all. She wobbled on top of Paul, rolled off him in slow motion. Panting, she lay flat on her back beside him.

Her belly a mountain he'd climbed, she thought dazedly. But of course, he hadn't. He hadn't climbed on her. She'd been on top the whole time, her solid belly bobbing between them.

"Does it hurt, was I too rough? Did I hurt you? Christ, did I?"

"It's, it's not that; it can't be. It's—you know what? I've heard, I've read that sometimes coming, the mother 'coming,' it triggers contractions. Not birth contractions but *like* birth contractions." Sarah faced the ceiling, hearing herself babble. "And those come-contractions make the baby *move* is all, I think is all. I'm all stirred up, so the baby gets stirred up too. It's just he's been so still all day. It's just it's been so long for us, it feels so, I feel so—funny." She couldn't stop talking, trying to convince herself. "Anyhow, we sure woke him up. Woke me up too, Saint Paul. Felt like I was *coming* for two. Plus, God, I'm *starved*..."

On top of everything (the cramplike post-sex-contractions fading; the familiar post-sex throb in her crotch; the baby clenching again into launchpad stillness) Sarah's stomach rumbled.

"You sure, Sare? That's all you're feeling—him moving?" Paul reached with his long arm for the bakery bag.

"I'm not sure of *any*-thing lately," Sarah mumbled, blinking.

Paul unrolled the waxpaper bag, releasing the super-sweet supergreasy aroma.

"My mouth's watering for two," Sarah announced, reaching.

"Women and children first." Paul tilted the honey-steeped bag her way. She plunged her hand in and seized two sticky pastry diamonds. Weighted with dates and nuts, slick with honeyed grease. Luxuriantly slow, she bit her baklava. Paper-thin layers of crust, then the rich inner mix of date paste plus chopped nuts plus achingly sweet honey.

Sarah wiped her mouth. The crampy sensation had subsided. "Doesn't your body just feel so—happy?"

"All over," Paul allowed, chewing. Sarah nodded, reassured, biting her second diamond. Sinking into a mini food trance. But Paul swallowed and cleared his throat, a professor introducing a difficult new topic. "Listen, Sare; this Review."

Sarah nodded, her mouth bulging with food.

"It's not so good. But that could be—ultimately—for the good..." Paul wiped his fingers and reached in the pocket of his unbuttoned shirt. He held out the unfolded paper.

Sarah was tugging her bra back on. "What now?" She bit another baklava diamond half. Paul leaned close so they read it together.

The complaints that Paul had 'fallen behind;' the list of paperwork deadlines and committee meetings missed; the warning that he would now be considered on Probation.

"They could've just fired me," Paul muttered over Sarah's shoulder, "So in a way, it's better than expected. But maybe what I need, really, is a change..."

Tick Tick like a timebomb outside: the ice storm kept coming down. Paul felt Sarah beside him sit heavily silent, chewing.

"Let's face it. What I think is—Being kicked up the ladder into Administration hasn't worked for me." Paul drew a husbandly high-dive breath; Sarah stuffed another diamond into her mouth, whole. "I was happier as lowly Supervisor. Working with the Severely kids themselves, instead of managing the 'Caregivers' and processing their paperwork. All the Incident Reports, the Co-worker Complaints. Hell, maybe I ought to look for something new—"

"Now?" Sarah managed, though it sounded like Ow.

She was chewing too fast, pastry flakes scattering onto her bared belly. As she wiped her gleamingly greased chin, she coughed. Paul stared. Her face deepened its pink; her eyes went watery. Christ, was she choking?

Paul clapped his hand on her bare back. Slap slap: both hard.

Sarah jerked away, glaring at him. Swallowing and gasping, wrist-wiping her chin. "God Paul—careful of the baby! And shit," she added with an attempt at a lighter tone, "did you have to wait till my mouth was full?"

She pressed her belly with both hands like it might be hurting again.

He heaved a contrite confused sigh. "Christ, Sare, I'm sorry. But I can't keep things from you. I—I'm thrown by this review too. It couldn't come at a worse time. And I know quitting right now makes no sense. Look, if we can just talk this out..."

"I can't even *think*," Sarah mumbled, rolling off the bed. Standing up naked except for her bra, she opened her arms as if in dismay. "God, look at me." She displayed it to him and to God: her voluptuous impossibly swollen body, dotted with flakey sticky crumbs. "I need to get clean. Then we can talk. After I think over this whole thing..."

She looked again at her body, as if it *was* the Whole Thing. And it was, for her.

"'You're dirty-sweet and you're my girl,'" Paul told her, low-voiced, echoing the old rock song he'd long ago declared was hers.

She laughed with him, her laugh still tense. "Just let me get cleaned up...." She padded barefoot and naked toward their bathroom, moving a little stiff-legged. Did something still feel not-right inside? Cramps, again? He watched her bare rounded ass, each slow step.

Christ, Paul exhaled as the bathroom door shut. She'd be the death of him yet.

Submerged in warm-not-hot water, her belly an island, Sarah shut her eyes. She'd fall asleep in the tub, if she weren't so keyed up. She swallowed hard, trying to gauge the state of her unsettled insides. So riled up after the shock and pleasure of sex; then so stilled. And now? That odd inner pressure rising again, like pre-menstrual cramps.

One day at the Center, before she and Paul had even

spoken, she overheard one of the female staffers praise his diaper-changing finesse. He'd make, the woman told Supervisor Stratidakis, a great Dad.

Not me, Paul had replied flatly. I'm too busy taking care of all o' you...

A sign, Sarah later believed. After she and Paul were married, she was relieved in a way to realize Paul meant it: he felt that he—with his inherited tendency to Depression—should not have kids. He believed Sarah's infertility specialist. He believed there was little chance of a miracle birth when she stopped using her diaphragm, when they decided against infertility treatments.

You were meant to be, Sarah thought in the tub. *I was meant to have you. To have and to hold—*

Her hand circled her taut belly, lightly massaging it. With this baby so close at last, Sarah couldn't upset everything by fighting with Paul. But Paul's mood shift, his impulsive desire to change jobs: were these positive signs or, somehow, further symptoms? If he left his job, would he find another? If not, would he sink into real depression, past some point of no return? Paul wasn't thinking clearly, wasn't thinking of—it still wasn't real to him—the baby.

Sarah slowed her hand, her circles. Despite her manic mind whirring away, her post-sex body was relaxing in the bathwater. Sarah pressed her back into the curve of the tub. She let her underwater thighs loll apart.

It rose from between her thighs: first cloudy white curls of Paul's semen. Then—Sarah felt her gut jump—a tint of red.

She stared dumbly through her stuck-up knees. Paralyzed, thinking at once: I'm bleeding; I can't be bleeding. Sarah hauled her body up, stirring a wave that sloshed the bathroom tiles. She gripped the slick sides of the tub, wobbling upright, climbing out, sloshing yet more water. A flood unleashed. Watery red streaking her inner thighs. Sarah lurched toward the closed bathroom door.

It's post-sex spotting. No, it's the first stage of Labor. My God, it's my Bloody Show. Sarah wrestled the wet doorknob, shouldered open the door. God, she was nothing but a big leaking sack of flesh.

Bloody Show, Early Labor, Hard Labor, Transition, Delivery.

The Stages of Birth ticked through her head in the rush of what happened next: Sarah slipping on her red-wet barefoot steps. Sarah freezing in her big-wet naked body, her legs streaked with blood.

But trickles of water and blood, not a stream. Premature labor maybe, but not—please God, not—Premature Rupture of Membrane?

So Sarah was thinking, stumbling through the darkened bedroom. She tripped on WHAT TO EXPECT. Then she kicked the damned book far under the bed.

Sarah staggered around the bed. Paul lay stretched out, unforgivably snoring. Panting, Sarah gripped the slippery phone. *Bloody Show Early Labor Hard Labor Transition Delivery.* She didn't need the damn book. She had memorized too the signs: how Bloody Show is light at first, a mere trace of blood signaling the start of Labor.

"Is it bright red?" Sarah's maddeningly placid ob-gyn Dr. Claire Lutz asked when she answered her pager, her question posed with a casual lilt.

"It's *red*-red," Sarah all but shouted.

Paul sat abruptly. He snapped on the lamp. In the sudden circle of light, he faced shivering bloody-legged Sarah like she was part of a nightmare he was already having.

"—well, see, Dr. Lutz, we were, like everyone does and nothing like this happens to them, we were having sex."

Sarah's voice shook as hard as her hands.

Paul pulled himself up. He draped over her shoulders the Birds of Happiness.

"—Sarah?" Dr. Lutz asked coolly, "Take some deep breaths. Is the bright red blood 'gushing' out or are you more—Sarah, are you there?—'spotting'?"

"It's—well actually there's all this water mixed in and I —I'm not sure what-all it's doing, my blood. But I do feel these, sort of, cramps..."

"Hate to say so in this weather, Sarah," Dr. Lutz's professionally soothing voice replied. A hospital elevator chimed in the background. "But you and your husband had best get down to the ER, just to check you out. Sarah? Sarah?"

"You were right, you bastard, you're always right," Sarah told Paul, shoving the still-talking phone at him. He took it; he pulled Sarah against his chest. She leaned on him, soaking his unbuttoned shirt. He spoke to the Doctor, his bearded chin bumping her head: *Yes* and *I understand* and *We will.*

"Screwing this kid up, but good, and he's not even outa the womb!" Sarah pushed away from Paul, dropping the chocolate-and-wine-and-semen-and-baklava-and-blood-stained Birds of Happiness. "You were right, Paul, we can't do this! How'd we ever think we could do this?"

She was rummaging in the mass of sheets for her sweatpants. Paul was climbing into his pants and snatching up his car keys. The car, he was saying. He'd start the engine while she dressed, warming it up; he'd come right back to get her. He was hugging her again, too fast. Then he was gone too long. She kept trying to suck in her sobs, pull on her inside-out clothes. Screwed up; she'd screwed up everything royally.

Would the baby come too early because she'd so impulsively pushed for sex?

RUTTING COUPLE LOSES BABY TO LUST.

Sarah rampaged through their closet, trying to shut up the manic tabloid-headline voice in her mind, pulling on a flimsy coat. Her fall coat; wrong fucking coat. Paul was thumping back up the stairs. He was leading Sarah through the living room. They thudded down the steep narrow stairs together, Sarah clutching her clunky Survival Bag.

She'd packed it over a year ago during a Hurricane Alert, based on TV News instructions: batteries, transistor radio, bottled water, underwear, Swiss army knife. All wrong for now but all she had at the ready. Metal clanked inside the bulging canvas satchel.

Sarah inched onto their un-shoveled stoop, her sneakers soaking up slush. The bath-dampened ends of her hair went stiff, instantly iced. Sarah and Paul bent together into the wind, needles of ice stinging Sarah's face. Tears welled in her eyes, too hot to freeze.

Their trusty Toyota was steaming, stewing in frost-whitened clouds of its own exhaust. It looked seriously stuck, the snow drifted high against their driveway fence.

Paul got out in front of the car, to push. Sarah wedged her belly behind the wheel, the car in Reverse. She pumped the gas, futilely. Paul rocked the car with his pushes. Had cramping started again? Was she too numb from cold and fear to feel it? Was Labor starting, ready or not?

Not if I can help it, Sarah promised the baby, clenching her thighs together under her coat. *To have and to hold; to hold, to hold.*

Paul shoved himself against the front bumper, his coat blowing open. Sarah felt him strain and fail to force the car from the drifted snow. Inside the car, she clutched the wheel. She should've packed a real overnight bag. She and Paul should've called 911.

Everything they should've done, they hadn't. Everything they shouldn't have, they had.

What the hell was happening in there? To her, to the baby?

Paul released the bumper he could barely feel through his gloves. Inside the car, Sarah stopped revving the engine. Everything—even Paul's panicky pulsebeat—seemed to stop.

The whole zany scene in which he'd felt like an inept Ricky Ricardo bumbling his attempt to get his wife to the hospital: hugely genuinely pregnant Lucille Ball with her red-even-in-black-and-white hair and her eyes ping-ponged like she felt both too happy and too scared for her face to hold it all. Paul could make out Sarah peering through the icy windshield with that same helpless hapless pop-eyed stare.

Shit, she was falling apart on him. Shit, he'd have to be the sane one.

Paul looked from Sarah to the snow-covered bumper. He brushed aside fresh snow, feeling his brain shift into his old Floor Supervisor mode, like when he'd race into a fight or a meltdown in the Severely ward. His mind and body suddenly charged up, on alert.

"We're gonna get *outa* here," Paul shouted toward Sarah, her head bowed now like she was praying or hiding. "I'm gonna get us out—"

Because I've goddamn got to, Paul with his lips clamped against the wind told himself.

What on earth was happening out there?

Sarah, in the vibrating driver's seat, hunched lower

with a cramp. 4:42 by the glowing numbers of the car clock. Maybe 20 minutes from the last distinct cramp as she'd dressed. A heated tightened sensation like PMS, only bigger. Another one: a whole-body menstrual cramp.

"But I can still talk," Sarah gasped, each word a puff of frozen breath as the car heater labored to warm her up. They won't declare you officially in Labor, she'd heard, till the cramps are so bad you can't talk.

"Sorry sorry," Sarah whispered, her cramp subsiding. The baby stayed clenched into his own stillness just like babies right before birth are supposed to do. *But it's too soon, you've got to hold on*, Sarah told her son, drooping forward. The cramp lessened.

She rested her forehead on the wheel, startled at the horn's half honk. Fumbling in her mittens, Sarah hit the windshield wiper. The latest layer of icy flakes swept away.

Do what he says, Sarah told herself. Dizzily, as the wipers pulsed together, Sarah swept her eyes to Paul. He locked her gaze like a traffic cop. You staked your life on such urgent commanding glances between strangers.

"Now—" Paul hollered. He pointed through the windshield toward the car's gas pedal. Sarah floored it, in REVERSE.

Later, years later, they'd both look back on that moment, the height-of-hopeless moment. Just before Paul finally—in a burst of strength neither of them thought he had in him—freed the car. This, they only realized later, was also the moment things shifted between them.

Because (Paul told Sarah in Neonatal ICU, as they sat vigil beside their preemie son in his glass cage) because seeing the pure panic in her eyes through the windshield made Paul see, too, that he had to pull himself together. Because Sarah was—the best medicine, they joked; married medicine—falling apart.

So Paul had to, and did, find the strength to push that car free. The strength, later, to begin a preliminary job search and preliminary parenthood all at once, in the first weeks with their fragile yet fierce-eyed son finally home.

The pay was lower in the hands-on job Paul later took at a Group Home; they struggled at first with the special care their Preemie son needed. As a family they watched 9-11 unfold as their toddler son, already catching up with other babies, careened about the apartment. After Sarah's cancer scare and Paul's occasional depressive bouts when their son was in high school, all crises had seemed to be behind them. Until their son arrived home from amidst his final year at college to hunker down with his parents in the long winter of 2020, in shared quarantine. Paul had high risk factors, Sarah as a cancer survivor did too. But they were together, the three of them. They would survive the winter, Sarah and Paul knew without saying so. All of that was long-distant from, and unimaginable within, the birth-night moment that seemed to both of them to set them back on track. Moving forward—or really, backward.

Paul outside gave a final heave; Sarah inside felt the engine lurch and the car give way. No stopping now. Suddenly it was, she was, moving: backwards with a screech.

The car rocked violently as if in a crash; ice crunched. Sarah kept pressing the gas as the car lurched further back. *Crack crack*; icy snow breaking at last. She rammed the brake: the car skidding, her heart pumping in that midair sensation as tires lost their grip.

Then it all stopped, halted with a quake.

"You OK?" Paul shouted in his big booming Supervisor voice.

She unrolled the window. Tall Paul, his beard sparkling, leaned down to her. Before she could answer —*No, you nut, I'm not OK*—Paul popped open the door.

He nudged her as if to wake her. Sarah managed with a last-gasp grunt to heave herself onto the colder passenger seat. Her Hurricane Survival satchel fell: a battery-and-can clatter on the car floor. Sarah rested her feet atop the bag: one thing it was good for.

A flurry of snow was sweeping into the opened door, flecking Sarah's cheek. Bracing stings of ice. Then the driver's door slammed.

"This—can't happen now—" Sarah shook her head, her tangled damp hair brushing her face, chill slaps. *It can, it can.* Another cramp coiled round her lower body.

"You all set?" Paul jerked the car into gear, his gaze brighter and sharper than it had been in ages. His face looked ruddy, ready for anything. More ready, in the end, than her. "All clear on your side, Sare?"

Sarah twisted her head, glimpsing only a whirl of white. Who knew what-all was out there? She almost couldn't speak, but she managed two words. "Just go."

WHEN YOU WATCH ME

Her first time, on camera.

Evvy at 17: flushed and sunburnt in her drenched bra and panties, riding her teacher in his twilight-cooled pool. She straddled his massive slippery shoulders. She clenched his neck between her thighs, hiding the shakes she was used to in her hands but not her whole body. Small-breasted long-legged virgin body she was just beginning to like, at least onstage. Evvy breathed chlorine and grapefruit, squinting in pool lights fuzzy bright like spotlights. Bear was slow-circling her in the low end; he was—Evvy sensed even before the first shot—displaying her. How, she would wonder for years, did she lose it in a flashbulb flash?

In August,1981; in Tempe, Arizona; in the eye of a Nikon.

"One time I rode my Dad like this," Evvy proclaimed shakily from Bear's shoulders as he halted his slow-mo. spin. "Fourth of July parade, when I was four." Her new stage-sized voice carried across his water, clear and quavery.

Loud enough, maybe, for the woman hiding on the patio to hear.

"Your first performance, then?" Barry Orr asked beneath her.

Professor Bear, Evvy called him like Katherine Hepburn in LITTLE WOMEN. Favorite film of the Shy Girl self Evvy Moore aimed to leave, spectacularly, behind.

"Yeah, my debut." She bent forward on Bear's shoulders, her long wet hair hanging down. Her breasts strained her junior-size bra. At last, she held Bear's bald head where she'd wanted it all summer: pressed to her heart. So close she sensed through his skull the heat and thrum of his (she felt sure) brilliant brain. "Up there on Dad's shoulders I was—" Evvy squeezed Bear's neck, savoring the sandpaper burn of his beard bristle on her inner thighs. "Huge."

Bear nodded against her heart like he knew that feeling. Like he nodded in Filmmaking 101 when she spoke. "So you enjoy it, Evvy? Up there?"

"I did; I do," she murmured back as Bear slow-spun her once more. That same heady parade sense of gliding along as if on stilts, impossibly tall. Same sense, too, of performing. Not for a 4th of July crowd on a leafy street. But for the hidden wife, hidden Izza, Evvy could feel stalking within the patio's potted jungle, watching. The Izza who had dared her to strip; who had supposedly, while Evvy swam laps, left.

"How about coming down?" Professor Bear asked, as casually commanding as Izza. "And having, since it's our last night, that first-ever drink? A whole glass?"

"You know I can't," Evvy protested, her one wine sip still flavoring her mouth. "I-I've told you—wine or even coffee is too strong for my system..." She hunched, thrusting before his eyes her shaky hand. "See? I'm way too wired already."

"Like Emily Dickinson." Barry Orr halted his underwater steps. "You only need to breathe to get high. You're so supremely—responsive."

She pulled back her hand. And wondered: would I, will I be? With him, tonight? She was twisting round on Bear's big slick shoulders. Graceful-for-once offstage, she was sliding down his broad chest and sandbag gut, splashing in.

How did it happen? Evvy Moore would try to explain for years, privately. To her usually one-time lovers, to her longtime therapist. I'm not sure I can say, she'd always start by saying. How later that night she lost it—her virginity—on camera. Sometimes, shakily, only in private, she'd show the photos.

Decades-old black and white pool shots. Evvy in the low end of the pool with a big bald man, his broad back to the camera. Yes, that's really me, at 17. My Sweet Look of Wonder, I call it. Not that I meant to have something so private filmed. It happened gradually, everything that led up to that night. But it all happened; I let it happen.

And the photos, she sensed even before she decided how she'd use them, were valuable. Because one thing, even in the jaded 2000s and beyond, retained its primal power. A girl's, anyone's (how had it happened; how had she let it) one and only first.

Evvy Moore arrived in the classroom half an hour early. She had signed up for this summer class at Arizona State University since she couldn't wait till fall to begin her film and acting studies. She'd graduated high school a year early, a month before. The empty ASU classroom reverberated with the building's central air conditioning. After the white glare of sun outside, Evvy blinked in the darkened humming room. She made herself sit up straight, not slouch like she'd done all through high school. Though she was still a too-tall girl in a too-small desk. Until Barry Orr entered with her dad's long strides.

He halted in front of her desk—fiercely bald, barrel-chested, his stern mustached face shadowed in the unlit classroom. Big blunt features; Bear's eyes sunken under his formidable forehead. His dark brows and mustache thick as fur. Fresh-looking scabs marked his jowly cheeks. Drawing a breath, Evvy tasted Barry Orr's frank salty sweat.

Why was he towering above her? Low-voiced, he said straight to her, "I'm called Bear."

She gripped the desktop, a shield over her tightly crossed thighs. "I'm Evvy."

He gave a brisk maybe dismissive nod. Theater majors in Ray Bans were filing in around him. Laid-back jocks sizing up too-pale too-intense Barry Orr in his odd collarless shirt. Bear flicked on lights, motioning them to hurry. "We've much to do," he pronounced with his clipped slightly formal accent. Britain? Boston?

Too pale for Phoenix, like her. Too big for his desk, like her. Bear didn't sit behind that teacher desk but leaned on it. Scanning tan bland classroom faces. His age maybe late 30s; his bald football-helmet head glazed as if from thinking too hard.

A clap like a gunshot. Startling them all, Barry Orr rubbed his hands together. He flashed a knife-bright grin. A wizard ready to conjure spells. "'Play,'" he told them. "The most important thing about filmmaking—about any art, boys and girls—is to maintain a playful attitude toward your material."

He bent, whipped a Nikon camera from his briefcase. He stepped toward them all, shooting. Whirs and clicks and everyone giggling self-consciously, sliding each other Is-he-nuts glances. Evvy stared straight into his

FLASH as he centered on her. He pivoted—his movements light, for a heavy man—to shoot the henna-haired Theater Major who'd jumped up, gyrating her flat tanned midriff.

"Need a belly to belly-dance," Bear murmured as if to himself. He backed away for a long shot, ignoring the class's uncertain titters. "I shot bona fide belly dancers, when I hitchhiked round Greece, reciting Byron for my meals…"

Evvy straightened, finding her old clear Speech Team voice. "'I had a dream that was not all a dream.'"

"Perfect." Bear lowered his camera. He nodded toward Evvy, a tip of a hat. "Perfect definition—courtesy of Lord Byron, circa 1786—for Film."

Evvy flushed with her mini triumph. The belly dancer slunk back in her seat. Evvy felt a familiar shift in the classroom air against her own Good Girl straight-A self. Turning, Bear attacked the blackboard. He chopped with smaller and smaller chalk the names of the filmmakers they'd study: Godard, Truffaut, Altman, Scorsese, Fellini. Dotting the 'i' finished off his chalk.

He tossed the spent chip over his shoulder. It landed by her foot. Evvy crossed and re-crossed her legs, her knees bumping her desktop. Was she only imagining that Barry Orr of the piercing gaze kept glancing at her long sunlit legs? The first part of her body Bear was to notice; to discover for her.

"Often using no script," he was winding up, shutting a glossy book of Godard stills. "He wanted, he said, to see. To create a more—intimate cinema."

Barry Orr flicked off lights, yanked down window shades. He brushed by Evvy's desk, her blank notebook page. But I've been listening so hard, she wanted to tell this breezily imperious man. In block letters, she printed, INTIMATE CINEMA.

"Note how Godard played with those possibilities,

virtually inventing the Jump Cut—" Bear flipped on a projector. Evvy penned in the dark the film title, the one other word she recorded on that day's pristine page: BREATHLESS.

Which she was, all through the first weeks. Gobbling up Bear's buffets of film clips—NASHVILLE, SCENES FROM A MARRIAGE, SEVEN SAMURI, TAXI DRIVER—then staggering out into sun like a drunk. Or struggling through her first Cut on Action exercises. Or hovering in the back of the ASU Dark Room for Bear's Editing Demo, not wanting him to notice how she stared at his strong hairy lit-up hands.

Would-be wizard, she told herself. Pretentious professor. Had he noticed her?

In the Girl's Room, everyone speculated about Barry Orr, especially when he ended the second week of class by inviting all his students to a Nouveau Westerns night at the Valley Art Theater, followed by a pool party at his and his wife's condo.

"He gives me the creeps," a pert blonde Acting Major declared. "He's such a cold fish!" No he's not, Evvy wanted to interrupt as she brushed her dark hair extra hard. He's the opposite; can't you see? "I mean," the blonde continued, 'o'-ing and glossing her lips. "he picks at those scratches on his face and watches those gloomy doomy clips like he's about to jump up and start humping the screen." The others giggled derisively. Evvy splashed her face to hide her flush. "I heard Bear's wife's foreign too," the blonde finished off, her lips agleam. "A real hot tamale; maybe a Lezbo. Heard she and Bear got in trouble at his last college gig 'cause of some photos Mrs. Bear took of Bear's girl students in, like, the nude."

"Hey, I'm up for it," Chrissy of the belly dance announced, adjusting her falling-off halter top. "C'mon, big bad Bear turns you guys on," she told the half dozen Theater majors huddled by the bathroom's one mirror. "With Barry Orr teaching, there isn't a dry seat in the house."

Evvy joined in the rowdy laugh, wondering if they'd all felt what she'd felt. That extra moisture between her crossed thighs. Especially when Barry Orr looked at her legs. There was, she reminded herself as the laugh died, nothing special about her tentative attraction to Bear. No reason to believe, with girls like Chrissy 'up for it', that he'd ever notice shy virgin Evvy.

Besides, Barry Orr might leave anytime for LA. This he kept mentioning in class, his future Feature Film deal. Everyone knew Phoenix was just his pit-stop. Everyone felt the impatience underlying his brusque student film critiques.

What a shock it was when Evvy's turn came. The rest of the class began by complaining her video short—a dreamy multi-angled study of her BFF Ramon in a deserted midnight pool languidly swimming laps—was too slow, too stylized. But Barry Orr stood up.

He stood up for Evvy, stopped class, paced the Discussion Circle of desks. Had we seen the same film? Yes; it was stylized, but he insisted they'd missed its—Evvy printed on her notebook page—meticulous intensity.

As class ended, as everyone filed around Evvy's spotlit desk, Barry Orr bent to give her his written critique. She pointed to one exuberant scrawl, asked in whisper what it said. He told her it spelled 'G-o-o-d.' "My apologies, but I don't often write that word. When I do—" Bear straightened to his full height. "—I'm excited."

Evvy was still high on that when she stepped hand in hand with Ramon B. onto the Orr's sunset patio, enclosed by Isabella Orr's potted trees. Orange and mango and chlorine scented the charged-up air. The Theater Majors were all asking each other, What's the name of your game? Everyone was supposed to answer in one word. Evvy—still afloat in nouveau—Westerns, MCCABE AND MRS. MILLER—hesitated.

Barry Orr answered for her with a glance like a wink. "'Trance.'"

Name of my game too, he murmured as he slipped inside to fetch his wife. Both Orrs stood in the patio shadows watching students swim and dance to genuine scratchy Jimi Hendrix records. Bear loomed huge beside his wife; Izza Orr so short Evvy wondered how their bodies fit together. Her face was shadowed by her hair.

Ramon and Evvy swam in tandem. He was her Pretend Boyfriend. They'd play-dated in high school for years, protecting Ramon from Fag rumors and each other from outcast status. Evvy followed the deeply brown sheen of Ramon's shoulders, matching her strokes and kicks with his. They bobbed to a stop, panting, clutching the deep end edge. Evvy leaned to Ramon's ear like she did at Tempe bars they'd timidly visited, she and Ramon eying the same brooding boys. "You or me?" she asked Ramon in a wet-lipped whisper. "Who is Orr watching so hard?"

With his new sure side-glance, Ramon whispered back, his retro-Afro sparkling: "You, Evvy; Mr. and Mrs. Orr; both yours." She shook her head no, her own wet hair throwing off starlets of water. But she knew Ramon's words marked a turning point for her. A new her.

Isabella—Izza—Orr. The one who shot the photos. The one who wound up, years later, mailing Evvy the shots. Deciding, in 1999, to try to make trouble for her then-ex husband. Evvy's ex-mentor. Izza had enclosed a clipping from a smalltown paper in Mississippi. Photographer Barry Orr appointed Professor in the Art Dept. of an obscure Bible Belt college. *Why not YOU*, Izza scrawled in lipstick-red magic marker, *play game on HIM? Why not you tell, on him, your story?* Izza had mailed the photos to Evvy at Boston University where Evvy held a Graduate Film School fellowship. These were the photos Evvy had begged for but never seen, except—imagined over and over—in her head. These black and white stills Evvy found herself studying at dawn after sleepless all-nighters in the film lab.

Her favorite time of day, holy 4AM. The hour, with its several shades of silence, when her best ideas hit. The pearly not-yet-polluted New England sun lit her narrow dorm room. Bare as a nun's cell, she was there so seldom and always alone. One October dawn, Evvy contemplated her Bear photos, deciding—as feverish peach enflamed the sooty windowpane frost—how she would use them.

As with all her boldest thoughts, Evvy had two feelings at once: No, I could never do that. And: yes, that's exactly what I'll do.

The third week of class, Bear asked Evvy out. Or no; not him. His wife.

Izza slipped clicking into class, her face armored in sunglasses and a gash of lipstick. She pulled Evvy aside.

Her red mouth told Evvy she must come see JULES ET JIM at the Valley Art on Sunday. Evvy stammered out a yes. She asked herself as Isabella swept off with her husband: Do we have—the Orrs and me—a date?

Never before she'd met 6-foot-plus Barry Orr had 5 foot 10 Evvy dared to wear real heels. Striding up glittery white sidewalk toward the Valley Art marquee on Sunday, she clicked in too, in new spike sandals. A colt, but a thoroughbred. Chestnut coat shining, legs strong, stance nervy and proud. Evvy caught sight of Bear's head, agleam in late sun.

She pulled a wobbly stop, facing him alone at the Valley Art Doors. He kissed her on the cheek. Then told her—lightly, like a movie line—"You can't look at a man with eyes like that and not expect to be kissed."

"'Eyes like that'?"

Barry Orr shrugged. "Actress eyes. Extra expressive. Not so much big as—bright. What I look for when I first see student faces. That extra light."

Evvy flushed in the marquee shade, studying the naked shape of Bear's head. His skull bones and veins showed. His mustache and dense shaven beard bristle glittered with sweat. One furry eyebrow was bisected by a white scar.

Close up, his green eyes held pinpoint pupils. Maybe he was, as Ramon had guessed after the pool party, on drugs.

"—first saw that light in the eyes of my first nanny. *Mon pere,* of Quebec, found one son inconvenient *in extremis* and turned me over—in more ways than he knew—to my French nanny. Then, eventually, disowned me..."

"Till I come a-long." Izza Orr materialized beside Bear in a lavish mix of scents. Cigarettes, citrus, jojoba oil. "Till I 'own' you." Izza's 'you' sounded like 'joo' with her Spanish accent. She wrapped Bear's arm in hers. Her black hair gleamed like licorice. Her white summer dress outlined her firm buxom body.

Bear joined Izza's laugh a beat late; Evvy rallied a smile. Was Isabella rich? she found her actress-eyed self wondering. Or did she 'own' Bear in other ways?

"I hear much about... Evvy." Izza held out her hand, red-nailed and short-nailed. Her tawny brown skin so smooth Evvy shook her hand slowly, not wanting to let go.

She could stand forever in this slanted sun, sandwiched between big sweaty Bear and his sly silky skinned wife.

Inside the fusty and buttery smelling Valley Art, Bear led Evvy and Izza to the front row. For maximum legroom and maximum impact. Izza Orr pushed Evvy in the seat between them. Izza held an invisible cigarette. Bear watched the screen, his forehead blue-white like a space helmet. His legs sprawled before him. He sank in his seat, an astronaut pitched back by the thunderous force of take-off.

In the tense end scenes, Bear picked at his unhealed scabs. Izza caught Evvy's eyes sliding to him. *Love scars,* she murmured. Had she made them herself?

Afterward, in the patchouli-scented Lady's Room, Izza surveyed Evvy. "What'll make the big difference for your face," she pronounced, holding out her own silver tube. "Is leap-stick." Evvy took the tube.

At first, at Bear's and Izza's condo after the movie, lipsticked Evvy felt she was interviewing Barry Orr. In Izza's little jungle, Bear called it. He led Evvy onto the pool patio. Izza was inside, changing. From the open sliding door, Izza's West African parrot whistled the first notes of the 1812 overture. Bear whistled them back, his own notes clear and hardy. He was, he laughed as he uncorked wine, always teaching.

"Might you try one taste?" He settled heavily into a chair, his knees spread wide. He seemed as low-key here as he was wired in the classroom. "Only if you want to," he added, half smiling under his mustache. Evvy shook her head no.

"I tracked down your first short film," she announced shyly. "The one you shot in Greece?" As Bear leaned forward, Evvy described how she'd viewed his Toronto Film Festival Prize winner at the ASU Library. How she'd been entranced by its sunlight-saturated look. By the scene where the street kids burned insects with sun and glass. "I have to ask about one other scene. Those amazing shots of the She Walks in Beauty Like the Night girl..."

"Ah yes." Bear sipped his wine, his mustache damp. "Not only did she walk in beauty like the night. She was a 'lady of the night.' My—first."

He met Evvy's stare levelly, adult to adult. Daring her to ask more?

"Your—'first'." Evvy drew a steadying breath of citrus trees. First prostitute? First lover? Or both? She heard Izza pad onto the patio, barefoot.

Evvy quick-shifted back (it felt like a long way) to Good Student. She asked Bear what had brought him to Greece. Izza sauntered by in a leopard-print bikini with her parrot on her shoulder. She carried a long-necked watering can, her ex-dancer's body trim. Her face thirty-something, set in an expression that said: Amuse me.

Izza posed before Bear. Nuzzling her parrot, her own nose hooked, she seemed a fellow sleek-feathered bird. Her lipstick outlined what Bear called, fondly, her Barbara Stanwyck sneer.

In early evening dark, Izza dipped from tree to tree.

"Well, I'd wound up dropping out of school. Cutting

short my Photography studies at Edmonton U., flying off to join my long-lost Mother—whom Papa called a dilettante debutant—at this artists' colony in Crete. By the time I arrived, though, Mother had departed for parts unknown. This was when I hitchhiked round Greece, renting a camera, reciting Byron—a national hero, it turned out..."

"I know! I used to 'do' Byron in Speech and Debate. I know a whole sonnet!"

"That," Bear told her, *"might* earn you, in Greece, un chambre."

Evvy nodded, a hitch in her heartbeat. I mean, she told skeptical Ramon excitedly in her mind, he said 'one room' in French the way Albert Finney said it in TWO FOR THE ROAD when he's checking Virgin Audrey into the seedy hotel. Which was—Evvy remembered as she held Bear's gaze the way Audrey Hepburn held Albert Finney's—the moment Audrey knows that he'll be the one. He'll be her first.

You're a Theater major and a virgin? Barry and Izza Orr teased Evvy early on. You're an actress and you've only had one other lover? Evvy's sole short-lived boyfriend at Brown University had asked two years later. You don't look like the type for this type o' thing, the bearded Irish actor from the EVITA Road Company would tell her later, in late '99 on one of her Serial One-Nighters. What Evvy described to the Boston therapist she saw her first year out of Film School as Serial First Times.

Making love that way—in the cut-rate Suisse Chalet favored by visiting Road Companies, in downtown Boston's Theater District—was a part, an essential afterhours part, of making her first real film. A dream-like collage of erotic snapshots: her and Ramon pretend making out; her and Bear, for real. Her own face after a one-nighter. Mouth raw and sated, eyes overbright and hungry. To her 3rd actor—amiable, Southern accented— she showed the black-and-white photos that had, she confided, re-awakened her sexual self.

"Having these photos sent to me—it freed me up. Having them to myself," she stumbled to explain. The actor flipped through them, just looking.

Evvy was standing before a mirror in Bear's at-home Dark Room, a week after the JULES ET JIM date, when he came up behind her. He shot stills for magazines while awaiting word on his film project. He was paying Evvy to be his photographer's model and Student Assistant. He faced with Evvy that mirror above the metal sink: a mirror she'd later imagine might be two-way, Izza Orr a wall away in their kitchen, frying chicken. Her cannibal parrot squawked, demanding scraps.

Evvy was washing chemicals off her hands, her muscles pleasurably sore from setting up Bear's lights, her skin aglow from his flashbulbs. He turned her around as if to kiss her. Instead he glanced at her sundress, unbuttoned her top buttons.

"You should never hide—this." He lifted out of his pocket his ASU film-lab grease pencil. "From here—" He pressed a smudgy black dot onto one knob of her collarbone. "To here—" He marked the other knob. "To here." He ended with a sloppy dot between her widely spaced breasts. Then he took one step back. Evvy straightened, stretching her long neck, basking in Bear's cool approval.

They both startled at the scolding shriek of Izza's parrot. Bear pointed with his pencil to his scarred eyebrow. "Damn jealous bird tried to gouge my eye once."

He smiled wryly; Evvy fumbled to button her sundress over his marks. Reminding herself that Bear was, however unconventionally, married. That messing with any marriage was, as Ramon kept saying, dangerous.

She and Bear blundered out of the draped door. Izza faced them, hefting a tray of chicken chili. She cracked a lewd lipsticked grin like she saw through Evvy's sundress. Like she had seen everything.

"How did you meet your wife?" Evvy asked on the patio after the chicken chili. The year his Greek short subject won the Toronto Festival prize, Bear explained, Izza was a judge. A professional photographer; a funder of offbeat films.

"She was involved, back then, with an actress I cast in my next Short." Bear set his drink down as if making a chess move. Why was he telling her so matter-of-factly his wife had been involved with another woman? "My New York Film Festival debut, a Short that Izza, to my eternal debt, wound up co-funding."

"Your own 'dilettante debut-tante.'" Izza slipped behind her husband's chair. As if sensing Evvy's secret desire, she took hold of Bear's head. Her thumbs smoothed both halves of his handlebar mustache. He rested against her breasts, plumped up in a black swimsuit. Izza's grip on her husband's head looked firm.

"And she's been judging me ever since." Bear turned his head—or maybe Izza turned it for him—toward Evvy. "Now, my dear, how about you?"

"Yes; do tell." Izza released Bear's head. Bending, she dipped one finger in his wine and licked it. She kept the finger in her mouth like its red nail polish was candy. Short well-tended nails, Ramon had told Evvy, were a sign of a lesbian. Maybe Izza Orr was coming on to her too? "Tell us all about—" Izza zig-zagged her wet finger. "You and that—pretty boy..."

Evvy blinked into the Orrs' inexplicably intent twin gazes. She stood up and breathed balmy night air, sensing she could take her time. She pictured, as she paced the patio, Jane Fonda in KLUTE. Jane pacing in her sparkly dress for the old man who paid her to tell him sexy invented stories. Evvy slowed her steps, trying to make her voice throaty and slow like Jane Fonda's. She told the Orrs how she and Ramon had been Thespians and high school theater stars; how more than once, knowing they were watched, they had play-acted making out.

How now that they were at ASU and Ramon was openly going after men, Evvy missed their old charade.

"Maybe I'm better at *play* making out than the real thing." Evvy fingered the buttons Bear had undone. "Guess that makes me a—what, d'ya think?"

"Born per-former." Izza Orr appeared at Evvy's side. She dove with barely a splash into the water. Evvy stood watching her swim, poised on the edge of the pool like— she dared to think—Jeanne Moreau balanced on the stone parapet on the Seine. Moreau's dark eyes teeming, dense and richly dirty like the waters below her. Jules and Jim and the whole audience wondering whether she will jump.

Opening night, at her first small Film Festival, when Evvy watched her intimate Short with a live audience, she started out scared. Her pulse thumped her throat all-but-audibly in the credit sequence silence. I can't keep doing this, she told herself. It'll kill me. But as the audience relaxed into the movie, its dreamscape spell, as they laughed and shifted and got so silent in the sexual flashes that Evvy sensed their mouths going dry, Evvy felt her heart swell. The theater silence grew absolute by the final photo sequence: black-and-white images frozen one by one onscreen.

17-year-old Evvy and Professor Bear.

The audience took it in solemnly, as if they knew by instinct what the photos showed. What one-time-only moment in Evvy's life. Evvy losing her virginity, she thought, to them as well as Bear. She smiled in the theater dark in quiet triumph. Had she ever felt—since that night with Bear—more alive?

In his Dark Room, after hours, late July. After Bear shot her walking the desert in a drizzle; after he and Evvy had clothes-pinned up his dripping prints; after Izza had begun frying supper, the sizzle of her pans reaching them through the walls. Evvy turned the water off at Bear's small sink. His steps, heavy and leisurely, rounded the partition. His hands smelled of chemicals.

"What're you doing?" Barry Orr murmured, his body not quite touching hers.

"I don't know—what you want me to do."

"You do." Bear eased back. His voice took on a coaxing tone. "Do what you do—when you're alone. In front of your own mirror. Show me."

Her teacher; his shadowed gaze in the darkened mirror intent on her. Waiting.

Breathless, Evvy raised her hands. She turned her wrists toward her chest. Against the nubby linen of her dress, she brushed her breasts with her inner wrists. Feeling through the cloth the hardened bumps of her nipples. Feeling, just as vividly, Barry Orr watch. Bear met her eyes as she raised her gaze in the mirror.

"Soup's on," Izza Orr called from the kitchen, uncharacteristically loud. A cupboard door slammed. That sound, too, louder than it should be. Izza knew, Evvy felt sure as she shuffled into the light behind Bear. Had she been watching them through some hidden hole in the kitchen cupboards? Izza stepped stagily from the kitchen carrying a tray, three steamy bowls. Bear greeted her with a nod, Bear all too convincingly acting as if nothing had happened. Had it?

They settled together at the low circular coffee table in the living room. Bear and Evvy dipped into their soup. A green bat swooped between them. "Pablo! Down!" Bear jerked up one elbow, but the parrot had already pecked his jowly cheek.

"Come Pab-a-lo," Izza crooned from across the table, crooking her own elbow. Nuzzling the bird as if her bidding had been done.

"Queen Isabella, meting out punishment." Ruefully, Bear unfolded his napkin and blotted his blood.

Isabella Orr wanted her to tell, Evvy knew. It was the week of Evvy's Film Festival splash. The week her Movie as Memoir won the Audience Prize, won her a single interview with a fledgling film magazine. Isabella would tell all herself, if she had this chance. To 'make trouble' for whatever was left of Barry Orr, clinging to his teaching job in the Bible Belt. If Izza was to be believed. If Izza was to be, Evvy thought as she dressed for the interview, obeyed.

A white dress, Evvy had chosen. She smoothed the skirt. Would she play the part of the virgin victim? Telling the earnest interviewer how big bad Barry Orr had 'taken' her—more than her—virginity? She fingered the photos she'd only shown to a couple one-night men.

Would 'telling all' in this interview give her a bigger

version of the thrill she'd felt then? Telling those men as she began undressing, as she may in minutes tell the interviewer. Look at me then, in those photos. You can tell, I can feel you can tell, it's real. My real first time.

What might she lose, here and now, if she did tell? Awaiting the interviewer's knock, Evvy typed on her new Apple computer, searching one word. 'Virginity.'

Mid-August afternoon, scorching sun. As they strode across campus toward the Film Lab, Barry Orr explained in his flattened professor tone that he'd write her a recommendation for the transfer to Brown University's Theater Dept. that she wanted. She gushingly thanked Bear, keeping up with his Dad-sized strides.

"Izza and I will be in LA by fall," Bear added matter-of-factly, leading her into the icy air-conditioned dark of the ASU lab. Then Bear said he had a meeting. He left her there, waiting in the dripping dark with panful of his stills, newborn wet.

Drifting back to her dorm at twilight, lightheaded and hungry, Evvy gazed at silvered palm trees arched above the concrete sidewalk. She imagined ivy-shrouded brick walkways at Brown, savoring her mix of exhilaration and pain. She imagined herself graduating from Brown, flying west to a silvery lit palm-treed future where she and an Izza-free Bear meet again.

Evvy phoned Ramon from the Student Union. She bought him a pack of his favorite KOOLS, met him in the courtyard of her dorm. Did Bear think she was talented, a future actress and/or director? Did he care for her? Or was Bear (Ramon in his Ray Bans speculated, stretched on his back beside Evvy watching his smoke unfurl) just out to cop a feel or a look. Or whatever it was this twisted dude was into copping.

They had worked late, as always. Their last day, Bear had been frantic to get his magazine shoot done. He let Evvy print her own name onto the 'credits' sheet; he packaged the shots himself, his back to her. Don't, Evvy told herself. Don't, your last seconds alone with him, play safe. "Remember when you told me about White Balancing?" she blurted out behind him. "How you said that once you show the camera one 'true white,' it can see all the other colors?" Bear turned, face deadpan. "I feel like you've been the, my, one true white..."

Like I never will be able to see any other colors, she didn't get to add.

He clapped his hands hard. Annoyed? Signaling Izza? He said, maybe playing a gentler man: "You've lots more ahead of you—trust me, love—than me."

That word, beating inside her chest. Love, love. That noble sadness in his eyes, like her Dad's eyes when he'd brooded and sipped his bourbon, his face Mount Rushmore motionless.

Evvy held Bear's gaze. Maddeningly breezy like Izza, he told her, "Come."

She followed him out to the patio. "Want me to beat to the bushes?" Izza asked Bear, mock polite, corkscrewing a bottle of wine. Izza gestured with the corkscrew toward greenery.

Bear asked, quick and low, "You got one of your girls hidden back there?"

Izza laughed, raising the bottle. "And your girl—your little virgin—" Izza was pouring three wine glasses. "She will drink? To-night?"

"Don't need much," Evvy decreed, meaning to sound breezy too. She downed a swallow, clanked the glass on the table. What next: now that Izza had upped the stakes in her Amuse Me game, now that she'd tossed into the night air the word 'virgin'?

"Me neither." Bear turned his back on Izza and Evvy; he padded to the pool. He unbuttoned his monk shirt; let it drop to the patio. He wore his swim trunks, his Strong Man chest overbalancing him. He lowered himself into the low end.

"You too." Izza poked Evvy's arm so hard Evvy startled. "Take a swim too? Take off your dress? You play like you two are in his... Dark Room."

With her free hand, Izza tugged Evvy's skirt, hard like she'd rip it.

"What're you do-ing?" Evvy jumped back from fierce-eyed Izza Orr.

Izza laughed louder. Laughed in my face, Evvy told Ramon in her mind. "You think I don't know what's going on in my home. And it is my home. I am paying the rent." From inside the house, Izza's parrot whistled the opening notes of the 1812 Overture.

Dramatically, Evvy bent and gripped the hem of her skirt. She pulled off her dress, her elbows poking up, the cloth tenting over her head. Why not? Izza had known all along. Night air felt fresh and warm against her bare legs, her sweat-glossed midriff. Evvy struggled with the dress, yanking her head free. She stood exposed in her panties and bra.

"All off—" Izza commanded behind her. "You dare?"

Evvy hugged herself. She couldn't face Izza's derisive face.

"See?" Izza called in a low jokey voice to Bear. "She won't; see? See?"

Turning to the pool, Evvy dropped her dress. She leapt in feet first. Her splash heavy and klutzy; deep end water sloshing all around her. Evvy treaded water, blinking and gasping. Her contacts blurred and burned with chlorine.

But she could see Izza had vanished from poolside.

You dare, Evvy heard Izza taunting as she dog paddled toward Bear. Did she dare? How could such a silly timid girl ever be bold enough for art? How could she not push for this last chance with the first man she'd loved? A man whose own wife had somehow been watching them, had practically been shoving her husband Evvy's way?

In the low end, in underwater slow motion, Evvy float-stepped toward Bear. Where was Izza? Feeding her attack-parrot, packing her bags? Or no; Evvy half heard barefoot steps. She was watering her plants. Slinking about behind her potted jungle as if meek Miss Evvy wasn't worth keeping an eye on anymore.

"Where is—she?"

"Izza?" Bear gave a mighty shrug, rolling his shoulders like he was inviting (from Izza, some evenings) a massage. His upper arms meaty; the hair on his chest kinky curly. Bear rumbled on in his low precise voice. "Sometimes lately, Izza's told me she was leaving. Think someday she will. For some woman. Izza's the one who usually—falls in love."

Evvy blinked hard. "If—she did leave," she managed, "Could I not?"

"Evvy." Again, that gentler gentleman voice; again somehow stagey.

The hibiscus bushes rustled. Evvy turned her head. "Is Izza still here?"

Bear gave his slow big-shouldered shrug. "If she is, she'll want a show."

"Oh?" Evvy rounded her mouth. She felt half disappointed (a show for Izza? Was that all this was about?) and half intrigued, relieved. Oh good; a show. A performance. Now that was something she knew how to deliver.

With his strong lazy hands, Bear stirred the water

invitingly. "Want to start with a—" He sank down so water lapped his shoulders. "Ride?"

I knew what kind of ride he meant, she could've told the interviewer when he finally arrived with his tape recorder. I knew what, or some of what, it would lead to. Just like I knew, at the first FLASH from the bushes, his wife was shooting us. Or, Evvy would've corrected herself if she'd wanted to be honest: No. I did and I didn't. I mean, part of me knew right off those were flashbulbs; Izza was shooting us. That part of me was thinking, See? No one ever wants me without it being—like with Ramon—some kind of set-up, some trick.

A trick, yes, here and now. That's what she knew she could play, if she told the interviewer her all. A trick *she'd* be playing, this time. On him; the Bible-belted Barry Orr. A trick on herself too, if she bought herself a flash of infamy; or more likely a spot amongst the half dozen websites claiming to show 'real' virgins losing it.

Who would ever know, besides her, that she among those cyber-virgins really had lost it on camera. Could she ever, she wondered as she let the interviewer take out his camera, lose having lost it that way? She posed, facing down the flashbulbs.

More FLASHes. 17-year-old Evvy thinking defiantly: *Let her.*

Meaning Izza, meaning me.

Me pressed against the Low End steps, Evvy did not wind up saying into the tape player mike, as Barry Orr pushed into me. Me gulping air, gaping into those final FLASHes. My eyes open wider than ever before. Me thinking to Bear, to Izza, to the invisible audience al-ways always watching. *See? See?*

A great shot, the interviewer told her. That last 'still'

shot in your film.

Yes; Evvy nodded. This was all she wound up saying of her most striking black and white still. The still the interviewer had only seen onscreen; the still she declined to bring out and show him; the still she'd shown to satisfying effect in her film, the one she decided as she spoke to keep. Hers; her own. A great shot I happened to have on hand.

"And so I had to—like my mentor taught me—use it."

These days—in the intense isolation of Pandemic times, which Evvy is better able than most to handle, having lived such a solitary life—she sometimes still remembers that long-ago pool night. She replays it in her mind as she works late editing her latest 'virtual festival' film; knowing she's long since missed the chance to contact the last obscure college where she'd tracked down Barry Orr—surely now retired or even dead; she hasn't checked in a long while. She doesn't try to imagine anymore the damage she could have done to him with her words, and with the photos to back it up. Instead, Evvy finds herself replaying the part before.

Because, she's told her longtime lover and sometime-film-collaborator, that's what interests her. She's followed her own interests and instincts into a career of sorts, as a respected if relatively unknown female film-maker, no more 'famous' than Barry Orr ever became. But no doubt happier in her lot, her work. In her innermost thoughts, following them where they chose to go. Not, these days, to the awkward painful low-end first-time sex.

But to the part before, the part not on film. When she still had a say. When she had just slid off his shoulders, just splashed in beside him. When Barry Orr, his furry brows beaded in silver, studied her afloat underwater in her underwear. Thinking, Evvy sensed, that despite Good Girl appearances she was crazy and craven enough to be an Artist like him, them. Barry and Izza; the notorious Orrs.

I'll show them, Evvy vowed to herself, floating up against him.

Bear wrapped his arms around her, his grand expanse of chest half submerged. Evvy took tentative hold of him, his beefy firm shoulders. His underwater hands cupped—a perfect fit—her ass. Had she ever felt so wholly *held?*

FLASH: his hibiscus bush exploded. Evvy startled; Bear laughed, an unsurprised rumble she felt in his chest. Was he laughing at Izza and her Nikon camera? Were the two of them, more likely, laughing at Evvy? Evvy's heart beat hard, wanting *out out out.* But Bear and his sloshing shimmering pool lifted her. Her head dipped back—her hair fanning out, a silent weight of water pressing her eardrums—then she whooshed back up.

A dare, she told herself. She curled against Bear, her wet bra straps sliding, binding her arms. Though Bear wasn't moving, Evvy felt like she'd felt on Dad's shoulders. Carried along toward something big and bright.

Another FLASH from the bushes behind her. 17-year-old Evvy didn't look back. She wrapped her long legs around Bear. Tighter than ever, because she was shaking harder than ever. She pressed her face into his damp hairy chest and strong heartbeat, wondering how far this game of the Orrs' was going to go. How far she was going to let it, let them—FLASH FLASH—take her.

ACT TWO

Arias

Tonya and Nancy: The Opera

Libretto for a Chamber Opera

OPENING/HEADLINES

(The headlines are displayed on banners or on video screens as the Chorus enters, chanting).

CHORUS:

SCANDAL SKATERS ON THIN ICE: TONYA TIED TO NANCY KNEE ATTACK

IS SHE HEADED FOR THE OLYMPICS—OR FOR JAIL?

TONYA DENIES ROLE IN ATTACK

TONYA & NANCY ARRIVE AT OLYMPICS—ARE THEY ON A COLLISION COURSE?

Enter TONYA and NANCY in warm-up jackets over their ice skating costumes, Nancy with a bandaged knee; they skate toward each other.
The Chorus are flashing cameras.

CHORUS:

ICY SHOWDOWN: TONYA AND NANCY MEET, SPEAK!

TONYA *(gesturing to chorus):*
Can you believe all this fuss?

NANCY *(icily):*
No.

Music resumes: Nancy turns and 'skates' away. Chorus/Journalists chase after Nancy as she winces, halting. She kneels, adjusting her KNEE BAN-DAGE.

CHORUS:

CAN NANCY'S KNEE HEAL IN TIME FOR THE SKATE-OFF?

NANCY DRAWS STRENGTH FROM FAMILY, PRAYERS!

Tonya on the other side of the stage climbs onto a small platform, motioning the chorus over to her side; they come running & surround her with cam-era flashes:

TONYA:

I just want to say
I'm sorry
I just want to say
I'm shocked and angry;
And I had nothing, I had nothing,
I had *nothing* to do with—
      (gestures toward Nancy)
It.
I just want to say
I'm pleased Nancy is recovering—
I just want to say
I'm pleased she's here too.
I worked my butt off to get here
and if anybody wanted to beat Nancy
it was me!
To prove I'm as good as her or better
Who wanted to compete against
her most?
It was me! It was me!

      (Tonya jumps down and starts 'practicing'; Nancy,
      visibly fed up, steps over and takes the 'stand' in
      front of the chorus).

      TONYA *('skating'):*

Whip her butt
I'm gonna
Whip her butt
Mom always told me...

      TONYA'S MOTHER steps forward from the
      Chorus, dressed in an apron, a 'mother' costume,
      shaking a hairbrush at Tonya, scolding her:

TONYA's MOM:
Whip their butts
or I'll whip yours!

(Tonya spins on, ignoring her Mom, chanting to herself)

TONYA:
Whip her butt
This week, this Skate-off
I'm gonna, I've gotta
Whip her butt

*NANCY has taken the stand; the Chorus is snap-
ping her photo;
She sings in a higher more girlish voice than Tonya,
but
she sends 'skating' Tonya icy glances between lines:*

NANCY:
It's quite nice
to be back on the ice;
I'm happy to be here;
my knee has a bump
on it but it doesn't hurt;
I can do everything I want to do.
I always hope everyone does their best.

(glares at Tonya, still practicing)

If I can't win it for our country,
I hope she does.

(glares harder at Tonya, shakes her head):

Yes, I would like to know how
she could do this to me, my knee
          (points to bandaged knee)
but I don't think
there's an answer
I think she needs
help in her head...
          (Exit Nancy, sweeping past Tonya):
Help in her head, in her head, in her head...

          Enter Chorus, brandishing a batch of Headlines;
many Headlines are chanted multiple times.

CHORUS:

GILOOLY COLLUDED!

EX HUSBAND GILOOLY PLEADS: 'FESS UP
TONYA!

          Enter GILOOLY, Tonya's Ex; he halts Tonya's prac-
tice, kisses her roughly as she struggles.

          Then he takes her by the arm, marches her over to
the Press Conference stand.

CHORUS:

GILOOLY ADMITS ROLE IN KNEE ATTACK,
IMPILICATES TONYA

ARRESTS EXPECTED FOR KNEE-ATTACK CON-
SPIRACY

GILOOLY SAYS TONYA OK'D ATTACK!

*Gilooly strides up onto the 'stand', forcing Tonya up
with him.*

*He sings to Tonya: he runs his hands over her as he
describes talking her into the attack;*

Tonya stiffens, looks both scared and defiant.

GILOOLY:

'Fess up, Tonya! 'Fess up, Tonya!
I said to you,
'Why don't we just kill her?'
I said to you,
Why don't we smack her in the leg?
I says to you, 'C'mon it's better than playing the lottery!'
*(Tonya tries to pull away from Gilooly's grip, shak-
ing her head NO)*
And Tonya, my wife, she finally says to me:
YES! You said: YES!
(Gilooly pulls Tonya to him and forces a kiss)
C'mon Tonya: Con-FESS!

*(Tonya sinks to her knees in front of him; the stage
darkens with a spotlight on Gilooly)*

GILOOLY:

I said to her, 'C'mon it's better than playing the lottery!'
An' Tonya said to me:
'OK, Let's go for it!'

*Gilooly grips Tonya by the ponytail; he forces her to
'nod'—*

*Then he forces her to rise as snaky Shawn Shane
music begins to play.*

Lighting suggests a shift back in time...

*NANCY enters WITHOUT KNEE BANDAGE
'skating' circles, confident and happy—*

GILOOLY:

So I hired,
WE hired
Shawn Shane—

*(Enter stocky Shawn, dressed all in black w/ black
face mask, holding a 'collapsible baton')*

GILOOLY:

He went to Spy School
He dropped out.
He drives an 18 year old Mercury
with a missing hubcap;

So I buy him
we buy him

SHAWN AND GILOOLY:
—a Collapsible Baton!

*(Shawn whips out the 'baton', fondling it as he
sneaks up on Nancy, still spinning away)*

GILOOLY:
So I said to Shawn Shane
we said to Shawn Shane:
'Hit Nancy above the knee
hit Nancy on her
LANDING LEG!'

(SHAWN looks confused by this last direction...

But he doggedly keeps sneaking up on Nancy, who is slowing her last spin, wiping her face with a towel, walking off the ice...)

NANCY's 'WHY ME' Aria music begins

SHAWN rushes up to Nancy, hits her knee brutally with the baton—
She cries out and collapses in pain onto the floor, spotlit.

NANCY:

WHY, WHY?
WHY, WHY?
WHY, WHY?
   (Pointing toward the retreating SHAWN):
He gave me a good whack!

CHORUS:

A good whack
He gave her
A good whack, good whack, good whack!

NANCY'S FATHER' from the chorus comes forward and lifts her up;
Chorus keeps singing 'a Good Whack as Father carries Nancy to
NANCY'S MOTHER, who bandages Nancy's knee
—

NANCY (in pain):
WHY ME? WHY ME?
My Daddy carried me
It was so unfair
I was more ready than I've ever
been in my life
I think it may all be over
I saw him running away
I don't understand
WHY ME?
WHY ME?
WHY ME?

NANCY stands up with effort, knee bandaged;
Nancy sings in a dreamier remembering voice;
Tonya behind her watches wide-eyed.

NANCY:
My Daddy carried me;
My Mommy cared for me...

NANCY'S MOTHER, lifting a hairbrush, steps
behind Nancy—
With loving care, she begins to brush Nancy's long
hair—

NANCY:
My Mom used to brush my hair every night,
used to count how many times...

NANCY holds a large hand mirror and gazes at
herself as her Mom brushes her hair;
Nancy's Mother counts the strokes:

NANCY'S MOTHER:

One, two, three...

*Tonya stares at Nancy and her mom. Bandaged
Nancy with help from Mom LIMPS offstage.*

TONYA:

My Mom hit me with
My damn Hair-brush—
My Mom always told me
Whip their Butts
or I'll whip yours

*Dreamy music ends—Chorus comes forward with
fresh HEADLINEs, chanted multiple times. TONYA
peels off her warm-up jacket so she is in her SKAT-
ING COSTUME:*

CHORUS:

SKATE-OFF DAY: CAN TONYA TRIUMPH?
SKATE-OFF DAY: THE WORLD IS WATCHING

*As they chant the headlines, Tonya 'skates' to cen-
terstage. Chorus members stand behind her as
Olympic Judges, including TONYA'S MOM.*

*The Olympic Judges are lined up watching Tonya,
writing numbers on cardboard squares as Tonya
starts to skate.*

*Tonya 'falls' on the ice in slow motion. She is
frantic; she crawls to the edge of the stage, address-
ing the Judges and the audience, pointing to her
'broken' skate lace.*

TONYA:

They won't hold me!
The LACES BROKE, THE LACES BROKE;
They won't hold me,
won't hold me!

(This is repeated multiple times)
*TONYA backs away; the Judges step toward her
stony-faced and chant, raising their cards:*

CHORUS:

5.5, 5.3, 5.4, 5.5, 5.5, 5.5, 5.6, 5.5, 5.4, 5.4

*Tonya turns her back on the Judges, addresses the
audience with breathless false bravado.*

TONYA:

I skated great;
        (Tonya breathes from her asthma inhaler)
I skated great
        *(She takes another gulp from her Inhaler; the music
grows dreamy again)*

*TONYA'S MOM steps forward from the Judge line-
up. She sneaks up behind Tonya and raises her
hairbrush like Shawn raising his baton; she starts
beating hunched-over Tonya with the hairbrush,
counting maniacally.*

TONYA'S MOM:
First, Second, Third—you couldn't even get fucking Third?
You fucked up your Triple Lutz;
You hear me?
(She knocks Tonya down)
You fucked up your Lutz!—

The MOTHER spits on Tonya as she exits; TONYA is left lying on the stage as the CHORUS re-enters.

CHORUS *(solemnly displaying headlines):*
NANCY GLITTERS: TONYA TOPPLES
BROKEN SKATE LACES AND BROKEN DREAMS

Enter Nancy, also without her warm-up jacket in her skate costume. She is poised and confident; Nancy 'skates' perfectly as the Olympic Judges, smiling, hold up and chant numbers.

CHORUS *(displaying the SCORES):*
9.5, 9.8, 9.8, 9,8, 9.9, 9.8, 9.9, 9.9, 9.9

Nancy smiles and waves and picks up a bouquet of roses. The Judges lower their cards; they become the CHORUS again, displaying and singing headlines.

CHORUS:
AMAZING GRACE: NANCY ICES TONYA
FIGURED OUT: TONYA BREAKS LACE; NANCY GETS—SILVER

*Nancy stops waving and freezes her smile; she turns
and faces the Headline that has just been read; she
reads it to herself, drops her roses.*

NANCY:

'Silver'? 'SILVER'?
Nancy gets SECOND-PLACE? Nancy gets SILVER?

*(Nancy mutters to herself as she steps on the roses
and approaches the stand, which is now clearly an
Olympic winner's stand with flags behind it)*

NANCY (to herself):

Why me, Why me, Why me?

*Nancy steps up on platform with big strained smile.
Enter OKASANA, pretty in pink, waving and weeping.*

*OKSANA elbows aside NANCY, flits to the winners'
platform.*

*She is now weeping copiously and gazing heaven-
ward. Judge drapes a 'gold' medal round OKSANA's
neck; Judge drapes a 'silver' medal on Nancy, who
is rigidly smiling.*

*OKSANA gives a wide tremulous smile as she
bounces offstage accompanied by several Press
members. NANCY pulls herself together and addresses the remaining Press.*

NANCY:

I was really proud of myself
I think I skated great
I was smiling; I was happy.
You have to deal with what you get;
I deal with it fine.
Just *fine!*
What? Did I know 'Tonya was watching me'?
      (angrily, tossing aside her silver medal):
Lots of people were watching me!

*TONYA elbows her way onto the platform; NANCY
stays stubbornly put so both are standing side by
side as TONYA addresses the Press:*

TONYA:

I skated great too. I skated great.
God had my life planned out for me—
I'm not bitter; not at all—

(NANCY beside her is nodding stiffly to herself)

TONYA:

The judges, they make a choice;
You have to live with it...

NANCY cuts in (to shades of her WHY ME theme):

NANCY:

I was made into something I never
claimed to be or wanted to be
Since I was young, I just wanted
to skate.
I never wanted to be famous...

NANCY and TONYA stand side by side and sing in mutual confusion.

TONYA and NANCY:
WHY HER? WHY ME?
WHY HER? WHY ME?

Tonya and Nancy step down from the platform together then turn to face the stand as a female Judge in Courtroom-Judge robes steps up onto it—

The Judge 'gavels' the court to order with the hairbrush. She addresses Tonya.

JUDGE:
For Conspiracy to hinder prosecution: 11,000 dollars in fines, 500 hours community service, 3 years' probation.

TONYA re-faces the audience with her head bowed, hands behind her back so the audience can't see them. JUDGE takes off robe; she is TONYA'S MOM in the TONYA'S MOM's apron.

She raises the hairbrush; again, she sneaks up behind Tonya, elbowing aside Nancy.

TONYA *(hands still behind her back):*

They make a choice;
you live with it;
You find something else...

Tonya's mom starts to beat her again; Tonya whips out her hands; she is in BOXING GLOVES. She 'slugs' her mother, who staggers, dropping the hairbrush so it spins across the stage.

Nancy watches in horror but also with a bit of admiration; Nancy picks up the hairbrush, and watches frankly, straightening her own spine.

The CHORUS, brandishing cameras, enters with a fresh batch of Headlines.

As the Chorus parades around the stage, Nancy dreamily brushes her hair on one side of the stage while Tonya continues beating her mother on the other.

CHORUS *(chanting):*
GO FIGURE: TONYA TAKES UP BOXING!
TONYA SELL$ HONEYMOON VIDEO, PHOTO$
HOMEWRECKER NANCY MARRIES MANAGER
HOMEMAKER NANCY EXPECTING FIRST BABY
IT FIGURES: BOXING IS A 'HIT' FOR TONYA!

Tonya knocks out her Mother. She raises both gloved fists above her head as her MOTHER slinks away. Nancy stops brushing her hair. The Chorus as Reporters surround TONYA.

TONYA swings at the air, singing lustily as if answering a question:

TONYA:

The biggest difference
between figure skating
and boxing
is you have to have the balls
to get punched in the face!

*TONYA 'dances' around NANCY, taking swings at
the air. As TONYA continues to circle the stage, the
reporters surround NANCY; Nancy sings into her
hairbrush as if into a mic.*

NANCY:

It's quite nice
to be on the ice
But the next day I'm sore.
I'm a Mommy now, a wife
            (She cradles her hairbrush, ignoring Tonya)
I'm a different person and this
is a different life;
I'm more friendly than I used to be
Because I realized,
with the press and all,
I have to be...

*NANCY rallies a big smile; she begins to spin slowly
while brushing her hair slower and slower. TONYA
herds the press her way, waving her boxing gloves;
gesturing at her nose.*

TONYA:

I broke my nose twice; first time it went
that way; second time put it back right!

Tonya steps forward and waves her gloves fiercely, mock boxing.

TONYA:

My brains are scrambled but not that much
I think I'm like the Energizer Bunny
I got a family now too; I got a life—
In the ring, I let everything out—
I think of my Ex, Jeff—
I want to pound him
I want to pound him
I want to POUND him—

(Breathless, Tonya waves her gloves over her head in victory)

I think of—

TONYA steps before Nancy; Tonya halts NANCY's dreamy spin.
NANCY lowers her hairbrush; TONYA comes at Nancy—backing Nancy across the stage.

Tonya takes a swing, but Nancy deftly ducks and blocks her with the hairbrush.

NANCY swings the brush at Tonya but Tonya ducks too and Nancy misses.

TONYA *(fiercely):*

The difference is, you have to
have the balls
to punch the other girl in the face.
The difference is, you don't get in trouble
for hitting her
for hitting her
for hitting her

> *TONYA keeps boxing the air, facing NANCY; NAN-
> CY raises her hairbrush/weapon to hold back
> TONYA. They freeze and face each other eye to eye.*

> *TONYA and NANCY sing to each other.*

TONYA and NANCY:
They make a choice;
you live with it
They make a movie—
You make some money—
You tell your side; I tell mine—
Why you?
Why me?
Who wanted to beat you most?

> *TONYA alone:*

It was me

> *NANCY alone, competitive:*

It was me

> *They are side by side, singing to the audience.*

TONYA:
Who wanted to beat you the most?

NANCY:

It was me—It was me

TONYA:

It was me—It was me

NANCY:

Who wanted to—

TONYA:

Beat you the most—

NANCY:

The most, the most

TONYA:

Beat you, Beat you

NANCY:

It was me

TONYA:

It was me

TONYA and NANCY face each other, singing into each other's faces with all their might.

TONYA and NANCY:

It was me.

—**END**—

NOTE

This libretto is based on public quotes
from the real 'Tonya' and 'Nancy'

Candidate's Daughter Tells All

Cristal, the candidate's daughter, sits on the bus with the baby. *I love you I have to love you,* Cristal whispers to Baby Troy. His black-haired head, still wobbly, rests between Cristal's achy mom-to-be boobs. *I love you I have to love you,* Denny her boyfriend had whispered in Cristal's ear when they'd hugged goodbye—the real time, the alone time in the hotel elevator. Not the crazy-big crazy-loud everyone-hugging lights-and-balloons onstage time.

Onscreen, on CSPAN, on the bus's giant plasma TV, Cristal's mother's face—all pinky orangey dots but still beautiful, still Mom—speaks to the crowd outside. The crowd's applause is muffled in the sealed air-conditioned bus, Mom's words MUTEd. Mom is wearing Cristal's favorite glasses, the ones with the coppery squarish rims that Cristal helped Mom pick. Mom's hair (richly reddish brown like Cristal's, but piled high) shines in September sun. How Cristal longs, suddenly, to feel that sun on her pale air-conditioned skin.

Her arms are stiff from holding her big baby brother in one position for way too long. Yet Cristal stays sunk in her seat. Wondering where, if she did somehow manage to step off this bus with no one noticing, she'd go.

"I love you I have to love you," Cristal whispers again into deeply sleeping Baby Troy.

What, Cristal has had endless numb bus hours to ponder, did her Denny mean by 'I have to' love you? *Have to* because she's 17 and he's 18 and the whole world knows their secret now. Or have to because Denny has decided—like Cristal'd finally done—to follow God's plan.

Cristal's new cell hasn't buzzed all day. Shiny cell with the new number she's only given out to her best friend back in Boise and to Denny.

Denim, the damn dumb newspapers and web reports have called him: Denny's given name, Denim Jensom; the name the whole USA can now make fun of like the whole Eagle High used to do, till Denny started knocking heads together on the hockey field.

Something she and Denny had in common besides just the way, since 10th grade, they couldn't stop watching—later couldn't stop kissing—each other. Yes, Denny hates 'Denim' like Cristal used to hate her own oddball name till Mom explained to her that she'd named Cristal after Christ himself, only she'd spelled it a special way, a Girl way.

Onscreen Mom waves: her mid-speech mini-wave, not her wide-armed end-of-speech Victory wave. Mom's lipstick red today and her suit navy blue, one of so many new suits Cristal's lost track. The day of Mom's Convention speech, an Aide took Cristal and her Dad shopping for their own onstage clothes, sneaking them in the back of the Minneapolis Macy's.

It's possible, if you're smart enough, to give the press what the Aide called The Slip.

Cristal pictures doing that now, slipping out of this luxury bus's secret back door. She could zap ON the TV sound to hide her own sound as she'd slide sleeping Troy into his bassinette; as she'd sneak first to the bus bathroom, then somehow—out.

Troy stirs, protesting even an imaginary Slip. He clings with stubby fingers to Cristal's drool-stained IDAHO IS GOD'S COUNTRY sweatshirt. Cristal lifts the bottle from the cup-holder of the throne-sized seat that's molded itself to her-and-Troy's joined body.

See? Cristal wants to shout to the reporters gathered outside the greenly darkly tinted bus windows. See: a bottle; see, I'm not nursing Baby Troy; see, Baby Troy is not mine. At least, Cristal thinks as she hugs Troy, he's not my secret baby in the way the nuts on the Net think.

She presses Troy's chubby boy-baby body even closer. He is what she holds onto all day, these days. What would she do without Baby Troy and his gummy smiles? And what—Cristal asks herself guiltily as she dozes off— what would Baby Troy do without her?

There is Witches. There is Witches among us! Who is the Witches among us?

The guest preacher shouted, but with an African accent that made his harsh words sound soft, lilting.

Let us bless this woman, this Mayor, this Su-zun, he pleaded at the end of his sermon, pronouncing Suzanne like 'un,' like 'gun', pronouncing the 'r' in 'Mayor' as a softly rolling 'r,' a way-different 'r' than 12 year-old Cristal had heard before. She rocked her head to his words, clutching Mom's arm like a kid though she was in Middle School, though she already had boobs. But she tried to hold Mom back as Mom started to rise in the pew beside her.

A candlelit night in Mom's Church, the First Pentecostal Church where they Spoke in Tongues which Dad said was too 'screwy' for kids. But that night—a secret; how thrilling to have secrets with busy Mayor Mom—Mom hustled 12 year-old Cristal in because she said that Cristal was hanging out with bad girls, that Cristal needed to hear this preacher, needed to see Mom get blessed and, Mom had added mysteriously, 'cleansed.'

Let us all bless her, our Su-zun Payne, the gentle-voiced fierce-eyed man implored. *'Our' Suzanne?* Cristal thought resentfully. Even though she and Mom had been fighting for weeks, Cristal felt like she was five again: No, it's my Suzanne; my Mom.

So Mom had to shake off Cristal's grip, shooting Cristal a pink-lipsticked it'll-be-OK smile. Left behind, Cristal watched raptly with everyone else as Mom stepped forward so graceful-like, Mom in her heels with her head and her teased-up hair held high.

But then Mom was kneeling between two other men and those men were touching Mom's head, her hair. Cristal's hands made fists. Ever since she was little she'd loved to touch Mom's glorious reddish-brown hair with its secret golden gleams; she used to reach up with both hands and sink them into Mom's dense hair—usually stiff with hairspray but always smelling sweet, gleaming gold and brown and red. Every color hidden in Mom's hair.

Who are the Witches? Who have the Devil's own power?

The two men, familiar town faces yet strange in their suits, dipped their hands into an urn of water. They rested their wet hands again on Mom's head, dampening her hair, flattening her perfect puffy bun. Scariest of all, Mom—Mayor of the town; Mom, who Dad said Took No Shit from No One—Mom was just kneeling there, stiff as a big doll, staring ahead through her best shiniest glasses. Her glasses dotted with water now,

Cristal could see from her front-row pew. But Mom's stare would not meet Cristal's. Mom was staring ahead at who knew what.

—Protect her, oh God, from the sinners, from the witches, whoever wherever they are...

Behind her water-dotted glasses, all glittery in the candlelight, Mom's unmeetable stare looked as fierce as the Preacher's, Mom's hair darkened by the water. Cristal, hugging herself in the front-pew chill, thought: *What if Mom is the witch?*

"Oooh," Baby Troy coos, waking Cristal from her doze; her dreamlike memory. Only it did happen. Troy coos again, louder—so Cristal knows what's coming, from inside his Onesie and diapie. She sighs, hoping his diapie won't overflow this time (she'd *prayed* it wouldn't overflow the first onstage-time: her clutching Troy wrapped in that huge blanket meant to hide Cristal's growing belly; Cristal scared in the stage-lights that Troy would stain the white blanket; a nationally televised stain drawing attention to her rounded then-secret belly).

"Nurse—Nurse—" Cristal calls, forgetting that woman's name. A brisk frosted-blonde who is super-snooty, like so many of the folks Cristal has met so far, so far from home.

"Oh my, not again..." Nurse whose-it pushes through the back-of-bus curtains with her fakey thin-lipped smile. Nursie bends for the baby. "My, my, where does it all come from...?" Nursie asks Baby Troy, who squirms in her firm hold, his floppy feet kicking air.

"Same place your and my poop comes from," Cristal snaps, a trace of her old smart-alecky Eagle High self shining through. "An' now I gotta pee."

Nursie, like Cristal's high school teachers, presses her lips in a line. Turning round with Troy; turning up her nose.

She thinks I'm super-slutty Idaho-ho trash, Cristal has confided to her best friend Jewel by cell. Maybe she can dial Jewel in the bathroom, the one damn place Cristal has any privacy. Jiggling Baby Troy, Nursie steps toward the changing table opened out like an altar by the Plasma TV. Nursie is skinny-thin like the wife of Mom's running mate. Both women give off, Cristal feels, the same frosty disapproving vibes behind their tight bright smiles.

Bracing her hands on the real-leather chair, Cristal heaves herself up, wobbling. Her already ample breasts big as melons and her belly growing by the minute and her once-trim ankles swollen like Denny's fat mom's. No wonder Denny hasn't called for days.

But his teeny tattoo, Cristal reminds herself to stop the sting of tears. Denny got that teeny tattoo of Cristal's name on his ring finger. The 'C' all curly, like the long hairs of Cristal's that he used to twist round his fingers back when they first started making out after his hockey games. In the hockey team van; while the other guys were showering. Denny always smelled of strong sweat and fresh ice chips; Denny's hands were strong too, cold at first.

That's how he got her to let him slip one hand between her thighs. Because his hand was cold, he said, and only she could warm it.

'Only,' ha. Cristal hugs herself against the bus's air-conditioned chill. The Campaign Bus, everyone calls it, but it is way fancier than any 'bus' Cristal's ever ridden; fancier even than the souped-up RV Mom got driven round in when she first ran for Governor. Back when that felt like a fun heady game the whole family was playing together, Cristal and her brother and sisters laughing and pointing and crowding round the van's mini-TV-screen whenever—a miracle—mini-Mom appeared.

Turning from giant Mom on the bus's giant TV, Cristal feels a pang of missing her pesky noisy siblings, way back in Eagle, Idaho with Grandma. Back in school and real life. Cristal's queasy yet hungry stomach gurgles. Before heading to the bathroom, Cristal shuffles toward the bus's shiny-countered kitchenette, over by the curtains she almost never opens.

"Noon, dammit; we add fucking Fayetteville at noon..."

Behind those maroon curtains: the low profane murmurs and the angry-fast laptop clicks from the front of the bus, where the candidate and his wife and always his Aides and sometimes reporters gathered. Cristal pops open the endlessly replenished mini-fridge. She nabs a cheese cube from a cellophaned tray meant for some Press Event.

The ones held without Cristal there. Never, Cristal has been told sternly by more than one Aide, never should Cristal talk to a reporter. No telling where that might lead. To the Fiery End of the World, Cristal thinks, chewing. What even the regular preachers at Mom's church warned about. Applause sounds like distant thunder. Cristal swallows the cheese in one lump.

Is someone gonna shoot Mom like Pres'dent Kenny? 10 year-old Pammy asked big-sister Cristal the other day by phone. Cristal pointed out that Mom was not running for President but for Vice. That no Vice had ever been shot.

But no Vice, Pammy countered, had ever been Mom.

The massive, muffled cheers outside die down. So the speech is still going on, or the cheers for the end would go on and on. Even though polls say Mom's ticket will lose. Some stories on the Net, some Aides in not-joking voices say: Mom should run herself, later, at the top of her own ticket. Cristal presses her belly.

She's sick of thinking about Mom. She presses her hand hard to try to feel the flutter, the 'Quickening' she might feel soon, sometimes maybe feels, but she's not sure. Not with her insides rumbling all the time, hunger and nerves.

Cristal U-turns from the fridge and inches past the biggest tinted window, peering out toward the field where Mom is speaking. All she can see is the sunlit parking lot packed with cars (barely any pick-up trucks like back home) and surrounded by skimpy Eastern trees. Lower-48 weed-trees, Dad who was born in Alaska says.

Where are they today? For a dizzy squinty second Cristal can't remember. New Jersey? No: Pennsylvania.

"My my, you've been busy little man," Nursie is exclaiming, mock surprised, over the astringent smell of Baby Wipes. "Yes, you take yourself a little break, dear," Nursie calls back to Cristal without turning her head, without meaning the 'dear'. Not the way folks back home do.

Cristal plods toward the bathroom, wishing her father was here today so she could lean on his strong arm. Dad doesn't say much, as always, but Cristal knows he loves Baby Troy, black-haired like him. Their unexpected blessing, Dad says like he means it. Means it more than Mom, maybe. But Cristal knows Mom loves Troy too, even as little as she gets to hold him.

It is a fact that Baby Troy will know from The Beginning that Mom, like God, is many places at once; she has to be.

Cristal halts before the closed bathroom door, not marked with MEN or WOMEN like on a public bus. She is sharing this bathroom with Mom and the Candidate and Nursie and the Aides like they are all one big family. But Cristal's been in a big family, for real, all her life. And this is nothing like.

Baby Troy bleats: his fussy pre-wailing where's-Cristal cry. One thing Cristal agrees with Mom on; it's best that babies are cared for by family. Cristal steals one last glance over her shoulder—not at him but at Mom onscreen. How much longer will Mom's speech be?

Mom is making a point on TV, shaking one manicured finger. It used to be Cristal who'd paint Mom's left-hand nails, and Mom'd paint hers. Mom is big and bright and commanding on the TV; she is smaller and sillier in the moments she and Cristal still share on the bus or in the fancy hotel rooms getting ready for Events —giggling like Cristal and Jewell; trying on cool lipstick shades. Trying to cancel out with those bits of fun the whole big bits of fighting and crying. How could Cristal have gone and got pregnant the very month that Troy was born?

The very year that Mom had the big chance Mom always knew she'd someday get. It was only after all the fighting and crying and late-night blackest-dark alone-time that Cristal had found herself praying *Help me please help me* and had heard God answer: *I love you I have to love you.*

Cristal slides open the bathroom door. Hadn't it been a sign to hear those same words from Denny's mouth? She feels her sweatpants pocket for her cell. If she can just talk to Denny again, she'll be OK; she'll stamp out her bad sneaky thoughts. But even now, stepping into the bathroom, Cristal finds herself calculating inside her head: *If* she were to give everyone The Slip, the best time would be right after Mom's speech, when Mom was coming back on the bus, the front of the bus. And everyone was focussed on Mom.

When Mom came on up front, Cristal could sneak off from the back. Stepping—just for a few fresh-aired minutes, maybe more—into sunlight. Is that, Cristal wonders in the disinfected bathroom dark, such a bad plan? She flips the bathroom light ON. Can't she— Cristal Lynn Payne—have a plan for once, not just Mom and God?

It is the best Bus Bathroom in the world but it is still a Bus Bathroom. Despite the little fan whirring away in the ceiling, despite the heavy-duty disinfectant, you can smell bathroom smells, magnified in the narrow windowless space. And Cristal can't help wondering, as she releases her own torrent of pregnancy pee, who she is sniffing: some lowly Aide or maybe the next President of the United States? At every rally those words thunder from the speakers, and they still seem unreal to Cristal, unconnected to Mom.

Yet, in a different deeper way: wholly connected to Mom. Hasn't Cristal always known deep in her girl-heart that her smart, pretty, determined Mom would someday rule the world? Or at least be in PEOPLE? Cristal flushes and maneuvers herself up to the spotless mini-sink, her belly pressing its edge. Oozy pink soap from a dispenser, only a little sweeter scented than the soap in the Girls' Room in Eagle High. Soap that chapped your hands when your hands were already chapped if you forgot your gloves.

Soap Cristal and Jewell sometimes actually rinsed

their mouths with to hide the cigarette smell back in 8th grade when they first started secret-smoking, secret-everything.

The cell buzzes against Cristal's thigh. Perfect timing! Has Denny sensed Cristal was just about to give in and call him? Sullen Denny with his Young Elvis profile and hair. Has he sensed from a whole other time-zone that Cristal is for once alone? Her fingers still slippery from the pink soap, Cristal fumbles to slip the cell—shaped like a bar of soap, itself—from her sweatpants. But when she answers breathlessly, "Denny?" she knows from the smoky-sounding sigh at the other end it is just Jewell.

"No, Crissy; way sorry. It's not him but it's, like, *about* him."

"How 'about'?" Cristal leans forward so the cold sink edge presses her belly, hopefully not hurting the baby inside but she needs the support, suddenly weak in her knees. Her stomach gurgling like Baby Troy's, loud even above the bathroom fan. Its relentless whir.

"It was, like, last night? At Idaho-Joe's? Me and Heather and them out on Heather's ID and Denny he was, like—there."

"Like, alone-there?"

A smoky pause at the other end; Jewell inhaling her forbidden cigarette so loud Cristal's mouth waters, wanting a hit so bad. She hasn't had a smoke in weeks, not since those sinful soggy late-night cigarettes when she first found out and she'd sit up crying all night after it got too late even to call Jewell on her cell, a different squarer cell. The brand-new soap-sized cell feels like it's going to squirt-slip from her hand, she's clutching it so hard.

"Um, Jewell? OK, I'm, like, on my pee break and Baby Troy out there's about to blow and you gotta just—say it, OK? He was out at 'Idaho-Joe's in front of freaking everyone all over who, WHO?"

Whoa; her voice got screechy-shouty there. Nosey Nursie will hear outside; who knows, some super-nosey Reporter waiting to pee might hear too and print it in PEOPLE-or-whatever: Cristal Payne, world-famous knocked-up-teen, Cheated On by 'Fiancee'?

Smoky sigh from Jewell. Jewell is cool; she tells it like it is. Her Dad is Black and she's used to standing up against bullies at Eagle High. It's made her strong.

"Not all-over her; not, like, in *front* of everyone and everything; he's not, like, a total douche-bag and not near as dumb as everyone says; *You* know that, plus he was prob'ly high plus drunk, *you* know..." Cristal is numbly nodding. Stone-Washed Denim, Denny got to be secretly known this year, for his pot-smoking. One of many things she never should've tried with him. "But, like—over by the phones? By the bathrooms? I, like, saw him take this girl's number; older girl from I think Snake River, down that way? And he—Denny—yeah, maybe he was way-wasted but I overheard—or anyhow Kimmy told me *she* overheard—his bro.s, from the team, like—betting how long till Denny, like—runs. Like in: away."

"Runs a-*way*?" Cristal croaks. That lying bastard and his Snake River babe don't know shit about running away, how bad you can want it. "But where'd he run *to?*" Cristal pleads, squeezing the damn soapy cell so hard it does squirt like real soap from her grasp.

It gives her The Slip; dropping down past the sink, clicking and spinning on the tile floor where Cristal, wedged up against the sink with her belly, can't bend to get it.

Can only hear Jewell's voice going on excitedly about where it is Denny might run to. Then everyone—maybe Jewell included, Cristal thinks, listening to her throaty miniaturalized voice—can laugh at Cristal Payne, only months ago the popular cool Governor's daughter. In Cristal's other life, her simple distant child life. Cristal is breathing heavy like in sex, only not.

Outside the bathroom—because he alone-in-the-world senses her distress—Baby Troy squawls. Jewell's relentless sure-sounding voice demands: *Crissy Crissy?*

But Jewell doesn't sound way-sorry like she'd sounded moments before. She sounds way-excited in that commanding *Crissy? Crissy?* Hadn't Mom warned in one of their lipstick chats that all Cristal's friends are jealous? Even her best? Maybe no one would be altogether sad to see the tears streaming now down Cristal's face, tears she angrily fist-wipes away. Then jams her fist knuckles in her mouth, stifling her sobs. Because Baby Troy's own sobs are coming closer, Nursie carrying him closer, Nursie calling through the door.

"Your mother's coming in, Cristal! When will you be out?"

"Not now, not yet—" Cristal manages to shout back, steadying her voice.

From the floor, hidden by the sink, the cell cuts itself off with a defeated *beep*—it's dead; Jewell far off in Idaho has hung up. Sauntering off to tell the other girls (if she hasn't already told them all) that Denny Jensom is going to run away, to jilt Cristal Payne?

Bastard, bastard! She never wanted to marry him anyway! Pot-head dick-head! Running away on her, leaving her trapped here where she can't even bend over and pick up her damn phone! She is staring into the mirror, eyes bright and fierce like Mom's got at the church, like Mom's get whenever she talks Politics.

Cristal's round familiar blue-eyed face is still pretty, though plumper than ever before. Mom's face, but with broader bones beneath. Dad's bones; Dad is part Inuit, from his own Dad back in Alaska. Cristal is fierce, Dad's always told her, making her proud. Though really

Mom is the fiercest. Mom 'coming in,' Nursie said, but it takes half an hour for Mom to come in through the throng outside. Cristal splashes her face vigorously. Thinking of Denny's cold-skinned ruddy-red face after hockey, those cold strong hands. Fine, Cristal thinks, hearing muffled voices rise from the far front of the bus, the biggest bus doors.

Fine, let some scummy Reporter come in and find her cellphone and call her so-called friend and print her whole sorry story. Fuck it all. Cristal shuts off the sink faucet with a sharp squeak. She never wanted to marry Stone-washed Denim Jensom anyway! But what'll he do with his Cristal tattoo? How will he hide that from his Snake River slut, by sticking that finger up between her legs? Busting Cristal's cherry that way, or that's how it felt the first time. Why did she let him be her first—that dumb-ass Denny she hopes she never does see again!

Cristal turns with a lurch and slides open the bathroom door hard. She bursts out like Super-girl to find— a sign from God—Nursie and Baby Troy and everyone gathered up front, behind the closed curtains.

"Your Mom's here! See her, see her?" Nursie is distantly asking Baby Troy above the small hubub of voices inside the bus. Without Cristal there watching her, Nursie sounds more natural, sounds OK. She can take care of cute cooing Baby Troy OK, can't she? For a little while or maybe much longer, can't she? Can't someone-the-hell else take Baby Troy?

Cristal gazes across the back of the bus at CSPAN, showing the throng outside this very bus; showing Mom or anyway Mom's perfect puffed-up hair; Mom still far from the bus, its front door. Cristal, on the other hand, is only steps away from the bus's back door.

Mom will want to hold Baby Troy when she finally gets in the bus; she will want to sit up front with the Aide who goes over every flub she's made after every speech. Mom listens and takes notes, while feeding Troy his bottle. It all takes time and sometimes, usually, Cristal fits in a nap in her chair after Mom's speeches. But she is not dozey now; no, she's wide awake.

She is stepping, as she's only imagined stepping before, toward the bus's back door. What if I do run away? she finds herself thinking. What would the headlines be? What would it do to Mom's race, to the history of the world? What she, jilted-but-still-pretty Cristal Payne, does right now? Her hand is on the rear-door handle, gripping it hard.

She is giving the door a slide, giving them all The Slip, facing the blinding bright light outside.

What if Mom is the witch?

In the darkest time, the time right after Mom found the number to the Women's Clinic on Cristal's old cellphone, Cristal worried as she paced her and Pammy's bedroom late into every night that having one bad-thought at Mom's church—wondering in Mom's church if Mom was a witch—maybe that triggered everything. Two babies at once, when no one expected any. Or wanted any, if truth be told. Baby Troy—and Cristal's baby too—'unexpected blessings.'

That's what Mom says, in the same firm voice she used when she gathered them all in Baby Troy's nursery to tell them she needed to go back to work. These words came out smooth as one of Mom's speeches, but slower because Mom who was never tired did look tired.

They all had nodded yet Cristal had felt her and Pammy and quiet Brooke all wonder: But how will we handle this, Mom, with you gone?

Cristal wondering it in a mad way, because lately she'd been so mad at Mom; pregnant irritable Mom forbidding her to hang out at the mall with Jewell, at the hockey rink with Denny. Mom making Cristal babysit Pammy and Brooke practically day and night. Now they had a darling helpless *baby* and Mom was still planning to go right back to work in the Governor's office. And who—Cristal was already thinking as she nodded dumbly—who was really going to be taking care of Mom's latest baby?

"You shouldn't go back to work yet, Mom," Cristal dared to blurt out. Mom turned a hurt teary gaze to Cristal. Mom, who rarely cried. "We should get a real nanny or something-"

"Don't you tell your Mother what to do." Dad clamped a hand on Cristal's shoulder.

"Yeah, even you can't do that," Cristal couldn't not mutter. Dad's hand felt heavier at that. She knew without Dad (as usual) saying another word that she'd let him down bad.

So Cristal in the coming crammed days had tried to make up for her selfishness by changing Troy's every diaper, by babysitting him all afternoon when she got home from school and Dad and the parttime Nanny needed a break. Cristal acted like it was all OK; Cristal missed two weekends in a row then Cristal begged for *just one* Hockey Game night out.

Just once, Denny coaxed her that night in the hockey van when she'd cried so hard because she'd drunk too much and she was trying to tell him about Baby Troy and how her Mom was never home and how Mom was all anyone cared about and Denny held her and told her no, he cared about her, not her freaking famous Mom. He held Cristal close, her head all dizzy with drink. Just once, he'd coaxed and she'd given in, all the way. Only it didn't turn out to be once, but twice more that week at school in that same van parked behind the gym.

Denny'd promised in his same coaxing voice he'd

'pull out' before any baby got made and he sounded like he knew what he was doing and Cristal's beer-befuddled head couldn't remember what Mom had said in The Talk they'd had except No; no, don't you ever before you're married.

But just once, Cristal decided dizzily, defiantly in the van's cramped backseat. Just this once she wasn't going to do what Mom said.

Then, as Mom's Preachers predicted, came the Fiery End of the World. Of Cristal's world, anyway, her Junior-year about-to-make-head-cheerleader world. Cristal told Jewell first and it was cool calm Jewell who dialed the phone, Cristal's phone, Cristal sobbing beside her in Jewell's bedroom, to make the appointment that Cristal never kept at the Womens' Clinic.

But I'm not a 'women,' Cristal was thinking; I'm a girl.

When Cristal couldn't tell Mom what was wrong, Mom had seemed as distracted as ever. But really Mom did Know All and Mom knew to check Cristal's cellphone while Cristal was sleeping. Mom woke Cristal at 4AM so she and Dad and Cristal could have a Family Conference at the kitchen table.

Only Mom did all the talking. No, Cristal was not going to any Women's anything. Yes, Cristal was going to be brave and have this baby. No, Cristal was going to hand over her cellphone and her car keys for what Mom called the Foreseeable Future. Then Mom took one of Cristal's hands and Dad took the other and they prayed together, Mom saying all the words. Trembly voiced; pleading with God like Mom never pleaded with anyone. *Help us, We are sorry, We have sinned, We shall be forgiven, We shall follow God's plan.*

In the sleepless school-less days that followed, Cristal had prayed and prayed. To accept her fate, her baby. Through the blur of doctor's appointments and vitamin pills big as horse pills that she had to force down each night, gagging, Cristal kept looking at the postcard Mom had given her to carry around with her:

I HELD YOU IN MY HAND BEFORE YOU WERE EVEN BORN, Isaiah: 45:12.

That same card Cristal slipped in Denny's locker when she finally went back to school, scrawling on the back that they needed to talk, her whole family and his. His Mom had gone to High School with Mom and was scared of Mom even back then. That's what Cristal kept thinking when they'd had the big Family Meeting with deadpan Denny and his hapless-looking doped-up but surprisingly stubborn Mom.

Suzanne was known as Suze in her days as Eagle High's fiercest girl basketball star. *Suze Can't Lose; Suze Can't Lose*—that chant haunted Mom because (one of those things Mom whispered to Cristal in their old confiding days) Mom knew some of them meant it like she wanted it meant—that she was such a strong player she could not lose—but others of them meant it another, meaner way. That Suze was a poor sport who'd do anything not to lose. Which wasn't, Mom had assured Cristal, true.

But was it? Cristal wondered all through the next few weeks, Cristal dazed and nauseous half the time, missing school half the time; Mom getting sad-eyed herself, saying maybe some people would say she 'made' Cristal keep the baby, but Cristal knew, didn't she, that wasn't true?

Mom even confided (as if Cristal hadn't heard this a million times at Eagle High) how she and Dad got pregnant too. We had to elope, Mom told Cristal, squeezing her hands. And Mom couldn't understand why this Denny boy and his dumb druggy mother didn't see—*not yet*, Mom insisted—that was the only way, the right path. God's plan. And Mom's.

Mom sitting on the phone talking with Denny's Mom or with the Pentecostal preacher Mom had talk to Denny and Cristal both; Mom in those phonecalls low-voiced and intent like she usually only sounded in work calls. Even sickly and scared as she was, Cristal kind of liked it: how she finally had Governor Payne's full attention.

At least until mid-summer when all this crazy (Dad thought at first) TV talk came up about Mom as a potential Vice President.

Then suddenly Cristal in September was stepping haltingly onto stage in front of more cameras than they'd ever seen even when Mom was inaugurated Governor; Cristal holding tight to baby Troy wrapped in that white blanket an Aide had bought them, the blanket hiding Cristal's new belly bulge. *You know how darn hard I've worked for all this,* Mom told Cristal almost pleadingly on the special chartered jet from Boise. *How nothing can distract from my message.* Mom sounding like Jewell talking about how bad she wanted to make cheerleading squad. And the plan, Mom had earnestly explained, the plan was that Cristal would appear onstage this one time then fade out of view; that Cristal's secret would stay a secret as long as possible.

But in those nonstop crazier-than-ever days after Mom's Convention speech, the Net began jumping with nutty rumors that maybe Baby Troy wasn't Mom's, was secretly Cristal's. And that her control-freak Mom wanted to hide this fact. And the only way to stop them saying that—Mom and a bunch of Aides decided at a meeting—was to tell the truth.

That Cristal's own big tummy was a pre-baby not post-baby tummy. Because otherwise, Mom coaxed—her voice soft but her eyes hard and shiny-bright—folks are going to keep saying such nutty things about us, you and me and our family. Especially you, Cristal thought.

Then as Cristal huddled over Mom's laptop in their Minneapolis hotel room, she Googled her own name and found 500,000-plus entries, some in languages she didn't recognize. She kept backing away, pacing round and round the room, staring dumbfounded again at the screen. Sick and not from the baby. Some bloggers on the Net said that Governor Payne had let her 17 year old daughter become 'tabloid roadkill' and one even said Payne 'threw her under the Campaign bus' by putting 'her situation' onstage. But really Cristal had agreed, right?

Mom and her secret powers; Mom taking charge like always. Mom deciding Cristal needed to be under her watch, on the Campaign Bus with her where Cristal could help with Baby Troy. As if it were planned, Mom tried to joke. But Mom wasn't good at jokes except onstage. The other side's top candidate, Mom joked onstage, he tries to sound like a preacher when he speaks but he almost never mentions God. *That's 'cause he thinks he is God.*

How would that feel? Maybe like this, Cristal thinks as she steps from the bus's back door into that dazzling September sunlight, so blindingly bright.

At first Cristal stands still, eyes shut like a kid.

Like Cristal as a sun-starved girl soaking in the thrilling first warm rays of spring after a long Idaho winter. How she and Mom and her sisters used to dance and bop around the yard, under the big Idaho sky. Sun, wondrous sun!

Outdoor sounds, too: how Cristal has missed during her whole days sealed in the bus real sounds—birds and car engines and, from the other side of the jumbo-sized bus itself, reporters crowding round Mom and Mom's

Secret Service men and Mom's own Aides. Reporters shouting questions but Cristal can't hear—doesn't want to hear—what.

All of that is far away and the woods (or what passes here as woods) are close. Cristal can smell the trees, the muddy soil. She doesn't dare glance back at the bus. Any second someone will spot her. She steps forward as if sleepwalking, moving slow.

She is stepping toward those skimpy green trees, smaller and less lush than trees back home, but trees. Cristal was a Girl Scout; Cristal and her family camped near Snake River every summer. Cristal could survive in the woods, at least for a day or so. She could find shelter; she could cut her hair and change her name and find one of those convent-style places for girls who want to have their babies but give them up for adoption. Then after, she'd be free. Free and strong and alone. This ridiculous yet real-seeming plan spins itself out like the whirring bus-bathroom fan. Going nowhere but at least the gears in her brain are moving, coming back to life.

Anyhow, she is moving, stepping carefully across the asphalt toward the edge of whatever woods this is. At least her skin is soaking in the September sun; she is breathing air tinged with brisk fall chill, waking her up like the first days of school she is right now missing.

"Cristal? Cristal *Payne?*"

The voice, strident with an unfriendly East Coast nasal twang, breaks Cristal's trance, halts her steps. She twists her head. A trim redhaired woman is creeping around the rear corner of the bus, then striding toward frozen Cristal with her hair lit up all orangey red.

Fake dyed-orange; not real rich auburn like Mom's hair. Thinner hair cut shorter, framing a professionally made-up reporter's face. Shiny-bright eyes and teeth, lipsticked lips forming a smile shape.

"Ms. Payne—what are you doing out here? I'm with

the Associated Press and are you—" A note of hope this New Yorky voice can't disguise, "all right?"

Am I all right? Cristal wonders, blinking. It seems like days since anyone has asked her that, asked her anything. Ages since anyone has peered at her with such singular interest, undistracted by Mom or by Cristal's uncomplicatedly cute unpregnant sisters. Cristal half wants to knock this perfumed-smelling woman down and rush for the woods. And she half wants to open her mouth and spill out everything, all her darkest thoughts.

"No," Cristal says clearly, half forgetting what the question had been but knowing that No is the right, the only true, answer.

"'No'?" the shiny woman repeats incredulously, again unable to suppress a quaver of joy. "You are not all right? Ms. Payne, do you need assistance? Ms. Payne, as I said, I'm with the Associated Press news service, and I wonder if you would mind telling me what exactly isn't 'right' with you...?"

How long've you got? Cristal thinks. She edges back from the leaning-forward woman. Who, despite the dyed hair and heavy make-up, does remind her of Mom. The fierce determined stare; that's it. The eyes deeply brown like real not-diet Coke. Eyes naked-looking without Mom's glasses. This woman meets Cristal's gaze full-on, the way Mom rarely does, anymore.

"I don't need your help." Cristal presses both her hands over her rounded belly, feeling like it holds more than just her baby.

I got the whole world in my hands, she wants to say, to sing. Because maybe what she says or doesn't say just now—this sunny green-buzzing moment—could affect the whole world.

Under both her hands, inside her belly, something new flutters. Cristal stiffens as if listening but it is something she hears with her fingers. A fish flutter separate from her and utterly unlike stomach rumblings. Her stomach is stilled inside now; she feels calm and powerful here in the sun with her baby held in her own hands. Maybe she had needed both hands to feel these early stirrings. My baby, she tells herself clearly, is in my hands.

I held you in my hands before you were even born.

"Cristal? Ms. Payne? You say you don't need help? But you wanted to say—something? Do you mind if I, just take a few notes—"

"Mom—" Mom won't let me, Cristal starts to say but she stops herself as her baby stops fluttering. Cristal is facing this reporter all alone and no one can stop what Cristal might say. "Mom made me," Cristal begins again, not sure why.

"Made you what? What, Ms. Payne? Made you—have this baby of yours?"

God. Has the lady-reporter really said that? Or are those words, those terrible true words, only inside Cristal's own head? Cristal presses her hands harder over her baby to keep him or her from hearing. What if she says yes?

What if that's tomorrow's Headline around the world? Just when Mom is already in trouble from flubbing that one big interview, from the Investigation back in Idaho into how she'd pressured the police to fire bad Uncle Roy. From accusations that Mom is out for herself, out to run as President herself. Isn't it simply true, that Mom makes everyone do everything she wants? But doesn't *Cristal* want this baby too, more than ever now, holding it in her hands?

"Ms. Payne, please. What do you mean?" The woman is fumbling in her small rectangular purse, tugging out a rectangular notebook. "Your mother, Governor Suzanne Payne, made you do what?"

Maybe I am the witch, Cristal thinks as she speaks.

"Mom made me; she held me in her hands before I

was even born."

Another truth, popping out of her. Whatever else Mom has done, Mom made her. Mom held her in her hands just as Cristal now is holding her baby—the baby she and Denny, not Mom and God, made.

"What? What do you mean by that, Ms. Payne?"

"I mean what I say," Cristal finds herself answering. Thinking: yes, Mom made me; and yes too: Mom made me have this baby. The baby I already love, more than anyone.

Behind them, startling them, the rear bus door opens. The voice that calls out—crystal clear; not angry but commanding—makes Cristal and the reporter turn their heads.

"Cristal? What on earth are you doing?"

Mom, thinks Cristal. And she hears too Baby Troy's thin distant wail.

"Governor Payne—?" The reporter drops her notebook. "Governor Payne I'm with the Associated Press and I wonder if you might—"

"Cristal, come here; come with me." Mom is standing above them, three metal steps above them, framed by the narrow rear door. Across the stretch of asphalt that Cristal feels she walked long ago.

"Cristal—come." Mom holds out one hand, her red nails gleaming in the sun. She stares, her glasses not gleaming because her famous face is shadowed by the bus doorway.

"Just a minute, Mom—" Cristal calls back shakily.

"Cristal—*Now!*"

Mom barks this last word: the same bark she had used to shout the same word across the High School's football field one September afternoon last year, when cheerleader Cristal had lingered by Field Hockey star Denny.

Cristal turns back to the reporter, who has crouched

to pick up her notebook. And Cristal remembers how glowing and witchy-powerful she'd felt in those last sunstruck moments saying goodbye to Denny Jensom.

Half whispering to Denny that day the same low almost unhearable words she breathes now to the kneeling gaping lady reporter.

"Talk to you later..."

Did I really say that? Cristal thinks as she turns away, just as she'd thought back on the sunny football field. Like then, Cristal marvels now as she walks toward her mother that she had said those simple yet significant words without Mom hearing, knowing.

Because even now, Mom does not see all, know all. Cristal steps back toward the bus, her head bowed but not in shame. Mom can't stop Cristal from talking, if Cristal decides to talk. If Cristal decides to say: Mom made me have this baby; Mom made me ride this bus with her; Mom made me want to run away, today.

CANDIDATE'S DAUGHTER TELLS ALL, the headlines might say. But I can't, Cristal reminds herself, hearing again Baby Troy's Want-Cristal wail, calling her back to him.

She can't abandon Baby Troy. Cristal halts at the bus, the metal fold-out steps leading up to the open rear door. She can't run away. But maybe, she's starting to think, there are other ways out.

Mom stands poised in the bus doorway, her slim strong body tensed like when she's hunting in the woods and about to shoot. Yet Mom's gaze as she stares down at Cristal holds new twin glints of fear: her blank TV stare when that one lady reporter stumped her. When Mom had had, for once, no answer.

"What did you say to her, that woman?" Mom demands from above in her lowest don't-mess-with-me Mother voice. Yet her gaze is an anxious almost-pleading gaze.

Make me, Cristal used to say when trying out being a bad-girl. And Mom would; Mom would make her do whatever it was; till now.

Cristal meets the glazed scared eyes behind Mom's glasses. Mom holds out one red-nailed hand again but Cristal doesn't take it. She hauls her body up the three steps herself, then catches her breath.

"Nothing," Cristal says. "I didn't say anything." And she adds silently like Mom used to add aloud when talking about Denny marrying Cristal: *Not yet.* Mom gives a slow—slow for Mom—nod. Her face looks frightened, resigned, stoically composed. Looks like she heard that silent *Not yet.*

Cristal steps forward, belly first, forcing Mom to step back, Mom unsteady for once on her high heels. What if Mom does run for President? What if, Cristal muses as she fully faces Mom, I turn out to be more powerful than the most-powerful-person in the world? Cristal stands eye to eye with her mother, the Vice-Presidential candidate.

What in the world will that make me?

Hamman's Castle:
Home Of America's
Second-Greatest Inventor
& His Wife

His family hated her, so he built her a castle. Hamman's Castle, it came to be called. A wedding present for her. In 1926, he began work on the meticulously designed replica of a 'medieval manor,' costing—as the New York News, America's Picture Paper reported in red-ink headline—'OVER $500,000.'

M'Lord, Iris called him in her new bedroom. *Bedchamber,* he corrected her, maybe in play. They were still newly wed the year they moved in and shut the world out. 1929.

The bedchamber, like the whole castle, was specially designed for her. Victorian-era wallpaper of a dense flower-and-vine design covered not only the bedchamber walls but the doors. Her husband the inventor contrived hidden slide-locks for the doors, so no knobs protruded. So there seemed to be, inside the bedchamber when the doors were shut, no escape.

He'd slip from the brocaded curtains, inch by inch, the braided gold curtain-ties. Gold rope, he'd say. To bind M'Lady.

No M'Lord, she'd breathe from the 400-year-old four-poster bed, though she meant Yes, still, in 1930, 1931.

He was James H. Hamman Jr, heir to a diamond fortune, onetime protege of Thomas Edison and eventually the inventor himself of such marvels as the RadioDynamic Torpedo System: the torpedo's course alterable by radiant energy emitted from a radio transmitter located at a distance of many miles.

She was Iris Fulton of the Newport Fultons. Nearly his match in money, so no one could say—though many did—that was why the black-haired violet-eyed Maxfield Parrish beauty married the pale and perpetually hunched and notoriously reclusive JH Hamman.

That was how outsiders saw him, saw them. But he didn't care, he'd told her from the start. Not about anyone outside them. Iris knew he meant it, too. She admired that in her husband. He seemed as independent as she'd always longed to be.

Since his twenties, JH had conducted experiments with radio guidance in Gloucester Harbor. In 1914, he had sent his pilotless 44-foot radio-controlled boat on a 120-mile round trip with no one on board. The US Army took notice.

Hamman's early experiments with radio control helped pave the way—only distantly, JH would always murmur, though she wondered —to World War II weaponry, even to the atomic bomb.

Those twin explosions he never in his later years mentioned, directly. Not even to her, except one time, in writing.

She was his match; his soulmate, he always said. In her post-debutante days, Iris had made a name for herself as a portrait painter and collector of early American artifacts. Her quilt collection rested under glass in one corner of the vast castle.

Hamman would not allow her to paint his portrait. He even disdained photos. Iris's favorite photo of him showed him at work in his basement laboratory, his high square forehead luminous, his hooded eyes downcast. Though he often told her he loved their unearthly violet, he only rarely met her eyes.

M'Lord, she would whisper when she wanted him all hers.

Because she did want it at first, newly wed: the gold braid cord knotted tight round her wrists and ankles, tying her to the alarmingly creaky wood posts of the always-faintly-musty 400-year-old bed. She would undress herself, first, slowly. She would lie on the bed, taking her time, arranging herself. Usually he'd tie her wrists first, then study her in that pose, then tie her ankles.

Sometimes that's all he'd do: tie her up and study her from every angle. As long and hard as she studied the people she painted. The braided ropes, really curtain ties, left only faint burn marks. The persistent musty odor and taste: that was what lingered. The sense of invisible 400-year-old dust drifting into her half-open lipsticked mouth, her bared stretched-open private parts.

Hamman's Castle. Hewn of Gloucester granite, it perched upon the rocky coast of Massachusetts near the Rockport line.

J.H. Hamman, her daughter's new husband, was 'mannered' and 'unsettling,' Iris's mother had decreed at her bridge table.

Iris, according to Hamman's mother, was 'ill-mannered' and 'decidedly chilly.' A joke between Iris and Hamman, those reported words from his mother, the

Diamond Queen, Ice Queen. Lording it over the 'help' in South Africa, where Hamman was raised. Where James H. Hamman Sr. made what Iris's mother deemed, sotto-voiced, his 'ill-gotten millions.'

Yes, Fair Lady, but I was but a boy, Hamman had told Iris on one of their earliest dinner dates when she'd brought up, perhaps too boldly, the diamond dollars. I was a boy buried in books about Camelot and castles. Yes, he allowed, later when his family moved to England he heard of the horrific conditions in his father's South African mines.

But it was nothing, he concluded, he'd seen for himself.

From various castle balconies they viewed, together, Gloucester's famous 'twin lights.' The two longstanding lighthouses were built in the 1840's, each occupying one side of narrow Thatcher island. Like us, Hamman told Iris grandly in 1930. Two brilliant lights, separate yet together. Enclosed on our own rocky island.

She nodded over her sherry, sipped. What she wanted too: hiding away from what her smallminded mother called The World.

A Great Hall with its enormous pipe organ, 16th century music echoing in the high-ceilinged stone-tiled space. A Bishop's alcove; a Side Chapel; a Renaissance Dining Room (she'd objected to the Italian tapestry hung above the table, depicting in fanatic detail a saint on his back, his mouth forced open by a flaming spear). A Library, a Map Room, later deemed a War Room. A Weapons Gallery; a Dungeon (Not really a dungeon, M'Lady, he'd told her with his dry chuckle, but she never descended that particular stone-cold spiral staircase to see for herself—especially not after he'd also told her, confessed like a sheepish boy, that he'd purchased, as red-lit centerpiece for the 'dungeon,' a genuine human skeleton from God knew when.)

A Butler's Office; a Butler's Room, a Drawbridge, a Bell Tower. The Early American Bedchamber (hers); the Medieval Bedchamber (his). A so-called 'secret passageway' between them.

So brutal, Iris breathed in 1933 when she first viewed the Weapon's Gallery. She stood gazing into a brand new glass case that displayed the medieval Spiked Mace, the Axe of Robert the Bruce. But M'Lady, Hamman answered in his distracted way, maybe joking or maybe not, It was all so very long ago.

"My subconscious is always working," he once told an interviewer, "No matter what else I am doing."

Iris had quietly shuddered, reading those words.

She loved best the dawn. In the mid-1930s, in her silk robe and nothing else, she began sitting at sunrise on the chill stone window seat of the dining room. She sat with her back to that dreadful tapestry and the diamond-patterned windows flung open to the sea air, the rising light.

She'd breathe deeply of that air, cleansing her lungs of the dank must that even three maids armed with ammonia spritzers could never wholly keep at bay.

It was 6AM; Hamman and the maids and the butler were all still asleep. So Iris would sit in her window seat with her tea, gazing out over the crashing indigo sea, the imperceptibly lightening pearl grey sky. The sun shone most blindingly orange as it flared between the distant twin lighthouses.

Iris would shift in her robe, savoring the feel of Chinese silk against her skin, of cold stone through that thinnest silk against her bottom. Her robe would fall open; her nipples would stand up in the sea breeze.

That was fine; there was no one for miles to see.

The richness of the sea colors; the brisk brackish taste of the air. Iris was too timid an artist to capture such splendor on canvas. She loved—in this, she was like him—just to look.

They'd been married for 12 years, the 1930's drawing to a close. No children, they'd agreed, and she douched herself with rosewater after each time. Then they would retreat to their separate bedchambers; their separate (this was what Iris treasured, as she sat up in bed sketching till all hours) thoughts.

This is our child, Hamman joked wryly when he brought it home for their Interior Courtyard, set before the echoey plashing fountain. Iris touched its chalky surface with wonder.

A genuine 5th century Roman sarcophagus; a carving on its lid of a reclining child, caressing a little dog. The carving represented, of course, a 5th century child who had died and been buried with his or her pet dog. The dog's face, miraculously, remained intact, foxlike and alert. The child's face had worn away through the ages, nose-less, the stone there (Iris's hand lingered) smooth as soap.

Hamman did not take a mistress, as many men of his means would have done when Iris declared herself too self-conscious for extended nude viewings. She was still lovely, though a few pounds plumper. And a few lines had invaded her face. Other changes were taking place that she wanted to keep (he'd understand) to herself. She insisted that the lights of bedchamber remain off, that the gold-braided cord bind only her wrists.

She still gasped, but she meant it now: No, M'Lord.

He did not take a mistress. Then again—Iris would confide in her mother's bridge partners in Newport, giving them her darkly lipsticked smile—the war was his mistress. The distant gathering war in Europe that Iris could only read about in the Newport papers during her extended visits there, since Hamman allowed no newspapers in the castle.

The castle's Map Room had become the War Room. Hamman gazed at constantly updated battle maps as intently as he used to gaze at her. Not that she wanted his fierce yet colorless gaze fixed on her that way anymore. Her fine white skin had been burned, if only faintly. The castle air gave her chronic bronchitis. It had infiltrated her, that air.

She spat dainty globs of phlegm into the lace-trimmed cloth hankies Hammond insisted they use instead of tissues.

He spent hours in the War Room, sometimes with grave-faced gentlemen visiting from Washington DC. They'd avert their eyes, trying to hide their respectful amazement or fainthearted horror as Iris would lead them through the Great Hall, her heels clicking smartly on the stone tiles.

She was proud of her husband, to be sure. She would

wipe her dark plum lipstick from the side of his mouth and remember to hand him both his bulging briefcases before she'd entrust him to the butler who'd drive him to the Rockport train station for his trips to DC. What went on in DC, so far away, she never entirely understood, or not until later.

Hamman would return too weary to talk. He'd smoke a single cigar in his library, brooding about God Knew What.

Iris, when she wasn't off on her own trip, would fetch him his velvet robe and sit with him in the library, coughing at his smoke and reading Trollope slowly as he rifled through papers. Then he'd kiss her still-smooth forehead and retreat to his basement laboratory, what he called his Night Shift. Of his work Iris knew mostly what she read in Newport, in the News.

DEATH BY RADIO? ARMY UNVEILS
NEW 'GUIDED' MISSILES
RECLUSIVE 'LORD OF
HAMMAN'S CASTLE' CREDITED

His Night Shift, indeed. Her husband did 'shift' at night, Iris began to imagine. She would sketch in black and purple ink Frankensteinian visions of her gentle detached husband in his basement lab, which actually was a clean and well-lit workspace, not the shadowy grotto of her own night mind.

Just as the entire Great Depression took place outside of Iris's immediate view, so too did World War II. She lacked a radio or paper when she was home. Not that she sought out either. And Hamman always sounded impossibly far away when she listened on her mother's crackling phone to his voice from his temporary 'quarters' in Virginia, near DC.

When in 1943, he finally came home for an extended 'rest,' Iris was off in Newport nursing—for nearly two years, it turned out—her dying Mother. Silenced at last; dear to Iris, at last.

So it happened that in August 1945, James H. Hamman Jr. was alone in his basement laboratory when he received the telegram from DC that the second bomb had been successfully deployed. Because, of course, Hamman allowed no telephone in his castle, and because there in his underground haven he was (or so Iris would later imagine) suddenly swept by a fierce loneliness, he sent Iris in Newport a telegram.

Dated 9/8/1945.

```
M'lady: Two Brilliant Lights stop
        Together Yet Separate stop
Just As I Told You, Foretold You stop
```

Holding the telegram in her shaky white hand, listening from her mother's bedside to her mother's tortured breaths, Iris thanked God her mother had slept through Nagasaki, had left Iris alone with her own thoughts and the terrible triumphant radio reports. To think her husband had helped control it all, at such a distance. Folding and hiding his telegram, Iris felt closer to JH than she had in years. Together yet separate, indeed.

Weren't they, wasn't it all, meant to be?

He seldom left the castle in his later years. By tacit agreement, she seldom stayed there. After the war that had so consumed him, Hamman spoke mostly to men who travelled from DC or MIT to share cigars and terse talk with him in his musty Library. Reporters were turned away at the top of the long gravel drive leading to the castle that later became a museum.

Hamman approved the plans for the posthumous museum with one condition. No visitors should tour the garden where he planned to be buried in a grave surrounded by (his final wry joke, Iris understood as she scanned his final will) poison ivy.

She declined to lie beside him, for good. Hadn't she spent enough earthly hours lying in his bed surrounded by painted vines and leaves? Now he wanted the leaves to be real, and poisoned. He'd gone too far, at last. He'd understand, Iris felt sure when she dictated her own burial condition in her own revised will.

That was the funny thing, she told herself as she sat in her private lawyer's office. Of all the people in the world, Hamman himself was the one who'd most understand and respect her wish.

Then she signed her name: Mrs. Iris Fulton Hamman.

So it happened that when Iris died, before JH, in 1959, she was buried in her family plot in Newport. Hamman, examining her otherwise unremarkable will, felt as he held the paper what she had felt when she'd held his

August, 1945 telegram. So close to her and so distant, both at once.

Following James H. Hamman's death in 1964, Hamman's Castle became a 'medieval museum' and a not-terribly-crowded tourist attraction in Gloucester. The castle was most often viewed from the outside, from the decks of Gloucester's wildly popular Lighthouse Cruise.

The line about Hamman being buried surrounded by Poison Ivy was always good for a laugh. Then the Cruise Director would point out the tree-shrouded castle itself to the tourists who had crowded onboard to see—further at sea, up close—the twin lights.

PANDEMIC PORN

Em waited for the WALK sign, noticing the black Jeep Cherokee only because its driver reminded her of herself. A thin-faced full-haired masked woman hunching over—no doubt clutching—the wheel. Her stare was scared. Her left-turn light stuttered; her windshield wipers scissored away at unnecessarily high speed.

Her whole throbbing vehicle seemed to signal help, help, help.

Get a grip, Em wanted to urge her. But who was she to talk, hidden behind her copper-infused mask-plus-filter? Drizzle misted Em's forehead. Her skin still ached and glowed from last night; her tongue still zinged from the Alka Seltzer she always downed before venturing out.

"Honk, honk—" a Honda driver shouted. Emasculated, Em guessed, by his broken horn. His candy-red car bullied its way around the timid Jeep; Em smoothed her rain-dampened skirt. Lightly, she pressed through its cloth the tender bruises on her ass. Maxi's marks; proof that last night had happened. Her most exciting night in ages.

WARNING: DRIVER DOES NOT GIVE A DAMN ANYMORE

The Honda's bumper sticker flashed by. Half-smiling, Em reached for the post beside her. Her fingers found WALK; her gaze snagged a tall tow-headed man on the opposite curb. Unmasked, through the hellbent Boston traffic, he half smiled back at her. Like he knew her. The hollowed-out DOES NOT GIVE A DAMN face of a homeless man; the stylish raincoat of a businessman. A thick shock of white hair. Em released the WALK button. A risen-from-dead Andy Warhol? Come back to mock 2020?

DON'T WALK, the sign kept advising. Help, help, the Jeep kept pleading.

Bowing her face, Em hid behind her brown cloud of hair, cotton-candied by the drizzle. No, she had to assure herself; no, of course, that man hadn't possibly seen the Film Festival film she'd appeared in last year. The title she avoided saying even in her mind, though she'd once typed it over and over in her diary. She carried her diary docs on Flash Drive whenever she left her apartment. Which these days, in dismal early Summer of 2020, was hardly ever.

Her Diary existed for her—not for posting online. She was an old-fashioned girl in some ways, she liked to say. If someone broke in her apartment and stole her computer, she'd care most about the diary docs. Perhaps foolishly, she typed Please Return/Reward Offered pleas atop those docs. She unzipped her mini backpack's side pocket, fingered her Flash Drive. Then, hurriedly, she slipped her hand from the pocket. DON'T WALK began to blink.

$$ REWARD offered for RETURN, if lost; It is of NO USE to anyone but me, Emmaline O'Neil; If found, PLEASE text 617-299-0030

WALK. As Em started to step off her concrete island, the Jeep driver started—with a lurch—to turn. Couldn't she see? Em froze, feeling the strangely sparse traffic whiz behind her. Everyone seemed to be re-learning to drive.

As if only now noticing the other half of Beacon, the impossibility of completing this left turn, the boxy Jeep veered from its curve. Aiming at Em. Incredulous, Em gaped at the masked driver's wet-windshield-blurred face. Eyes panicky wide. As the Jeep zoomed toward her, Em thought: this can't be happening.

June 4, AM, 2020 (THE Day I've Been Waiting For?)

PM: Maybe because my luck may've changed today, just as the state of MA begins re-opening, I keep imagining my accidental death: how I'd be found, what those who'd care (Mom&Dad; Maxi&Jeff&Daisy;Sue too) might conclude based on the clues: those odd mixes that trigger, in the 1st place, in the start of my 3rd full month of so-called Self-Isolation, my Death Reveries.

Example #1: suppose I'd electrocuted myself as I poked into the jack-hole or whatever it's called of my phone w/ a Q-Tip after I'd dropped said-phone in my shampoo-y bath puddle?

Would anyone notice the phone jack-hole (??) clogged w/ shampoo slime?

Would anyone guess I'd accidentally dropped the whole phone in sheer shaky-fingered joy after still-naked me checked my message post-bath & my FilmFreeway Submissions Update informed me HER BATH has been chosen as finalist for the N.E.N. V. 2020 Film Fest's top Prize?

Or if, my robe flapping open, I rushed into my living/bedroom, beelining toward my laptop to check the super-familiar FilmFreeway site for its ranking of this Fest? And if in my rush I tripped on DanielDog's old leash, dropped the Q-Tip & toppled to the floor, not banging my head on the corner of the desk though I might've. Might've died there: leather leash & robe-tie & soapy Q-Tip scattered beside me. What would an outside observer make of that scene? That evidence of self-isolated drama?

What, based on it, would they make of the late Em, aka Emmaline, O'Neil?

The hurtling Jeep crashed into the signpost. Staggering backwards, Em felt but couldn't hear herself scream. Drowned-out sound was yanked from her throat. Metal shrieking; shards stinging her skin; Beacon Street shaking. Then not. Em was still standing, stiffly swaybacked, limbs electrified. *No,* she told the Jeep's shuddering mass. And the more subtly shuddering pole, tilted like a chopped tree, beaded with quivering raindrops.

Em's throat ached; her scream had been swallowed whole by this crash that couldn't be. But—the split front grille of the Jeep creaked like a cage door shoved open— *yes.* Matter-of-factly, the grille collapsed at her feet.

As if part of her were detaching in turn, Em's mini-backpack, her *bag,* dropped from her shoulder, plopped on the ground. Yes, this has happened.

January 1, 2020- new yr!

NewNotebook/NewYear/NewMe: Saying it Out Loud at Least; a First Step

Last Night/ 'First Night': In crazy-crowded Venus D. Milo; Me & Daisy bemoan being alone, being #1 to no one; We watch Maxi dance w/ the girls & Jeff w/ the boys; Daisy confides over our shaky table: "The thing about feeling like a hopeless—" (in stage-whisper under K-Pop beat) "loser" (back to shout) "is you do things you wouldn't've dared to, because: why not?"

Later, downing what I make her promise will be her last

beer, D. tells us her last guy warned her, as if apologizing for his gender: Men are such pigs. Maxi shakes her head, her cool new Fulani braids, decreeing: Even men who say 'men are such pigs' are such pigs; & I laugh too, but I don't meet Maxi's eyes like she wants. Don't want her thinking I want her like she wants me. Back home, in brand-new 2020— maybe high on being wanted that way; for-sure high on beginning HER BATH at last—I tell J&M&D how I want HER BATH to be about Safety and Pain, how I want it to go beyond Fifty Shades of Grey's prettied-up-porn. How I want to film a mind & body stripped. Then I—the director; the boss— tell them casual-like, business-like: here's what we'll do for the Final Fantasy Sequence. Which'll show only my face, close-up; not my body, not what's happening to my body. Which'll be what I acted out in SICK PLAY, only real. So the pain on my face'll be real; so I'll have to have, whipping me, someone I trust.

Gentle Jeff is the one to nod. To slip off his belt & double it in a loop. No, no, I tell him, laughing like I'm drunk too. I've got something better'n a belt; Whatever you want, Jeff tells me. He's willing; he's done it with/for guys & he's Gotten Off too; he's done it onstage & he hasn't; So what'll it be like —he's curious; I act merely curious too—with/for my camera?

With/for me?

After, alone; asking myself: but should I? Telling myself: but it IS for my film; I'd only—this part IS true—do such a thing in/for my film-life, work-life. Not that I've got, these days, much of a life-life. Not that that bothers me much as I pace & plan camera angles & sing along w/ the drunks in the street.

AM, first of 2020: So below-frozen cold it hurts to go outside.

A short curly-haired unmasked man leapt from a dented car that had rear-ended the crunched Jeep. He branded Em with his confused, accusatory glare.

"Outta lane—" he bellowed, unmuffled, swiveling his head so fast he erased Em from the scene. "That fuggin' *Jeep*—" He galloped up to the Jeep's window. Above the broken wave of her bumper, the driver sat upright, seemingly unharmed. Still masked; still clutching her wheel; fixing on the madman her dazedly wide-eyed gaze. You, Em thought, pressing her cut finger to her thumb. Almost killed me.

"Yer outta lane!" The man swung his arms like a crazed umpire.

Em—scared to be drawn into this scene; taken, God forbid, to a Covid-swarming ER; her scratches sending out unseen sparks of pain—lifted her bag. Shakily, she made her way across the crosswalk. The drizzle had stopped. DON'T WALK blinked again. Drivers poked their heads from their cars. Em drifted in front of their bumpers. Weightless as a ghost, she felt as she crossed, even as one pedestrian noticed her. A stout Grandma in a flowery mask stood beside the unmasked tow-headed man. He no longer stared at Em, but at the wreckage.

"Ya all right, dear?" the Grandma asked.

"Yes," Em answered faintly, gratefully. She stepped onto the other curb as the ghost of Andy Warhol stepped off. Em had read Vanity Fair pieces on the infamous Warhol crowd because she resembled—her own un-famous crowd had told her, back when her hair was short—Edie Sedgewick. A tabloid-celeb heiress of another era. Not that Em was any heiress, though she was less penniless than some of her own crowd. If you could call it a *crowd:* her filmmaking friends. She found she couldn't stop walking.

"Ya might've been killed," the flower-muffled Grandma called after her helpfully.

The 'might' confused Em so much she forgot to answer. She walked down two blocks, passing the jammed-up cars, playing the words like different line-readings: might have been killed; *might* <u>have</u> been killed; might have <u>been</u>. Em shook her head hard to change its channel. Her finger was bleeding.

"—Family Sleeping style," a stylishly masked plummy-voiced woman ahead of Em was saying, pushing a baby carriage. "Since the lockdown and all, we just let it happen and it feels, like, so natural. Joshua Jr. cuddled between Josh and me..."

Oh what was I *doing* with my life? Em thought in past tense. Picturing herself and pale blue-eyed Jeff and buxum chunky black-eyed Maxi and the camera crammed together in her bathtub. Em a reckless waif: doomed like Edie S. to die young, only unlike Edie un-famously?

"...Heard it can keep the baby from developing—what's it called?" a second plodding kerchief-muffled Mom answered. "Self-Something-or-other Sleep Skills..."

Em skimmed past the Moms, guiltily glad to feel so unencumbered, so light. Whatever else she'd done in life, Em had maintained her skinny high school body: its effect considerably different once she'd baked off her acne in the sun of UCLA, permed and bleached her plentiful baby-fine hair and transformed with contacts her starey eyes. Doe eyes, when made up. Shoot you through filters, Maxi told her, and you look 20, honey. Which'd serve you well if you'd consider more (Maxi had silently mouthed the title Em hated) Sick Play. Maxi joked via their latest ZOOM 'meeting' that she and Em and Jeff ought to start a podcast, broadcasting their (ironically) Safe Sex escapades—which all could be per-formed masked and at a certain distance.

They could call the site (Em had jotted this down, though she felt sure this name must already be taken) *PandemicPorn.com.*

Em had laughed gamely, not saying aloud: *But it wouldn't really be Porn, right?*

They made what used to be called Art Films, right? What were those called now? Em sucked her bloody finger, Bank America within sight. Self-Soothing, she told herself. Her empty stomach rumbled. Her gait stiffened, delayed-action shock setting in. She never had learned, she thought as she lurched forward, how to soothe herself. Booze or weed or Zoloft or even cigarettes too strong for her hyper-sensitive system.

Your body creates its own Speed, Maxi had once told Em, admiringly.

Em shouldered the glass Bank America door, asking herself—everything from before the crash seemed so far away—why she was here.

Feb. 14, 2020:

AM: On T-train, on Day 1 of HER BATH, I shoot on my phone a sign on train door: NO PASSING THROUGH rubbed out to become: NO ASSING ROUGH. Ha- I'm still thinking of that, wondering if we can work it in somehow, when I walk up the sidewalk past faces wearing these weird Chinese-flu medical masks, making me afraid even to breathe today—

PM: Maxi & our rented Artifex & her grout brush. M. insists on scrubbing soap scum I'd not noticed—in hour-long showers—before she'll shoot my tub. We clean to her vintage Bloody Valentine EP; I say she reminds me of my bossy sister; Of Sweet Sue? Maxi demands. The Do-Gooder? She faces me w/ her brown tattooed arms akimbo; Sue's tomboy pose, Sue's See-Through-You stare. But I love Sue, I protest & Maxi's black eyes spark at my careless 'love',

Scene One; Take One: in spanking-clean (M. jokes) tub, in bubbles, in only bikini-bottoms-that-don't-show; only Maxi crammed into the bathroom w/ me. Her Fulanis pinned up so no mini bead-clacks sound as we film. Maxi with her ever-steady hands aiming the Artifex, filming me: she pans bubble-glints of my body; she fixes a tight Close-Up on my face, my eyes half-shut behind my old stop-sign glasses, lenses fogging. My expression shifting as I picture each Fantasy we'll cut to; Great Takes, Maxi tells me after; Amazing how relaxed you get, Miss Too-Tense-to-Live, soon as the camera rolls. I give a giddy nod, still hot from its lights.

PM: I phone Sue in AZ; she's breathless from visiting Mom & Dad in Sun City, driving Dad to the doctor and drugstore; I offer our code for Selfish: good thing you're not a Shellfish. Like me.

PPM: in bed at last; I sense in my room movement, sense another intelligence. Another being in my isolated apartment/ life. Turn my head super-slow & I see in corner of my closet a mouse head, walnut-sized. Twin glint of eyes. Then—as I startle—gone.

In Bank America, in line, Em's legs still vibrated. Light scratches crisscrossed her ankles. She touched her face, felt a fresh droplet. Was her cheek, like her finger, bleeding? She shuffled forward, breathing slowly through her mask, tasting its cool copper-infused cloth. Feeling the dull ache of her ass. An aged hippie stood in front of her, his ponytail limp and greyish blond. Em remembered her dad's doting depressing phone message last night. How she'd been crouched on her hands and knees before Jeff as it played; how Maxi had teased her after. Daddy's pampered white-girl princess. *Will you be getting another Stimulus check, Emmaline? Do ya need anything to tide ya over till ya do?*

A little, she would make herself say when she made herself call back. But how much longer, she asked herself yet again, could she live on Dad's loans, on her strung-together part-time jobs? The best of which she was still secretly working despite filing a claim for Unemployment. Tutoring English as a Second Language, directing Massachusetts Edu-Film videos, recording books at the Massachusetts Association for the Blind, closed down since March. She'd asked her ESL students to pay her in cash, for the foreseeable future. Which was, she reminded herself now, why she'd taken her place in line at this bank. So she could deposit her two months' worth of cash into her anemic account. Just so she could keep paying her bills electronically, from said account. Just so she could keep the account 'active.'

"Next?"

The elderly hipster approached the bank counter like a supplicant. He'd have some complicated complaint or request, Em guessed grimly as she stepped into his place.

"There's, um, an issue with my account," he began, his voice and the counter woman's both muffled by their masks. Good; Em did not need to hear anyone else's woes.

She pressed her thumb to her cut, a tiny mouth she was trying to silence. Suppose she had been killed? What was one wanna-be star, more or less? One shellfish? She pulled her own envelope from her purse. Her paltry fistful of tutoring twenties. Would the disapproving-looking counter lady think Em was turning tricks, or whatever that was called these days? Mentally, Em imagined reciting to this woman—visibly frowning behind her mask as the whiny guy with his droopy grey ponytail droned on—the few prizes and professional gigs that separated 'Emmaline Moore'—didn't they? —from true losers.

Second Place last year in Boston's First Annual 2019 Femme-Flicks Short Film Contest; paid acting appearances in five film-fest. films: the last the title— SICK PLAY—she skimmed past fastest; Director of an Edu-Film podcast on STD and Skateboard Safety; First Prize last year at the Mass. Arts Video Expo., where she'd met Al and Phillipa Ray, producer/ composers who'd financed and provided an eerie soundtrack for Em's Short Subject, HER BATH.

"I really don't think we can help you with that, sir," the fed-up sounding counter woman was explaining, the customer slumping in sullen defeat.

Em gazed restlessly out the bank's giant glass windows, glimpsing in the far corner of her eye the white-haired Warhol man. He passed Bank America briskly, swinging both his hands in fists. As if holding tight to something. His walk hypnotically intent; something had woken up that guy, charged him up. Maybe the crash itself? Em's crash?

"Next," the counter lady was announcing, Em's turn at last.

But Em was stepping over to the windows. Something about that man, his swinging fists, woke her from her trance. *Woke,* everyone was always chattering about in the Twitter-ized world Em avoided. Yes, she'd marched with Maxi in the Black Lives Matters rallies out on this same stretch of street, in the spring. Feeling like a masked impostor. Just another self-loathing white girl awaiting another Self Stimulus check from her Dad. Outside, moving in the opposite direction as the now-vanished Warhol man, a police cruiser whizzed by, its orange light revolving slowly. Its siren half-whooped, then died down as if embarrassed. By the paltry size of her crash? But still it was her crash, whatever size! Em spun. She almost ran into the glass doors, thinking, Wait! They can't have it without me!

Damp wind in her face woke her further. How could she sleepwalk away from it, her crash? Its real-life drama, however small-scale; its images? Finally, something real had happened in her life and she'd sleep-walked away from it! *HILLARY 2016,* a way-faded bumper sticker proclaimed, its arrow pointing nowhere.

Em half-ran, half-chasing that car.

Wait, she wanted to cry out, pounding down the sidewalk toward her intersection. Her mini-backpack bumped her lower back, lightweight bumps.

An orange-lit truck parked importantly askew on Beacon, blocking traffic. One policeman and a few onlookers stood scattered round the wreck, disorganized, like extras awaiting the arrival of the star.

March 10, 2020

Heady giddy AM: in new paper medical-mask I bought on Amazon, I buy fizzy Alka S./Ginger A. breakfast at aSeven-11; the shelves cleaned-out by folks expecting to be Locked Down any day now, if that ever really happens. I shoot the emptied shelf on my phone, then the hand-printed sign taped to Coke can stack:

WARNING: CANS OF CERTAIN LOT #s MAY BURST & PROPEL

PM: Maxi & me & Flashback #1, Tight Shot: me w/ ponytail & my years-old stop-sign glasses and my brand-new face-mask; I fondle our old DanielDog leash; I unfold its metal-buckled harness, my hands trembling: the harness-leash our dog died in, irresistibly drawn to chasing cars. Straining that leash so hard he broke away one day from Mom, who never talked about his death with weepy Sue and me; who wouldn't let us see his body but let us keep his leash.

March 31, 2020

PM: Despite our warnings, Daisy's posted on MeetUp.com for a Discussion Group on Quarantine Depression; She's looking, Jeff claims, for Mr. Sad-Bar; M&D&I laugh, me glad to be looking for no one, to be immersed in HER BATH; We cheer & boo the T. Awards; We remember one speech from Nathan Lane years ago & award it BEST speech of all awards ever: "...& most of all I thank you because I'm an emotionally unstable desperately needy little man."

Post-T.-Show; 2AM: How in high school, as PUNISH-

MENT, a teacher made me WRITE 100 TIMES what I'd never do again. 4-eyed Goody-Good me; caught lying to the gym coach about a phantom fever; I slashed I,I,I down the page: I WILL NOT PLAY SICK;I WILL NOT PLAY SICK; But now—because I can't stop worrying that I'll like it too much, The Scene I'll be shooting in mere weeks—now I reverse the words; I write over&over the title I rarely say out loud: I WILL NOT SICK PLAY; I WILL NOT SICK PLAY; I WILL NOT SICK PLAY; I WILL NOT SICK PLAY

3AM: correcting ESL papers on my computer screen, in Docs, my comments in blue sidebar cartoon-balloons—twitching as my Mouse Companion scrabbles in my walls—tears wake my sleeplessly dry eyes; I promise to promise Jin extra help: "My name Jin Yong. By the boat I come. In the boat, the mountain waves. We afear much. Here I most of time make my English better than now. I also am to try to learn the culture of America how they have been living so far. When I leave your country, I would expect myself to be different much."

Panting through her mask, Em alighted the concrete island. Taking her place centerstage, so to speak. What a tableau! If only she had her real camera, not just her phone! The pole-warped Jeep Cherokee was turned around like a bad child facing a corner. The Jeep driver stood on the very curb where she'd almost flattened Em, watching the tow truck hook her bumper. Em stepped up behind her, staring too at the Jeep. Inside what Em as a kid had called the 'way-back,' she saw a tidy jumble of rolled-up woven rugs and large wooden spoons.

"Excuse me?" Em tapped the driver's tensed shoulder. She pivoted lightly as a dancer. Clutching a fuzzy shawl, still masked, her fine blonde hair vibrating with its wool, she studied Em as if trying to place her. "You—" Em began with shaky indignation, wishing she could tug down her mask and displaying her cut finger. "You might've killed me."

The woman gasped under her mask like Em had declared herself dead. Above her maroon mask, her irises swelled: wet blueberries.

"I'm *sor*-ry," she told Em. And Em blinked, hearing her own forgive-me whine when she apologized to her friends or ESL students for spacing out.

"Me too," Em answered illogically, studying the woman studying her. Her fragile good looks did remind Em of her own: just pretty enough to get away with being a Space Case.

"That's all that saved me—" Em pointed to the tilted iron signpost beside them. "It blocked me from, from—" She gestured to the overcast sky, dizzy as if staring from that great height. No: as if feeling someone stare down at her.

"Actually," the Jeep woman cut in earnestly. "The policeman, he told me that that signpost *causes* crashes at this intersection! It's so far *over* you can't see the No Left Turn sign till you've already started the turn—which I *tried* to stop but it was like the Jeep, my father's Jeep, was *driving* itself—Like those new cars are supposed to do! Drive—"

"Itself? Oh, come on," Em waved a hand, disapproving of her own disapproval. Who was she to feel superior to this 30-something daddy's girl? Or—Em caught herself by habit—superior for not letting herself feel superior? She sighed, sick of her own useless hair-splitting scruples. "*You* were driving. Unfortunately. But—I guess we were both just—lucky."

"I *am* sorry." The driver fingered her mask, then her hand-knit shawl, looking relieved.

"I know, I know." Em backed up another crunchy step. On impulse, she bent. She lifted one shard of Jeep headlight. Orange plastic: brightly faceted, sharp-edged. "Souvenir," she murmured, slipping it into the unzipped pocket of her backpack.

That pocket otherwise—Em waggled her fingers in sudden alarm—empty.

"Oh my God—" Em turned her back on the driver. "Officer?" A cop stood a few feet away, his firm meaty arms folded. Em ran up to him, picturing the ghost of Andy Warhol passing Bank America, swinging his fists as if clutching something valuable.

Why does she feel so suddenly sure what he gripped in one of those fists?

April 20, 2020

3AM: At last, I pour the poison I purchased on Amazon, at Maxi's recommendation. RODENT CONTROL: turquoise granules, a color they must've test-marketed; it must look good to a RODENT, look EATable. Granules like chippy colored sand in the terrarium of my childhood chameleon who'd turn green on the turquoise, turn I-forget-what on the yellow. But who looked sad on either side. I sniff the bitter granules, imagining their burn on my tongue. Calmly— thoughts are only thoughts—I set the bait in my dark closet. Where his (or her) nightly gnawing has been driving me crazy. Or keeping me company. Or both.

4 AM: Sleepless still; guilty about more than my mouse, I replay for comfort Jin Yong's lovely 2-week-old phone message, left after our first—so far our only—extra session: "Miss O.; you are helping me most-much."

Faint-light AM: Fingering DanielDog's leash in bed, pulling it taut. Snapping its leather on my arm. Then thigh. But going no further. God, will I finally get all-the-way off with someone to—only Maxi and the camera, only days away —watch?

"I *lost* something in the crash! It fell outa my purse pocket then might've got *stolen* by this man; it's my, my —" Em formed a tiny rectangle with her fingers, mentally flipping its doc pages. Her name and number so insanely typed on top; then all her worst secrets.

"Phone, Miss?" the cop asked, his beige eyes bored.

"No no; more important!" Em pressed her hands to her chest, feeling her heart thump, remembering a story she'd heard at a party: a South American poet losing his own diary notebook and rushing to his doctor, complaining of pains in his chest. Told it couldn't be his heart, the poet asked the doctor to draw an X on his chest where his heart was. Late that night, aiming at the X, the poet shot himself. "See, it's my *flash drive;* my whole—life."

"Your what? Whole what?" the Jeep Cherokee woman piped up behind Em as if fearing she might be accused of near-murder after all.

Em repeated it as carefully as Jin Yong, trying out a new word. "Life?"

May 18, 2020/ The Scene/ aka: Final Fantasy Sequence

AM: How much—I admit only here—I've wanted exactly this. Play; it has to be play; can't be 'real' or I'd be real scared; it has to be Play & I have to be Directing. And Acting but acting in a mask. Somehow the paper mask—virtually all I was wearing—makes me feel hidden. It has to be hard enough to feel real, I've instructed Maxi; It's how you get off is all, Maxi would say, matter of fact; So banal & Fifty-Shades-ish that the act itself, we agree, won't be shown; only its effects. Only my face. Is all, is all (I tell myself, half-stripped for the shoot).

Jeff is more than willing; he says he's half turned on & half not, acting; I'm half & half too at first which's how I like it, the best part in a way: I'm on my hands & knees, breasts pointing down, ass up; I'm at home in the lights, the Artifex steady in Maxi's hand; she's crouched by my dry tub; & it still feels like Play, Play-Acting, it's a Fantasy Sequence after all, doubly unreal:

Me doubled-over the tub & Jeff bunching up DanielDog's leash, the harness end, its buckles clicking & Maxi's camera fixing on my face, tiny in her lens; all flushed; half hidden by the mask. All of us masked, of course, so it's all supposedly 'safe.' My final clear thought.

Then the tail of leash snaps; I flinch at leather-on-flesh; SMACK, SMACK; Hard enough to hurt but not to mark; My first moan pitched for our mike but not my next & next; I'm gone but not; I'm counting is all, 6, 7, 8 licks; by the end, by 10, I'm whimpering & gasping & flushed in the way that can't be faked.

Once the lights are cut—after a dark dripping moment when we're all hushed, recomposing who we are—I can stand, I can laugh, I'm whipping off the mask; we're laughing together, I'm high-fiving first Jeff then—harder—Maxi in this drippy dark; I'm high, I've come & come back & We got it, Maxi enthuses; We got it all, kiddies; it's a Take.

Striding away from the scattered crash scene, from the policeman who'd abruptly turned away from her incoherent babble to direct traffic, Em had ducked down a familiar tree-shaded sidestreet. Taking the long way home to calm herself, to pass by the Massachusetts Association for the Blind. Wishing the Recording Studio was open so she could hide in one of the familiar sound-proof booths where she recorded books, where she could freaking think.

What-all was *on* that damn kidnapped flash drive? Striding by the heavily shaded MAB compound, Em imagined she heard from a distance the heavy-metal clatter of the Braille machine. Torture Typewriter, Em thought, picturing reems of paper imprinted with stiff permanent goosebumps. She sped her steps, moving to that harsh imagined beat.

She marched past the wooded MAB grounds, past a distant tied-together group of masked young students walking a path in the woods. No—Em did a quick double-take—not tied. Each of the children had a grip on a long rope, led by their plodding teacher.

Oh God, what had she written on her flash drive diary about her real leash, her real date—if you could call it that—last night? Em kept moving faster as if chased, aware again of the fading ache (maybe only imagined now) on her haunches. That faint ache reminding her that it had been—everything she'd so foolishly written down—all too true.

June 8, PM, 2020

PM: Jeff & Maxi & me celebrate HER BATH being named a Finalist; They drink & drink & tease me for not; not drinking, not social media-ing; you guys do that, I tell them like I'm the boss; so Jeff wields Daniel's leash half in fun & half not, our encore; Maxi plays Director this time; Maxi seizes the leash, saying she'll show Jeff how it oughta be done, how Daddy's white-girl wants it done; & she makes me—I knew she'd make me—wear it first; the adjustable harness that could not save DanielDog from chasing danger. Its worn leather cuts into my breasts, its buckles strapped round my skinny ribcage; Maxi tugs my leash, making me crawl; & then when she roughly unbuckles me, when she flourishes the leash like a lion tamer, I know she'll whip me hard enough to mark; & as soon as I know that, I can't not want it; at least down on my hands and knees like a dog I can't; Maxi playing regal Butch Dom, aiming to scare wimpy White-Girl Sub (me); But maybe I'm the one who scares her, takes her aback, whimpering for more & she hesitates, panting, asking: Em? You sure? She looks down at me and shakes her own head No, her silver Fulani beads clack-clacking. Which wakes us both from the spell; So I make myself say: No I'm not; No I don't want—but I always want—more.

Reaching the end of the MAB's quiet sidestreet, approaching busy Beacon Street, Em heard above the renewed traffic clamor her phone beep. She stumbled on the uneven sidewalk, tree roots having pushed through the grainy old concrete. A new message?

Em halted on the deserted sidewalk. She fumbled in her backpack—first—for a Tums tablet. Slipped it under her mask, into her mouth. Then she stood still, leaning on a rough but comforting tree trunk. She gripped her sleek sweaty phone and pressed it to her ear and heard her new message. A voice she'd never heard before.

As Em listened, as her cherry Tums turned to chalk on her tongue, she remembered one of her UCLA mentors. Whenever her Films screened, this mentor had confided to Em, she found herself wondering if it all wasn't happening only inside her own head.

"Hurts you to go outside, Miss O? Don't know if you'll hear this message, but I'm giving you the—chance. Your friend's right, y'know. The good thing about feeling like such a—" (in whisper) "loser" (coolly expressionless again) "is you do things you wouldn't've dared, because, Why not? Why not rough her—rough your—ass? Harder'n your little friends'd dare. None of this half-acting half-not crap for me. None of that 'PandemicPorn' but-you-think-it's-not crap for me. For you either, if you'd give it half a try. I could tell from across Beacon, babe, you're a born actress. All normal-nice, but with me you can drop that act. Drop your fancy-pants. Get real. Maybe I'm not, babe. Maybe I'm just a—crazy voice on your messages. Or maybe I'm a—real man. Wearing a real old-fashioned dead-leather belt; waiting for you, maybe, at the address printed right, er, smack next to your name in the Brookline Directory, Miss Director. We'll wear our masks so it's all safe, right? Can't hide from me. Come on home, babe, and we'll climb those mountain waves. Burst and propel; burst and propel. Tell me: have you ever? When you leave my country, Miss O., you'll be different much."

Em turned onto Beacon and tried to slow her headlong steps down its long straight sidewalk. She knew she should—maybe—find another police officer? Tell all? Walk to the police right now (where were they on peaceful Beacon?) before heading home. She should tell them that a stranger knew where she lived, knew her secrets. But would they then demand: what sorts of secrets? Em's emptied-out guts fizzed. Would they insist on hearing the whole message?

So unreal, it felt: that whole message she just heard. Or maybe it was the most real thing to happen to her in ages. In– ever?

Em walked at a brisk clip, passing sleek doctor's offices and Kosher delis and Turkish rug shops. Slow down, she told herself. Distant flimsy words, as she left behind Beacon. *None of this half-acting half-not crap for me,* he'd told her. Not acting out for some film project; not—how close was she to this next sliding-down step?—for some pathetic Pandemic Porn site scheme. Had she been considering performing such acts for money?

Why not just for her, as a person? A flesh and blood body. Who might die, like, now? Wasn't that what was missing in her Self-Isolated life? She bumped off the curb, forgetting to stop. God; what was she thinking? Her helium heart, full yet light, bopped with her steps. She was heading home as automatically as she'd headed to Bank America after the crash.

Her skirt brushed her dulled bruises. She was picturing that Warhol stare. Seen it all, tried it all. *Have you ever?* he'd asked. If he whipped her already-bruised ass, whipped her for real, would she finally totally lose control? Bucking and flailing, her whole body straining to burst into violent flight? Would she, in fact, be *different much?*

Em marched faster to her inner braille-machine beat. She veered onto her quiet side street. The apartment she couldn't afford without Dad's checks. What if—at last, she slowed her steps—he told? Posted her shit on Twitter? Could she somehow stop him if she met him face to face? Would he—surely not, she felt deep down—be there at all? But what if he was? What if that Warhol man, if that was even who he was, wouldn't—of course he wouldn't—stop? No safe words; no calling the shoot to a halt. Not with this utter sidewalk stranger who now knew her secrets.

She half-staggered onto her block of dingy yet sturdy brick buildings. It was dusk, she noticed, panting. The time of day for window-peeking. Each one Em passed flashed its story: a woman sorrowfully adjusting a lamp-shade; a young shaven-headed couple chattering with aggressive animation. Hoping to be watched. How done she felt, just now, with all that.

Em gazed up into their window, picturing audiences gazing into their computers at HER BATH. If she even made it that far. To a real screening at a virtual film festival. How real would that even feel, in the end? Any more real than anything else, these self-isolated days?

Em fingered her sharp-edged headlight shard. A lucky charm, now. Reminding her that she'd survived a crash; survived the pandemic, so far. So why not take a real chance, for once?

Have you ever? Em stepped toward her building. Ready for anything, she half believed, provided she lived. And she was unkillable, wasn't she? She tugged down her mask so it covered only her mouth, so she could breathe real air through her nose. She kept step-ping forward like a car driving itself. No one was going to take it from her: this day she deserved.

She halted across the street from her entrance. Her heart was hammering out its own hard code, sharpening her boldness and her fear. Both at once. A car whooshed by; Em squinted after its flashing, vanishing lights. Anything might happen. To me, she thought. Today. She eyed her building's glass doors, its number. Then her unlit 2nd floor window. Did its shade stir?

Stiffening like a soldier, Em imagined him watching her across the street. *Can't hide from me,* he'd said. That much felt certain. Whether, she thought clearly, he was there or not. Em touched the throbbing base of her throat, pressed with her slit fingertip.

No missing it now; no wondering where it was. Her heartbeat filled her chest and head. She blinked, remembering the too-timid Jeep driver. How she'd tried too hard to stop the dangerous turn she'd already started to make. Em drew a diaphragm-deep breath. Looking both ways, she stepped off the curb.

ACT THREE

Finales

THE ONES WHO ARE GONE

The men woke early to take the boys shooting. I stirred, awake before my husband's alarm. Through the knotty-pine walls, I heard my brother-in-law Hal's heavy shuffling steps. Maybe I could still talk Jerry out of going? Hal had reserved the firing range for his own private party, for the purpose of letting his boys and my boyish husband practice shooting. Because, Hal claimed, we might need shooting skills here in our family quarantine; in early June of 2020, in the largest of Hal's Woodside Family Cabins. But who made my brother-in-law our boss?

Who, I wondered groggily, did Hal think he was: Trump?

I burrowed into my pillow, trying to fall back asleep. Trying to delay the start of this day when everything would wind up changing—or starting to change—in ways I couldn't imagine back then, two years ago. I lay beside my steadily snoring husband, my own slim body already defensively tensed.

I rolled over, facing the many-eyed wall. Knotty-pine already driving me nuts. And it was only Day Two of the Flynn Family Quarantine. Wasn't I a Flynn, too? Sylvia

Szot Flynn. Though some Flynns, I believed, still regarded their liberal Boston-born sister-in-law the way the Goat Guy had yesterday. Our last gas stop: the man pumping our gas glancing at our faded HILLARY bumper sticker, then glaring through our car windshield at me as if at Hillary herself.

Worse: a defiant dark-eyed Hillary who stared right back.

Jerry stirred beside me in bed, restless, then lay so still he might be feigning sleep. Was it time yet? Dawn yet? Strident birds chirped in the chill pure air outside our cracked-open window. Small sounds magnified by the vast countryside silence all around us.

No reassuring rumble of traffic nearby; no Boston. I blinked, my curly black bangs—uncut for weeks—fringing my sight. And I shivered under the musty quilt, chilled. I'd lost weight these past tense weeks, our seemingly secure jobs suddenly up in the air, like everything. I pulled the quilt closer, moving carefully, so as not to wake Jerry.

Maybe his iPhone alarm wouldn't go off, I hoped. All our devices went wonky out here in the Greene County sticks, like our GPS yesterday before that final gas stop. I shut my eyes, trying not to picture it. The damn gas-station goat.

We'd been driving for hours, crossing the border into New York state, passing TRUMP 2020 yard signs, looming billboards for the THUNDER MOUNTAIN MOTORCYCLE RALLY, and a handprinted posting: WE BUY & SELL & LOVE GUNS. Trying not to feel we were driving into a Stephen King novel (Jerry's guilty pleasure) or a campout horror flick (mine).

Mid-afternoon, a cheerful boy walking along the

highway with his MAGA-hatted Dad in a matching plaid hunter jacket gave our car a friendly wave. I waved back, feeling suddenly hopeful. Reminded—as I reminded Jerry at the wheel—that we weren't just visiting Hal and Sharon but the kids too. The boys who loved Jerry, plus Mia. The niece I called 'my Mia.'

But just as we both relaxed a bit, our cell's GPS cut out. So, we stopped at a gas station. Jerry ran in to ask directions. I wanted to stay huddled in our Toyota while that glaring guy filled it. But I had to pee. And to check that I wasn't bleeding. My period promisingly overdue.

I ducked his glare, slipped on my mask and scurried to the sour-smelling bathroom—no doubt seething with Covid virus microbes. Then, relieved to pee and find no blood, I hurried back out, turned the wrong way and stumbled upon the goat pen.

Through my mask, I breathed the stink of goat shit and mashed muddy grass. The lone goat stood on stiff peg-legs in a wire-fenced pen along the weedy backside of the gas station. Eyes on the sides of its head. One eye fixed on me. Half a hex stare. I bent to meet that un-blinking gaze, remembering from my Mythic Creatures thesis research how goats are said to have the Devil's eye. That eye stared blankly back at me.

The eyeball piss-yellow; the pupil a sideways bar. A floating minus sign.

"I bet *Trump* has goat eyes too," I told Jerry as we drove off, as the Gas Guy watched us go. "Bet that guy has them. With the weird sideways pupil—"

Jerry, at the wheel, gave me a look, his glasses flash-ing and his curly auburn hair blowing sideways. "C'mon Sylvie, maybe he's just a crabby old man sick of pump-ing gas—"

"Especially for us 'Mass-holes,'" I admitted, using Hal's name for Massachusetts drivers.

"And with that HILLARY 2016 bumper sticker still

plastered on our car like a target—"

"Not the best look for good ol' Greene Country," I had to agree, though sullenly. "Look, maybe I'll be ready to peel 'Hillary' off our car after the Democrat's convention..."

Jerry nodded with another wry sideways glance, then switched to a more serious tone. "Speaking of the future, Sylvie—When you made that bathroom stop—"

I patted his knee lightly, keeping my voice light too. "Nothing, future Daddy—so far, so good. God, maybe all those shots in my ass actually worked—"

"It's too soon to tell, Syl. Anyhow, with the world going like it is..."

As Jerry trailed off, eyes fixed again on the road, I burst out, *"What?* Will you ever finish that sentence? You keep saying stuff like that then cutting yourself off."

"Because I don't know how the sentence finishes. No one does—"

I could only nod. This trip to hunker down together with our in-laws had been prompted by the abrupt cratering of our summer travel plans. With Covid numbers spiking in Boston, fleeing to rural New York seemed to make sense, at least to Jerry, who missed his big brother.

He pulled our car onto a long dirt road, a sign pointing the way to 'WOODSIDE FAMILY CABINS.' Beneath it, Hal had planted a TRUMP 2020 yard sign.

Jerry paused the car at the two signs and gave me one quick warm-lipped kiss.

"It's just for a couple weeks. And remember, Hal and Sharon—they're family."

He started driving forward, the dirt road bumpy, lined with the cabins Hal managed, while living with his family in the largest 'cabin'—really a house—at the end of the road. Big enough for Hal and Sharon, their two boys and baby and our niece Mia. Plus, in these past weeks, after Hal rescued her from her Covid-ridden nursing home, Jerry's and Hal's mom.

"Hal always looks out for his family, Syl. Remember, he used to protect me from bullies—" Jerry drove past the deserted cabins, the tourism biz having dried up in lock-down.

"I know; he's your family. Our family," I added as we bumped onto the gravel driveway to the Main Cabin. "I just wish Hal and Sharon would start seeing *me* as family..."

In our last moments of sleepy peace, I eased backwards toward Jerry's reassuring warmth. I pressed into his pajama'd crotch. I felt reassured, too, that I sensed no ache inside of me; no pre-menstrual cramps. Could it be that our first round of shots in my ass had 'taken'?

Such fertility treatments were considered non-essential medical procedures, I knew. Another worry I hadn't yet mentioned to Jerry, already stressed over the rumors that Boston College would slash its Humanities faculty. He had wanted us to wait on treatments till his job was 'secure;' this had been his—our—official excuse. Had that been a mistake too?

On the other side of our wall, the baby had not yet woken; FOX News was not yet cranked up. Still, I reminded myself, we were lucky to be out here. Though I'd rather have spent the first weeks of Summer locked down together in our condo, as we'd been all Spring, I sensed I needed to let Jerry win this one. After all, the fertility treatments were, really, my idea.

Outside, Hitchcockian bird twitters rose. Groggy Jerry wrapped his arms around me, clasped his hands over my still-flat stomach. Our usual spooning; our slender, strong jogger bodies fitting as perfectly as ever. Jerry tightened his sleepy yet sure grip on me.

Why did I still feel so tense? What had Jerry's Mom said last night as I'd helped Sharon tuck her into bed? I rocked against Jerry, recalling his mother's ominous sing-song words.

Out here—out here is emptiness in its frightening.

Jerry and I startled together at his alarm, pulling apart. The pulsing beep chimed over the high-pitched birds. Jerry sat up first, so abruptly that I rolled to the edge of this saggy unfamiliar bed. I shot him a plaintive semi-seductive look over my bare shoulder.

"'s time..." Jerry fumbled with his phone, his hands always shaky when he woke.

"Hope Hal gets you some coffee. Shit, one twitchy finger and—what?" I sat up, raising my hands to mime quotation marks. "'American Carnage at Catskills Shooting Range'?"

Jerry allowed a crack of his usual crooked smile. "Hey, duty and Big Brother call."

"Can't you say you're sick or something? Fake a Covid cough?"

But Jerry was already rising like a stoic soldier. He'd showered the night before, as per Hal's orders. A toilet flushed from the bathroom in the hall. Sounding extra loud, like the Angry Birds outside. Hungry baby birds? I wondered, remembering in a fuzzy flash that I'd dreamed my niece Mia had slipped from my hands in the pond and sunk like a stone.

"Wonder if Mia's up yet," I mumbled aloud. "And your Mom..."

"Hal's taken good care of Mom," he reminded me. "He probably saved her life..."

"I know." I lay back down. "Rescuing her from that Home. And you're going to talk to Hal about us contributing more, right?" Jerry nodded but evaded my gaze, guilty when his Mom came up. He'd always paid for over half of her Nursing Home costs. How would all that work now? I faced the darkened ceiling, its judgmental knotty pine eyes. Jerry sighed and began dressing in his methodical way, as if—if only—for another day of teaching.

Jerry and I been in our mid-thirties when we'd met at a BU alums mixer, our five-foot-five heights and curly hair matching. Assistant Professor Flynn's gaze shone behind his glasses, blue-grey, watery yet intent. Had anyone ever stared at nerdy me with such fascination?

I told him I was Sylvia Szot. Rather than asking about my Polish last name—a source of endless teasing in my childhood—he asked: Sylvia as in 'sylph'? Then he'd shown me on his phone, our shoulders and heads pressed together, the official definition: "a mythical air spirit."

"Ha, you got me," I murmured back. "My secret identity."

For years I'd been moving so lightly through life, almost invisibly; now someone had finally spotted me. I raised my eyes from Jerry's phone to his waiting gaze. Caught.

Soon we were jogging together along the Charles, then later racing each other home on our bikes, along the Chestnut Hill Reservoir, up Mass. Ave beside the treacherous T track. Always crash-landing on our comfy condo couch. The two of us gaming away on our tablets at either end, our bare feet meeting in the middle. Toes touching, castle battlements falling.

"Syl?" Jerry materialized above me, dressed neatly as ever but in plaid flannel and jeans.

I took his hand, wishing I could pull my wiry-strong husband back into bed. "I know you've gotta go. We girls will be OK here. Just watch your back around your *Kar Darig.*"

Red-bearded domineering Hal, Jerry and I had long joked, was clearly the mythic Evil Twin of Jerry, the mild-mannered Leprechaun—Hal his nemesis and 'Red Man.'

"Don't worry about me, Babe. I'll shoot straight. It'll all come back to me from those Bad Old Days hunting with Dad... Not exactly how I thought I'd be starting this summer."

I squeezed his hand, still feeling a pang at our June travel plans shattered. We'd finagled an LA Gamers' Conference presentation on a fledgling shared research project examining the 'Pop Gothic' texts Jerry taught and their roots in my gaming design inspiration: ancient mythologies. I'd been researching Celtic myths the past few months, working 'remotely.'

I released Jerry's hand as if sending him off to teach, not shoot. He kissed my forehead. Through the walls, the boys were now thumping round. The Master Bedroom TV was on, grave-voiced anchors reciting muffled facts about new Lockdowns. Jerry headed to the bedroom door, opening it and turning back to me.

"Listen, Syl—" He nodded toward the News voices. "The way things are going—The way that gas-station guy looked at us. Maybe Hal's right that we might need to— buy a gun."

"'We' as in you and me?" I sat up, hugging the homemade quilt in the window breeze.

"Plus a baby too, maybe..." Jerry turned away as I

smiled. "I really gotta go—"

"Wear your damn mask," I told him mildly, pleased that he'd mentioned the baby.

"Hal says we don't have to around here, but I will." Jerry slipped out, adding our usual farewell phrase, which sounded serious here in the actual wilds. "Hold the fort."

"Uncle Jer-ree! Daddy says you're LATE!"

"What took you, Wall-eyes? Chicken-shitting out, already?"

"Daddy said 'shitty'!"

"Whoa, big brother, watch your big mouth-"

"Screw you, Professor Prick—"

"Daddy said 'Dick'!"

"No, boys, he said 'Prick'!"

Through the shaded bathroom window, I overheard the men and boys bantering outside. I bushed my teeth as Hal's Ford Ranger truck roared off down the long dirt road. On schedule at 7AM; heading toward the Firing Range. Where Jerry might purchase a gun, for real?

I spat in the sink. And I dressed slowly before stepping out into the larger cabin.

I was used to small apartments shared by two introverts. Before Jerry, I'd only lived with my earnest workaholic Mom, struggling to raise me alone. She'd put my skinny brainy dark-haired Dad through Law School only to be abandoned in favor of a younger Paralegal wife. Don't marry too early, Mom told me from early on. She took back her Polish maiden name and worked overtime as an Accountant, crunching numbers on her calculator on one side of our kitchen table while I labored over extra-credit homework on the other. At school, I didn't fit in on the rowdy playground; kids pronounced Szot 'snot' and called me 'Snotty Sylvia.' I must have seemed standoffish, because I was shy and studious like Mom. I snuck off to the library during recess, immersed in fantasy sagas. Mom hung my ink sketches of girl warrior-princesses all over the kitchen walls. Together—over scrumptious Nut Kolachi that Mom baked for her skinny ever-hungry daughter—Mom and I finished daily crossword puzzles.

Only at home with Mom was it OK that I always knew all the answers.

After Mom's death, her big heart giving out shortly after she'd retired, I'd numbed my own heart, submerging myself in the fantasy gaming world, both in play and work. Having written my feminist Comp Lit thesis on Warrior Princesses in ancient epics, women who took charge, I'd parlayed my BU degree plus my ability to sketch out heroines and plotlines into a career. Never wanting a husband, much less—until I fell for Jerry, almost too late—a baby.

A door thumped across the cabin. Muffled movement in the Common Room? My Mia? As a modest act of rebellion against my Trumpist sister-in-law Sharon, I slipped on my black 'Nasty Woman' tee shirt. Dark memento of my days as a Hillary volunteer—when I found myself taunted by haters online, who mocked my last name as if I were back in grade school.

Hal mocked me too, phoning me on Election Night to gloat. I'd promised Jerry I wouldn't even mention Trump to Hal, this trip. We've gotta stick together now, Jerry decreed. Our family. Eschewing my usual red dash of lipstick, I padded barefoot down the wood hallway.

"Mia?" I stepped into the Common Room with its worn but vacuumed carpet and its comfy corduroy couch. The pool table—Hal's pride—always looked good as new. Its wood legs shone, freshly polished. How, I wondered absently, did Sharon have time to keep the house tidy?

"Auntie Syl-vee?" Mia used her proudly precise pronunciation. From across the shadowy room, she peered at me through the pink-rimmed glasses that matched her pink sweats.

I stepped up to the pool table, feeling like it was just Mia and me: two barefoot kids alone on a deserted island. The grown-ups off on some vague scary mission.

"Wanna play our game?" I prompted Mia. Under her straight-cut blonde bangs, her eyes lit with the promise of forbidden fun. "But," I reminded her, "we'll have to *whisper*-shout."

Mia nodded solemnly. With a flourish, I lifted the metal triangle, let loose the multi-colored balls on the green felt tabletop. They scattered, making satisfying clack-clack-clacks. Mia bounced on her heels with painstakingly restrained glee. A stifled teakettle squeal. Could Jerry and I hope for a child so dear? Was it even right to hope for one, in this wicked world?

"Cats-Kills!" Mia whisper-shouted to me—the word that had first set our game rolling in our last visit last Fall. She'd wanted to know if cats got killed in the nearby Catskills; I'd assured her it was just a funny word. Thus we discovered our mutual love of shouting absurd and (to Mia) new words. Whilst randomly rolling and clacking pool balls.

"Cats-Kills Ca-tas-trophy," I whisper-shouted, my opening gambit.

"Cat-ASS-tree!" Mia sent a red ball whizzing my way, hard and fast.

Catastrophe!

Pandemonium!

Ricochet!

I threw out words as Mia and I rolled the glossy wood balls super-fast, not using what Mia called 'the sticks.'

She squealed as balls collided, bouncing, clack-clack-clack.

"Ricochet," Mia exalted as a fresh ball whizzed.

"It's a *catastrophe!*" I slowed my own ball rolls. So Mia wouldn't get too hyper.

"What's cat-ass-tree again?" She widened her already-magnified eyes.

"A catastrophe," I explained, "is when everything goes wrong!"

"Everything goes WRONG!" she agreed with edgy*f* escalating glee. "Like NOW- When everyone goes SICK!" She hurled the red #2 ball. It bounced toward me across the green felt.

I ducked as it bounded off the table, cracking to the floor like a gunshot.

"Mia?" Sharon stepped from the hall in her pink bathrobe, "What are you two up to?"

I froze in my foolish crouch, peeking over the pool table at Sharon, her shoulder-length dark-blonde hair already neatly brushed. She looked incomplete without the baby in her arms.

"You're not scared of Mia are you, Sylvie?" Sharon asked me flatly.

"No one's scared, Sharon!" I straightened, sheepish, shaking back my wild curls.

Mia studied her Mom to gauge how mad she was, behind her wearily patient smile. Then Mom Flynn creaked open her door and shuffled down the hall, halting beside Sharon.

Mom Flynn gazed from Sharon to me, seemingly confused. Did she know anymore which daughter-in-law was which? Which one had given her oldest son three children plus the late-in-life gift of her namesake granddaughter Mary? In Mom Flynn's permanently fogged-over mind, were Sharon and I now the same, equally unrecognizable?

A secret relief, I recognized in my heart, to face Mom Flynn and not feel that she was wondering when or if I'd be able to give Jerry a child of his own.

"You girls." Mom Flynn shook her head of dandelion-fluffy white hair, tinged with a rusty trace of its former auburn glory. "The men took the boys away—"

"They went SHOOTING—" Mia blurted out, then clapped her hand over her mouth.

Mom Flynn nodded, taking this information in stride. "They aren't coming back, then."

"Of course the boys are coming back." Sharon shot a reproving glance at Mia.

"No," Mom Flynn corrected Sharon, a spark of mischief in her foggy-pale eyes. "Only the ones who are here will be back. Back in two shakes of an old man's stomach!"

After Sharon had helped Mom Flynn dress and we'd fed Mom and Mia breakfast; after Sharon planted both of them in front of the Common Room TV blaring with a FOX morning show that—luckily, in my view—neither of them seemed to be watching, Sharon and I cleaned up the cramped kitchen. Our first time alone. Rinsing the breakfast cereal bowls in hot water and handing them to Sharon as she loaded the dishwasher, I asked how things were going, really.

Sharon answered in her flat faintly accusatory way. "Not so good." She was wedging a final bowl in place in the dishwasher's wire rack. "Hal's been busting his butt to make this Cabin gig work, but folks keep canceling trips in this crazy pandemic-or-whatever. And now we've got Mom Flynn too—" Sharon straightened and shut the dishwasher, switched it ON.

"Which is why we want to help *more,* Sharon." I raised my voice over the churning mechanical chug, meeting

Sharon's skeptical pale-blue gaze. "You're doing the work of that whole Nursing Home now. Jerry and I agree. We need to find a way to give more—"

"'Find a way,' Sylvia? When you and Jerry both have those fancy Boston jobs—?"

Behind Sharon, visible steam began to rise from the throbbing dishwasher. I turned to the sink, wiping my wet hands, buying time, taken aback by Sharon's blunt tone. I re-faced her.

"We *will* help more with Mom Flynn, Sharon. I promise—" I found my voice rising defensively. "But those jobs? Jerry's might get cut any time, the way things are going. Honestly, we can barely pay our Boston rent. Plus, we still owe a ton of student loan debt—"

"Yeah, we've got a ton of debt too," Sharon mumbled with an edge. "Real debt."

A pause, filled by the chugging old-style dishwasher —sounding ready to burst—plus the strident FOX voices. Over Sharon's shoulder, I could see Mom Flynn slumped in her chair, Mia on the floor by the TV scribbling impatiently with Sharpies, waiting for the grownups to finish talking. In the back bedroom, baby Mary was asleep for now. What on earth was it like to take care of four kids and a senile old lady? What was it Sharon really wanted—deserved—from us?

"I didn't mean—I'm sorry, Sharon. That was a dumb thing of me to say." I reached out and touched Sharon's rounded-down tensed-up shoulder. "I can't even imagine what the last few weeks have been like for you! Taking in Mom Flynn when you've got the four kids—"

"And you haven't got any," Sharon cut in, still flat-voiced. "Any kids."

I pulled away at that, lowering my hand and stepping back, bumping the counter.

"But we're *trying*," I blurted out foolishly. Shit, why had I said that? Jerry and I had agreed to keep our fertility treatments secret for now. Yet here I was telling Sharon with her smoothly unreadable face everything. "We've—I've—been getting some treatments—"

"I had an Aunt who had to have those—" Sharon waved one hand dismissively. "But she only got pregnant with her twins after she and my uncle stopped all that 'trying'—"

I turned back to the sink to hide my face. I seized a sponge, gripping it hard. Remembering as I wiped the sink a TV comedy skit in which a defeated Hillary Clinton is told she simply didn't 'try' hard enough. She smiles stiffly while quietly ripping a wood panel off her podium. Yes, the TV Hillary makes herself agree. She just hadn't 'tried' hard enough.

"Look Sylvia." Sharon spoke in a slightly softened tone. I made myself turn back to her, still gripping the sponge. "All I mean is, you and Jerry don't have any kids yet, right now—"

I nodded dazedly at this undeniable truth, as the true point of this whole awkward talk—and maybe this whole visit, which Hal had proposed—hit me. Inside my spacey self-absorbed mind, I realized that Sharon and Hal wanted Jerry and me to take her in: Mom Flynn.

"MOMMY—" Mia called out, startling both Sharon and me. "Can't we get out-SIDE?

I wound up leading Mom Flynn out while Sharon, inside, helped Mia with her sneakers. Outside on the sunny wood deck, Mom Flynn studied me with her eyes widened like Jerry's round eyes in a photo of Baby Jerry she'd shown me once. His first time in a highchair.

But he was always staring at us like that, Mom Flynn had confided. *Appalled, like: what are you people doing to me NOW?*

We'd laughed fondly that day, the day Jerry first brought me home to meet his family. Witty Mom Flynn had been my ally among the gruff close-mouthed Flynn men. She'd scolded Hal for asking me 'what kind of name' was Szot. Today, though, Mom Flynn faced me warily.

Sharon opened the sliding door, balancing the baby on her shoulder. "Mia's coming out."

"I've got this," I replied with more confidence than I felt. Baby Mary gurgled. Mia ran by in a bright blur, thumping down the deck steps as if some other little girl awaited her.

"She's got this baby," Mom Flynn stated brightly to Sharon. Sharon shot her a rare genuine smile, beaming over baby Mary's downy sunlit head, Mary's sparse hair blonde too.

"Someone needs a burpy, don't you sweet-pea?" Sharon jiggled baby Mary.

"Sweet pea," Mom Flynn repeated. Or, I couldn't help wondering, did she mean 'p-e-e'? God, would I need to change her bladder-leak pad? I'd noticed a box of those in the kitchen bathroom. Sharon was stepping back behind the glass door, about to disappear.

"Oh, and Sharon, I brought some masks in case Mia wants to take a walk." I pulled two paper masks from my pocket. Sharon nodded. Was she not dismissive of masking like Hal? Or did she not want to fight me on this when she'd gained points for her agenda in our kitchen talk?

"Fine, Sylvia. But there really shouldn't be anyone around. The cabins are all empty—"

"It's a Ghost Town," Mom Flynn observed, Sharon talking on as if she hadn't spoken.

"Let me know if you go walking and I'll watch Gran. But don't go near the main road—"

"Yes. No—I mean, I won't." I turned to Mia out in the

yard, hearing Sharon slip inside. Bright-haired Mia was kneeling in the tall grass, picking wildflowers and weeds.

"I need a tissue, Miss," Mom Flynn murmured, maybe thinking I was a Nurse from her old Home. Would I wind up being her new Nurse? While trying to work remotely in Jerry's and my one-bedroom apartment? Too small for three adults. What would Jerry say about this possible plan? Mom Flynn rubbed her eyes.

"I have no eyelashes left." She sounded choked up. "I cried them all away…"

I smiled but Mom Flynn didn't smile back, irritably lifting one mask. "What on earth IS this?" she demanded, surely remembering MountainView Nursing Home. How scary her last weeks there must have been, so many sick and dying in May when Hal checked her out.

"Face-MASKS—to cover our mouths and noses in case someone sneezes." I lifted one mask and held it up over my nose and mouth to show her.

Gram pointed at my half-hidden face, bewildered. "Who ARE you?"

I lowered the mask. "It's just me, Sylvie… One of your daughter-in-laws—"

"The one who's here? But the ones who are gone…"

"The boys? They'll be back soon—"

"No. The other one—"

"You mean," I twisted in my seat, scanning the empty yard. "Mia!?"

I stood up, shading my eyes from the sun. Wind-ruffled grass; no Mia. And over by the gravel driveway: the handful of daisies and dandelions she'd picked, abandoned. Oh God, had I already lost Mia? I scrambled from the table and ran down the wood deck steps.

"Sharon, you've gotta *watch Gran*—" I shouted toward the open bedroom window.

"OK—" Sharon called irritably through the window. I

was hurrying down the driveway toward the dirt road which led to the main road, its truck-heavy traffic.

Not seeing Mia, I broke into a run.

The first time Jerry and I jogged together, after our first night together, we fell in step side by side along the Charles River, the waters reflecting the gracefully arched white elms and the early spring sun. I could feel something big and invisible turning, a wheel of fate.

We'd both lived in our heads for so long, lonely without knowing it; we wanted time to live in our bodies, just the two of us. We took that time, knowing—or I knew—we were pushing our luck in terms of babies. The baby I'd imagined all through our first two years of marriage. After we'd 'tried' for a year, Jerry hadn't been too enthused about embarking on fertility treatments. But I felt hopeful that once I was carrying our child, my doting husband would be happy too. *Make a plan and make God laugh.* One of my Mom's old favorite sayings.

In mid March, 2020, as the first Lock Down orders kicked in, I'd taken a solitary masked jog past an elementary school, running—literally—into afternoon pick-up. A couple teachers wearing medical masks stood by the parking lot entrance, looking stressed as they waved in cars. I slowed to jog past and gaze in at the kids lined up by the chain link fence.

A teacher spoke to me sharply, asking: "Excuse me? Whose mother are you?"

"No one's," I told this masked woman. Then I turned heel and ran on.

"Mia—" I raced onto the dirt road—pounded up toward the main road that rumbled with trucks. "MIA," I hollered, scanning the empty cabins and empty yards. God, where was she? And I wondered, as if pursuing an elusive gaming foe: where would she *want* to go? Based on previous clues? My thudding steps stumbled. I aimed toward the stone chimney of the middle cabin, picturing it in a flash: the swing-set Mia loved. "MI-A—"

I beelined toward the cabin, catching a glimpse of Mia's pink jacket. Relief buoyed me as I bounded into the overgrown side yard. But Mia stood stock-still by the chimney, staring at something in the cabin's back yard. I scrambled to her side; Mia grabbed my leg, gripping me.

And I saw him too, the stranger. The man stumbled to his feet from the rickety wood picnic table by the swing-set. A scruffy black-haired guy with a sunburnt unshaven face. Middle-aged, but sullen as a teenage punk. He held a cigarette in one hand. With the other, he patted his battered camouflage-jacket. Feeling his pocket for a gun?

"Who are you?" I made myself ask, hoping this disheveled unsmiling guy might somehow be a co-worker of Hal's. Or a cabin-renter Hal had failed to mention?

"Just stopped for a smoke—" The man raised his cigarette, half smoked, its tip lit. "You the owner?" He nodded toward the cabin. Asking this question curtly, as if I were the intruder.

I glanced at the cabin, noting a back window half-open. God, had this guy crashed here overnight? I inched back a step with difficulty, Mia attached to my leg.

"Yes, I am," I lied, nodding. Glad that he was bending to heft his backpack.

"No, she's NOT," Mia burst out, releasing me to proclaim this proudly. "My DADDY is!"

"That so?" the man asked me, sizing me up from across the small yard. He hoisted his pack on his shoulder, started to trudge toward us. None of us, I realized, in masks.

"Yes," I told this guy, backing up and pulling Mia with me. My back pressed the cabin's chimney, its cold stone. I felt trapped as the man with his slept-in sweat-smell shuffled closer.

He came to a halt, only about three feet in front of us. Too close for comfort and for Covid safety. He glanced at my Nasty Woman tee shirt. Looking nasty himself. Yet I kept trying to explain why *I* was here. "Her father owns these cabins and—this is private property."

"That so? Think I can't figure that out?" He glared at me, his bloodshot eyes red, white and blue. "You don't need to get all *nasty* on me—"

"Listen, sir." I met his narrowed gaze. "I'm sorry but —You need to get going."

In reply, the guy lifted his cigarette to his lips and sucked in. Leaning forward, he exhaled a mouthful of smoke right at my face. I ducked down, bowing my head, holding my breath. And I pulled Mia even closer, cupping her head, pressing her face against my thigh.

The man laughed, a hoarse satisfied sound. "Don't lose your shit, lady. I'm going."

He tossed his cigarette on the grass beside us. I watched it smolder, tasting its acrid smoke. I heard and felt the man stride away from us. Mia un-froze, squirming against my hold.

"Let GO—" She pulled away and stared up at me, her hair mussed, and her glasses crooked. "Why'd you DO that? Why'd he say 'SHIT'? Where's that man GO-ing?"

Shakily, I smoothed Mia's hair, trying to sound calm. "Away, I hope."

Together we peered around the cabin corner. Thankfully the man *was* stalking away, his pack thumping his back. Heading off to hitchhike? Near the end of the dirt road, two cabins up, he turned around. He called out to me mockingly, his ragged shout loud and clear.

"Might be back later, BITCH!"

With that, he tromped on toward the main road. I felt jolted inside, frozen outside.

"Why's he so MAD?" Mia found her voice before I did.

"He doesn't have a place to go," I told Mia, voice shaky. "A lot of people don't, right now. Because of—the way things are going..." I took Mia's hand, tugging her away from the lingering trace of his smoke. "We need to go and tell your *mom* about that man—"

"No. I wanna SWING!" Mia strained toward the swing-set, but I yanked her back.

"Mia, I mean it!" I darted another glance at the cabins' half-open window, a glare of sun on the glass. In games, such clues were never nothing. Who knew if someone else might be hiding in there? In any of these cabins? I tugged Mia's arm urgently.

"Stop!" Mia insisted, jerking back. "You're NOT my MOM!" She pulled free of me.

Then she burst into tears. Breathlessly, I knelt to pull Mia into a hard hug, feeling her hot tears dampen my tee shirt. "I know, I'm sorry—But Mia, this isn't a game. That man might come back. So we need to go back and —wait for your *Dad* to come back—"

With his gun, I thought but didn't say. Mia snuffled. And she patted my back lightly with her stiff-fingered hand. Such comfort in those few soft pats. Then she pulled away and regarded me seriously through her crooked glasses. "You're still—not my Mom."

I broke into my Fun Aunt grin, leaping to my feet. "Yep, I'm not! Because what a CATASTROPHE that would be!"

Mia hopped up too. We walked back to the main cabin hand in hand, me leading.

"Catass-Trofee," Mia repeated as we reached the driveway, pronouncing it perfectly.

Never had I been so glad to hear Hal's truck pulling in. Its guttural unmuffled roar usually irritated me but today it elated me. I rushed from the kitchen to greet the men.

After I'd described to Sharon what had happened and she'd texted Hal about the trespasser, we'd whipped up an early lunch of grilled cheese sandwiches. When we heard the truck, Sharon stayed back with Mom Flynn and Mia while I jogged out onto the driveway.

"I'm so glad you're all back—" I burst out to Jerry, breathless.

He hopped down from Hal's truck and pulled me into a hug. I breathed the woodsy smell of his hunting jacket. And I felt grateful for Hal's gruff calm. He ruffled his youngest boy's curly red hair. Then told Hal Jr., "You're in charge, pal." Hal Jr. beamed as he did whenever he's given a task. The boys went running inside for lunch so Hal could go check out that cabin.

But first he had one question for me. "This guy you saw—he was Black, you said?"

"Um, no. I told Sharon he had black hair. Like me. He was a sunburnt white guy, Hal."

"But you think he had a gun? In his pocket or whatever?"

I bit back my reaction to that 'But' and simply nodded. "I—think so, maybe."

"I'll come with you, bro." Jerry stepped up beside his broad-shouldered brother, looking less boyish in that boxy hunting jacket. He patted its large pocket the way the stranger had patted his pocket. "I got us one today," my husband announced, following my gaze.

"A—gun?" The word stuck in my throat. Yet I found myself feeling a sick rush of relief.

Hal answered for Jerry. "Just an old-lady pistol, Sylvia. The way things are going, he—you two—you need one. So yeah. Your hubby's now armed and considered dangerous..."

"You really think we need our own gun?" I asked Jerry, but Hal again replied.

"You really think you need to wear that damn Hillary-shirt 'round here?"

I took a step back from the men, looking down at my 'Nasty Woman' tee. "Yeah, well, this shirt did seem to get that guy riled up. You're right about that, Hal."

Hal gave his firm fatherly nod. A good Dad, I reminded myself. A family man, no matter what his politics, right? We did need to stick together, we Flynns—right?

"C'mon, Jer." Hal turned on his boot heel and started striding down the driveway, crunching gravel. Jerry leaned closer to me, his hand cupping his pocket. Our hidden pistol.

"Sylvia." Jerry hardly ever used my full name. "Hal, he talked to me about Mom—"

I nodded, feeling as if walls were closing in around me though we were outside. "Yeah, Sharon—she talked to me too. I think she wants us to—take Mom Flynn back to Boston—"

Jerry nodded back at me, hard. And I could see in his blue-grey eyes—unblinking like Sharon's bluer eyes—that he felt we should do it, do our share. How could I argue, really?

"Let's talk about it later—" Before I could say more, Jerry nodded again and turned away. He jogged ahead, light-footed as ever. He caught up with Hal. The two of them headed down the dirt road, Jerry standing straighter, more square-shouldered.

The short brothers walked briskly, casting tall shadows in the sun. God, what was happening? Were we really going to take on Mom Flynn? And what if Jerry or I did get laid off? What would this mean for our baby plan? I wondered all this all at once, suddenly queasy. Plus, I was feeling a different ache, down low. Crossing the backyard, I noticed the face masks had blown onto the lawn. I retrieved them, remembering how close that man had stood to Mia and me as he'd breathed smoke at us. How trapped I'd felt. I clutched the masks, climbing onto the deck. Hoping Mia hadn't breathed any of that smoke. Hoping that guy wouldn't come back. Maybe that encounter with him had been nothing. Or maybe—everything?

Please just let Mia be safe, I thought as I pulled open the sliding glass door, turning toward the bathroom. And please let this not be my period, starting up inside. I stepped across the kitchen, hearing the boys call from the Common Room: "Uncle Jerry got a GUN!"

"I *know*," I shouted back above their Mario-Kart game music. "I want to see it," I lied, darting into the half-bath. I shut its door, facing the knotty pine, those watchful dark scrolls.

Minutes later, though it felt like more, I shuffled from the bathroom into the empty kitchen. Then I slipped—unnoticed by anyone—back outside. Numbly, I stepped onto the empty deck and sat at the redwood table. I shifted, uncomfortable with one of Mom Flynn's bulky pads in my panties. My tampons were stored in the other bathroom. Faintly, I heard from the dirt road Hal's booming laugh. Good. He and Jerry were safe, so far. I shut my eyes.

Behind my closed eyelids in the sun, I saw only red. Pulsing red like the menstrual blood draining from me now. A floater appeared: a minus-sign, the goat's eye pupil. A floating red minus sign had appeared in the tiny window of each home pregnancy test I'd taken this past year of 'trying.' Jerry always sympathetic yet (I let myself think now) relieved.

The way things are going, he kept saying. When he really finished that sentence, would the end be: we can't start a family now, in this crazy world? Especially, I thought clearly, if we're going to be caring for Mom Flynn? For who knew how long. Because who knew how long the pandemic would last? Or what more it might bring with it? So much already slipping away. I was almost 40. Was our best chance to have a baby slipping away, too?

Eyes still shut, I remembered my first time jogging along the Charles River with Jerry, sensing a giant wheel of fate turning. Something unspoken already decided, between us. Was a wheel of fate turning now, too? Silent minutes passed by before the glass door slid open again.

"Mom's coming out," Sharon called to me. I blinked, thinking for confused moment she meant my mom. As Sharon settled Mom Flynn beside me, I wished my own clear-headed Mom were here, alive. So I could hug her; so I could hear her sensible, soothing voice.

Instead, Sharon's flat voice asked me: "You OK, Sylvia? OK to watch Mom?"

I blinked up at her, squinting in the sun as I told her, "Yep." Then added: "Jerry—I think he's open to the idea of us taking in Mom. I—I'm sorry I seemed closed to it earlier. Honestly, Sharon, I was thinking then I might be, y'know, pregnant. But—turns out I'm not."

Sharon nodded slowly, taking all this in. "I'm sorry about that, Sylvie."

Was this the first time she'd ever called me not 'Sylvia' but 'Sylvie'? Stiffly, she reached down and patted my shoulder, like Mia had done. Then Sharon gave one of her rare yet warm smiles. "And Sylvie? I—we—appreciate your offer. If you two could just take Mom Flynn this summer, while the kids are home. We can work it all out later." I nodded; she nodded too. And Sharon hurried back inside to her kids, her steps maybe lighter. The door slid shut again, sealing me in—or really, out—with Mom Flynn. Her fluffy wispy hair blew in the breeze.

"Will they come back?" she asked aloud, musingly. "The ones who are gone?"

"They did come back," I replied, studying the yard. "The boys came back. But some," I added to Mom Flynn in her sing-song rhythm. "Some who are gone never got going...."

She nodded, mulling my words. I nodded too. Staring into the sunstruck grass, sitting silently beside Mom Flynn, I stiffened against a forceful cramp.

Two years later, now, as Covid fears begin to lift, I still don't know when or how Jerry and I might start our own family. But I do know—after working together with Hal and Sharon to keep Mom Flynn safe from Covid, only to lose her this past year to Alzheimer's—that Jerry's family and I have come together in ways I wouldn't have thought possible. Not back then, in the bleak fearful beginnings of summer, 2020, as I sat on that deck beside Mom Flynn.

I kept my eyes fixed on the sunny grass. Beyond the cabin yard, I knew, so many people were dying. So many souls lost already, all around us. And one soul never to be born? I squinted in the sun, peering out across the yard toward the darker woods. Jerry had always been uncertain about us having a baby; I admitted that to myself, at last. And I felt sure that if his mother came to stay with us, a new excuse, Jerry would want to put off more fertility treatments.

I tensed up against the rising pain of another cramp. And I kept studying, as if for an answer, the backyard. The grass: its delicate unreadable patterns in the capricious breeze.

A hand touched mine. I startled slightly, then turned to Mom Flynn. She pressed my hand, her own hand scaly-dry yet warm. As the wind blew my hair sideways, I looked at her deeply lined sunlit face. Her eyes the same blue-grey as Jerry's. Only in hers, the grey had won.

Within that foggy grey, I caught a spark of understanding. I met Mom Flynn's saddened gaze, neither of us speaking. For some sorrows, there are no words.

THE QUIET CAR

"Ma'am? You may have to leave."

The deep Godlike voice from the train's loudspeaker, only live. Anne stiffens in her seat in the Quiet Car.

"Me?" She gazes up at the conductor in his policeman-blue uniform. His shaven jowls quiver with the train's ratchety motion.

"We got a report of a disruption here," he informs her in his announcer voice. God with a chowder-thick Boston accent. "You're aware, Ma'am, of the Quiet Car rules? If you'd step aside with me..."

She started it, Anne wants to blurt out childishly. But the girl has vanished; the one who'd begun the (what was Anne's mother's old-fashioned word?) *altercation.*

"Ma'am?" The conductor takes half a step back, expertly steady on his feet. Meeting Anne's stunned gaze with his sorrowful blue-green Irish Sea eyes.

Shakily, Anne makes herself rise. The train lurches, but Anne edges out of her seat. Because if she does not move, this man might make her.

Only an hour—or a third of the ride—before, Anne began her trip as she had begun many. She stepped onto the Quiet Car quietly as ever, an extra-stilled waiting silence in her mind. Though she walked as briskly as ever. Relieved to have made it, before the train rolled forward, into her favorite haven.

Anne Marie Malloy always felt happy—or close as she came, since hitting fifty—on the Quiet Car. But she wondered as she made her wobbly way down its aisle if maybe she should change her plan. Her non-plan, for not checking her messages. Her old-fashioned purse-shaped purse bounced on her hip. She passed mini screen after mini screen, most headphoned passengers already plugged in. Staring at celebrities Anne was secretly proud not to recognize. Anne followed all Quiet Car rules religiously. Her cellphone was already on Mute.

So if the call she was awaiting today came, the ring would occur unheard. Her day's voicemail remained unopened. The cell itself was tucked away in her purse, closed up. Waiting too. Anne intended to keep it that way, for the three-hour ride. Her test result report could wait, whatever it might be.

Anne halted, mid-aisle. "Let me," she murmured like an automatic prayer. And she helped a stoic older lady with her old-fashioned suitcase. The thin-lipped lady offered a shy Quiet Car smile of thanks. Then Anne stepped forward toward her reward. One blessed doubly vacant seat. Her heart gave a familiar little leap. She reached the mid-car seat with a held breath. As she edged in, she exhaled.

A window seat, all to herself. Heaven. Maybe, Anne thought, it *was* here, safely ensconced on the Quiet Car, that she should slip out her cell and make herself listen.

To the message likely left already in the final afternoon hours when she'd been teaching her semester's final Intro to Lit class. Possibly her Farewell to Intro to Lit. Or maybe the message was left while Anne was rushing to catch her train, then racing the last underground lap to outpace fellow plodding mid-afternoon commuters and gain (*Second cah to the rea-ah,* the conductor called after her) the Quiet Car. Fifty years old, five foot two, her greying reddish hair bluntly cut, her fiercely blue eyes lowered so not to alarm, Anne always sailed past Security.

As she set her purse on the vacant seat beside her, she felt sure that her shut-off phone did hold, by now, a message from Dr. Kumar. The message due by today, Friday. Anne's gentle soon-to-retire gynecologist—plus the nurse who'd held her hand through the in-office 'procedure', urging Anne to let out her moans—had both assured Anne the results of the 'scraping' would come within the week. By today.

Here in the Quiet Car, maybe more than inside the emptier quiet of her Friday-night apartment, she could surely bear to listen. To the good doctor's voice, which—if the worst was true—would probably not give the diagnosis via phone but instead instruct her to come to the office in person, post haste.

Right? Wouldn't that quaint tradition of telling the worst face-to-face still be followed? It had been for Mother the week Anne had accompanied her first to her CTSCAN and days later to her longtime physician. *I'm afraid, Mrs. Malloy, your CTSCAN did reveal, as we had feared, what we call a 'nodule' on your left lung...*

Luckily, if there was any 'luckily', Mother's diagnosis came down in the days before Google. So Mother never visited the circles of Virtual Hell that these days precede an actual diagnosis. Late-night Googling: Anne's timid fingers tapping in OVARIAN CANCER, pressing

'SEARCH' only to find herself unable even to open the link, its first chopped-off line revealed to be: *'What makes ovarian cancer so particularly deadly...'*

But open it she did, next night. Among the all-cap RISK FACTORS for OVARIAN CANCER were NEVER HAVING GIVEN BIRTH. And—listed as a whole separate risk factor, just to rub it in—NEVER HAVING NURSED A BABY.

The train jerked and rattled into life. At first it seemed the darkness was moving, but no, it was the train itself. Trundling through the dank, permanently dirty Penn Station tunnel. Anne shut her eyes for this part, to avoid glimpsing on the rails the skittering rats. The seat beside her remained empty. *May it stay that way, please.* That's all she dared to ask God or whatever she sometimes talked to. Whoever it was she thanked, now, for this empty seat. On the righthand side of the train (left side, leaving Boston).

So she could see the ocean, come Connecticut.

"God," Anne finds herself saying, facing the conductor in the windy accordion-floored between-car space. The non-quiet non-car. With his sad canny gaze fixed on her, he does look in the shaky sunlight like a God her fearfully Catholic mother might somehow have concocted.

"Sir. I—you see, the, the altercation in the Quiet Car— Yes, it happened but I didn't start it; I wasn't the one *shout-ing—*" Though Anne is shouting now, against amplified Amtrak clatter and a damp rush of wind. The conductor shakes his head (again Anne hears her mother's voice), *more in sorrow than in anger.*

"—should know from my announcement earlier that there is never no shouting, by anyone, at any time in the Quiet Car. Now, there is no call to get upset. I am not puttin' you off the train, dear—"

Dear; like she is already her mother's age. Anne presses her lips tight and swallows. Mother dying at 70 and now Anne may not even reach 51. Ratchet ratchet ratchet; the miles clipping by. 48, 49, 50. The conductor's deep loudspeaker-worthy voice continues, his delivery as deadpan as his jowly face. Jiggling flesh lit by jittery sun. "—So maybe they were shouting too, that lady who reported this and her daughter? That's what you're sayin', Miss? OK, but they de-trained—at Greenwich. Ya see."

Does he wink? Greenwich; rich bitch. That's what the conductor's comradely gaze tells Anne. So he'll let her go back? But his voice plods on. "... And ya see, Miss, there *are* plenty of seats in Coach—"

"No." Anne leans closer to this conductor though his gaze goes stony gray again. "The Quiet Car is 'Coach'! Don't send me to regular Coach—"

"Bob—" a young-conductor voice calls from the Coach Car behind the older conductor. "Bob, need ya in Cafe Car; got a Code Two; need ya NOW—"

"COMIN'—" Bob bellows over his big blue shoulder. Then he turns back to Anne. Rowdy laughter behind him in Un-Quiet Coach. "I'll find ya a nice new seat, dear—"

"But I—can I at least go back and get my purse?"

"Yo, BOB—" the younger voice calls, closer. Conductor Bob gives one curt nod. Then he pivots again on the heel of his shined shoes (he must get them done at Penn Station). He shoulders past the stinky open-doored bathroom into the louder car marked COACH.

Anne pivots too. Emboldened, she faces the closed labeled QUIET CAR door. Deep breath, count to five, exhale. Mother's old formula to calm her high-strung girl in the years after Anne's aging Dad died in his sleep. Young Anne prone to fits of anxiety, late-night reading binges, fear of sleep itself. Anne Marie hiding out for hours in the library at Waltham High, then walking to the redbrick Public Library. Opening books and (as Anne's one serious semester-long love put it so well) 'falling through the page.'

Into—what? Other worlds, other lives.

Anne blinks back more tears. Mustn't cry or draw attention. Must walk into the Quiet Car and listen to the complete cell message. Those last words that the shouting 'Samantha' had cut short. What more did Dr. Kumar's aide have to say besides telling Anne she must meet with the doctor tomorrow? Not 'at your convenience' or 'next week' but tomorrow, Saturday. Had the missing words told Anne to bring a 'significant other' with her? Not that she has any to bring. Unless you count her colleague Cara, the Women's Studies Professor. Anne had somewhat awkwardly accompanied Cara to Cara's own colonoscopy. Anne draws another deep breath. Yes, chubby overly chummy Cara. Cara owes her. But would she even want Cara with her to hear her own worst?

In the Quiet Car, even if someone sat beside you, you were alone. Alone with your own thoughts, in the quiet of your own mind. Anne's favorite place, Heaven help her.

Anne takes a last lurching step toward the Quiet Car, invisible as a Ghost Girl. She cracks a slight smile. GHOST GIRLS had been the title of her well-received essay collection. Published back when collections were 'received' at all. GHOST GIRLS: CATHY/CATHERINE IN WUTHERING HEIGHTS AND OTHER ROMANTIC REINCARNATIONS.

Back then busy young Assistant Professor Anne Marie Malloy would sometimes pause in her jam-packed days of teaching and reading to think how lucky she was. To have found a niche in this noisy world where she could be her quiet self. Independent, intelligent, intense. Or intense on the inside. While luck of the bigger variety deserted Anne in her later years, with her tenure bid denied and her mother so painfully dying, small-scale states of grace remained.

Anyway, no one stops Anne as she punches her small bony-knuckled fist onto the square button of the door. It jolts open. She slips into the Quiet Car as if she owns it.

I get so much reading done on the train, she'd told the Barnard colleague, a true admirer of her book, who'd gotten her this latest fill-in job. *I get so much work done.* But she didn't, really. Unless you counted staring intently out the window work. Anne half-smiles again as she edges back into her seat. Yes, *hers.* She settles in as if at the start of today's ride. Before the non-ghost girl and her mother disrupted everything.

Absently, Anne reaches beside her. She pats the second seat. Then looks at that seat, stunned. Blinks her eyes hard though no tears are left. Her purse—it's gone.

This trip had seemed so promising at 2:10PM as the Northeast Regional train had rattled its way through the Penn Station tunnel. No one in the seat beside Anne, thank God. Not that Anne believed in God, exactly. God as Omniscient Narrator, Anne the eternal English Major imagined when she imagined anything of the sort. An all-seeing Narrator who somehow still watched Anne and judged her even though no one left alive now did. Her own life hardly the stuff of stories. Surely this Narrator did not really exist, outside her mind.

But at least she did have her mind. Plus a window seat to herself. *At least for another three hours,* Anne had told herself happily (well, contentedly) as the train burst from the tunnel into May afternoon sunlight. Something no one could take away, today. Her splendid solitude.

Or so Anne believed as she faced her window hungrily. The train whizzing past, first, New York City's extravagant rail-side trash. Look! An entire exploded mattress and its violent rusty-springed history retreated along the tracks. Yes; she'd wait till they cleared the cityscape in all its graffiti-decked grandeur.

Obama Is A Suit. Obama Is A Sellout. Then in a seemingly different angry red scrawl, on the same soot-charred concrete wall, the hopefully unrelated sentiment, 'Death To-' followed by an unintelligible word. Or name. Gone in a garish flash. Writ as if in giant grainy lipstick. The waxy overbright kind Anne's mother wore even in her coffin. Making her face look—in death just as in life—worse, not better.

Death won't be so bad, Anne tried telling herself as the last of Manhattan barreled by. A thought that had first started sneaking into her head ten years ago. After the year of her last lover. In Mother's version of Heaven, another better life did exist. If not, Anne dared to think now, at least Death would share the biggest benefit Anne savored in this, her favorite earthly perch. No one can interrupt you.

But of course, there is no 'you'. You yourself have been interrupted.

Shoshanna I XX U!!!!

The Devil Wears Sunblock

Obama = Bush

Anne leaned closer to her window. Starting her spring semester's final New York to Boston run. The train was ratcheting rapidly past the flat yet antic rooftops—the crammed-in gardens and above-ground pools—of Queens. Then the stark brown-brick buildings, so many anonymous windows uncurtained.

Some flashing colors, mini-flags of defiant brightness.

"If you can hear my voice," the Boston-accented conductor announced over the crackly intercom, "you ah on the Am-trak Qui-et Cah."

He let those words, sink in. Anne nodded like a parishioner in a pew.

"In the Quiet Cah, a li-brar-y like atmosphere is maintained. Turn off all cell phones and all sound-emitting devices. Keep con-ver-sation to a minimum..."

Anne gave another reverent nod. Heaven could not be much better than this. She patted her purse on the seat beside her, like a mini watchdog. So later down the line, strangers filing on would be less likely ask the dread question, Is this seat taken?

"—If you have boarded the Quiet Cah in er-rah, please move forward and there are plenty of seats in Coach Class on this train..."

Thank you, Amtrak Gods, Anne thought as the announcement ended there. No additional warning this afternoon of a 'full train,' no specific request that passengers keep the seats beside them clear. This could be Anne's last ride, for a long while. But it would be—Anne vowed to herself—perfect.

And it was, at first. The city retreating, the leafy suburban trees emerging in spring afternoon sun. Anne watching, her tired mind a sun-dappled haze, till the train trundled into New Rochelle. A tidy commuter station; Anne stiffened as if at a battlefield. A fresh crop of passengers straggled aboard and haltingly advanced down the aisle. Anne made her curved back rigid as a turtle's shell.

She focused on the train window reflection when shadowy threatening figures behind her hesitated, then inched forward. Anne exhaled in tentative relief. She pictured Mother clutching her metal-clasped purse, clenching shut her Irish mouth. Anne loosened her own tightened lips, her creeping Mother Mouth. Though she missed and mourned her mother—and felt every day the lack of someone watching over her, even disapprovingly —Anne found it a relief not to have to deal with their phone calls. Not to have to report to Mother on what Anne herself wryly deemed the 'pale excitements' of her academic life. Fielding the sighs and tight-lipped silences as Mother the Martyr would 'not even ask' (she'd point out if Anne indelicately brought it up) about the lack of a man in Anne's life.

The affairs Anne had had—such as they were; her Spring semester of love with a Visiting Professor of Comp. Lit.; her various wine-fueled flings at MLA conferences—she kept from Mother. Most of her romantic life few people knew about. Years later, it felt almost like it had happened only in her own head. Which was exactly where Anne wanted it, right?

Exactly my point, Anne once said to her lover, the Visiting Professor, who liked being right almost as much as she did.

And that *'exactly,'* he'd cut in, gimlet-eyed, *is exactly why you are so unlikable.*

How that still stung, all these years later, that 'unlikable.' Not even 'unlovable.' It had not even gone that far, with him. This was their last full conversation, his final jibe. The week that Spring semester, 2003, ended. Only weeks after her tenure bid had been officially denied. The two rejections had felt connected, in the sweltering summer quiet of her apartment. A one-two punch which had weakened her. That summer, Anne first felt the sinful sneaky lure of leaving life. This life, anyway.

The train lumbered on forward at its Northeast Regional slow-fast speed. Anne began to relax, when two late-coming strangers, burdened with crackly overstuffed shopping bags, appeared. Intruding in Anne's window reflection. Worse: audibly talking. Worse still, one of them was a child. Or a teen. Halting beside the just-emptied seat in front of Anne's own.

Please don't sit there, Anne silently begged. The younger stranger nodded up at the discreet Quiet Car ceiling sign. "'*Quiet*' car, Mom, like: Really? *Real*-ly??"

This delivered in a parody of a whisper. The second 'really' drawn out, sitcom style. Anne stiffened her spine again; not like a turtle's this time but like a cat's, its territory threatened.

"Shush, Samantha."

The mother sounded pleased to have an excuse the tell Samantha to shush. 'Samantha;' how Anne had tired over the years, teaching each generation of trendy names.

"Sit," the mother commanded as if to an unruly poodle, her massive bag crackling louder. Bowing her head of blonde-highlighted hair so her chin doubled, Mommy Dearest started edging into the the seat in front of Anne.

"At least lemme have the win-dow," Samantha whined in her stage-whisper.

Clumsily, like two people not used to moving in close quarters, the mother and daughter shifted places. Buxom Samantha plunked down into the window seat. Through the sunny reflection, Anne saw Samantha fumble with wires, eager to plug herself into her iPhone or (as Anne's most annoying students said) *whatever*.

Exhaling at last, Anne unclenched her jaw. Relaxed her crimped Mother-mouth. Silly to worry that a teenage stranger would—of all lost arts—talk on a train. Especially not to the Mom she clearly hated; the Mom who'd already jolted her seat into the furthest-back sleeping position.

As the train clattered forward, deeper into greener pricier Bedroom Communities (Mother would say, as if it were still the 1950's), Anne decided it was time to hear her damned Voicemail. Now, because the ride was disrupted anyway. Its perfection marred.

If only, Anne wished, it could start all over.

New ride, new life. Was that so much to ask? The faint tinny beat of the whatever-girl's music, too loud on her earbuds, entered Anne's sensitized ears. Its insistent drumtrack buzz like a bug. What in Heaven's name was Anne waiting for? That sharp annoying buzz in her brain; that dull annoying pain in her heart. The same old pain she'd felt in varying degrees for years whenever she glimpsed mother-daughter duos. Laughing or quarreling like she and her mother would never do; like she and the Ghost Girls who could've been her daughters never got to do.

In another life, Anne automatically comforted herself as she slipped her hand in her purse. She flipped her phone open, shaky fingered. The cell lit up. DR KUMAR; the top name on VOICEMAIL glowed green. 1:35PM. No more foolish hesitation. With a spasm, Anne's littlest finger pressed PLAY.

A young-woman's voice; not Dr. G. herself. Anne pressed her cellphone hard against her ear so it would not 'emit' sound. She listened intently to the words she'd dreaded so much she felt she'd already heard them.

"—a message for, for Anne Malloy from Dr. Kumar's office. Ms. Malloy, Dr. Kumar requests that you meet with her tomorrow so she can—explain the results of your initial uterine lining tests—I repeat; Dr. Kumar does need you to come in, in person, tomorrow—you can call the office at eight and—"

A pause in the message, a silent roar in Anne's head. She'd known it, really, as soon as she'd seen in the Faculty Restroom's glaring light the first flash of red, of *post-menopausal bleeding.* Requiring the in-office 'test.'

Anne could barely hear the next words as the untroubled young voice on the phone went on.

"—and when you come to the meeting, Ms. Malloy, Dr. Kumar wants you to, to—"

Samantha's live full-throated voice interrupted.

"No—Mo-om, come ON! I need YOUR phone cause MINE ran out of BAT-teries—"

Jerkily, Anne yanked her cell from her ear, the message still talking in its tiny unhearable voice.

"—you DRAG me along and won't even LET ME CHECK MY EMAILs, it's like, like—"

"Shut up, Samantha," the mother cut in. A stagey hoarse whisper. Anne stuffed her phone into her purse. She zipped the purse in fury, her face going hot with years' worth of rage.

"Ya know what, MOM?" Samantha fired back. "YOU shut up!"

Anne stood shakily on the shaky floor so her head poked above the seat-top. She was so short she barely had to stoop. The blonde pink-faced daughter stood too, twisting awkwardly to face her seated mother. Samantha's earbud cord bounced on her shoulder. Her voice the strident whine of every lazy loudmouthed student Anne had ever tried to teach.

"—I MEAN IT MOM! I am so freaking SICK of you telling ME—"

"Shut up, Samantha," Anne Marie Malloy cut in, quietly. It felt good to say it aloud—say it as if to every Samantha and Heather and Britney.

"Who the Hell are YOU?" Samantha turned, her blue-lined blue eyes popping. Her mother twisted round to glare up at Anne, from under her hairsprayed bangs. Other heads turned in other seats.

"I am—we are—passengers on the QUIET CAR." At her own Teacher Voiced pronouncement, Anne felt other riders craning to see her, appalled. She could feel the others thinking she was a part of this commotion, not the one trying to control it. But so what? She was dying and she damn well didn't care.

"You hear me, young lady? *This* is the—" Anne pointed at the sign above the central aisle, jabbing her finger at its words. "QUI-et CAR! Can't you—any of you—*read?*"

With this final foolish question—of course the young people could read but they didn't want to; no one wanted to read anymore—Anne collapsed back into her seat.

"Is she CRAZY?" a still-loud but abashed-sounding Samantha asked her mother.

"You don't talk to my daughter that way," the mother rallied to reply, rising in a bag-crackling hairspray-smelling flurry. "Come ON, Samantha. We don't have to put up with *this*—"

Finally silenced, Samantha followed her mother. Or Anne assumed Samantha followed; Anne did not dare look up for fear she'd see some concerned or annoyed or concerned-and-annoyed face staring back. Anne's own face felt numb as if freshly slapped. Not that her mother had been the slapping kind. Or the shouting kind.

Tears Anne hadn't realized were there spilled down her cheeks. *Dr. Kumar requests that you meet with her tomorrow. Meet tomorrow. A Saturday. Sometimes,* Anne's mother had said of church friends who died before her, *they sock you into the hospital right away.* Hadn't one of mother's oldest St. Mary's pals gone dutifully to a face-to-face with her doctor then been shipped to the hospital that same day for a mastectomy? Then died, horribly, anyway?

"Greenwich, Greenwich. Next train stop is Greenwich, Connecticut..." Boston-accented God on the loudspeaker announced with his low no-nonsense voice.

A blur of sprinkler-fed landscaper-trimmed greenery

and McMansion type homes unrolled in the window, in the corner of Anne's eye. But she kept her head bowed as she used to do in St. Mary's beside Mother. Please, Anne thought, but she felt no answer. She couldn't even bring herself to reach into her purse, lift her phone, hear the damn words all over again, to the end. The train stopped, then started. Familiar train clatter filled her paralyzed mind. Until she heard it above her, a few minutes and miles past Greenwich.

The voice of the Amtrak Announcer, only live. *Ma'am?*

Where in Hell is he? God—no, Bob. Anne pats the seat beside her again, frantically; with both hands now, as if she is blind. Her purse-shaped purse must be there, after all. Hidden somehow in the fading sunlight flashing through the window. Where is Conductor-Cop Bob now that she needs him?

Anne bends over, squeezing her head low, breathing stale below-seat air, groping on the gritty rubber-matted floor. Under Samantha's seat. *Everything I have is in here,* Mom in her quavering old-lady way used to say of her purse. As Anne straightens in her seat, her hair mussed, she feels she's lost everything.

Not only her credit cards and library card and University ID and cellphone but the Health Card that her longtime yet untenured teaching gig does not provide. Will it be sufficient to cover cancer costs? The train is blasting past the bombed-out buildings, city outskirts.

"Bridgeport," Conductor Bob's voice intones over the loudspeaker, perhaps a note of warning in his words. "Next stop is Bridgeport; BRIDGEPORT, Connecticut."

One stretch of so-called scenery Anne usually avoids studying. She squints down hopelessly at the empty darkened floor below the seat beside her. Too tired to bend and twist again. She turns instead to the window. She faces from afar those giant abandoned factory buildings, shells of buildings, leading into Bridgeport. Mammoth sinister structures that seem only to exist so women can be raped and murdered within.

God, Anne thinks or maybe prays as she slumps in purse-less defeat. Facing the trash-strewn streets of outer Bridgeport; deserted, post-apocalyptic. Even the train clatter seems to grow louder and harsher. Anne feels the added vibration in her gut, her tensed empty stomach. God, will she wind up losing her cozy Back Bay apartment to health care costs? Wind up living out the rest of her cancer-ridden days on such bombed-out streets?

Eyes shut, wishing she can just fall asleep—just die and get it over with—Anne pictures herself breaking under such a fate. Like the Edith Wharton heroine of Anne's favorite novel, The House of Mirth. Dying alone in her rented room. Abandoned the way Anne had felt all during the long hot hollow summer of 2003. Hurt less by the lover she'd known would never last than by the college she'd been convinced would be her home. Her prospects in work and love shrinking so drastically that summer, when she'd first secretly begun to think that death wouldn't be so bad. That maybe some other better life did await her.

"Excuse me?" Voice of an angel this time, not God. Polite, kind, shy.

Anne startles. She turns from her window, smoothing her mussed bangs. Gazing at a young woman with smooth black hair and clear black eyes and wire-framed glasses. Her smooth brown face calmly concerned. "Are you looking for this? It must've fallen—under the seat in front of me—Under the seat behind you, that is." The young woman holds it out to Anne by its straps: Anne's purse, miraculously zipped and intact. "There you go," she adds, like a gently coaxing mother.

"Thank you," Anne chokes out. She snatches it back, her tightly packed purse. "Oh thank you. Thank you so much. I—I can't tell you..."

Perhaps taken aback by Anne's near-tearful delivery, the young woman nods stiffly. Yet she keeps her shy smile. Dressed in a modest mauve spring raincoat, the kind of coat Anne would pick out.

"It's OK, it was nothing, really..." The girl slips back into her seat behind Anne. Hidden, but there.

"Bridgeport, train now approaching BRIDGEPORT, CONNECTICUT."

Protectively, Anne clutches her purse and watches the aisle, hoping the sweet-faced young woman behind her won't be de-training here. Wanting her close by a little longer.

A few passengers Not-Her file by, chatting cheerfully. The train heaves to a halt. The Bridgeport station, softened in late sunlight, bustles at this rush-hour; everyone but Anne eager to get home. Anne loosens her hold on her purse as the train pulls away again. The young lady is still there; Anne can feel her. Something to be thankful for.

Plus, they are heading toward the most picturesque part of the journey. Coastal Connecticut: the ocean Anne loves to see any time she can. How has she lived in Boston all these years and so seldom visited actual nearby beaches? One of many regrets Anne feels gathering in her mind as she creeps with her purse down the Quiet Car aisle, visits the bathroom, returns to her seat. Drained, dazed. Who knows how many miles pass? The cloud-streaked sky is beginning to flush with a spring sunset. Dense darkly green trees rush by.

A pulse in Anne's throat flutters. The Connecticut stops and then Providence, Rhode Island. After Providence: the Boston stops, the end of the line. No, Anne tells her spaced-out self. She can't listen to the full Doctor Kumar message all alone in her apartment. At least here in the Quiet Car, there are kindred souls around her. The young woman behind her. The heads around her bent over computer screens and magazines. Even a few brave books. No one noticing Anne at all now. The earlier disturbance forgotten if not forgiven.

The Irish never forgive and never forget, Mother used to say as if that were something to be proud of. Hasn't Anne wasted way too much energy not forgiving? Envying her tenured colleagues the way some students she'd secretly scorned—and maybe that was why she'd been denied tenure—envied shiny celebrity lives. What had made Anne think, all these years, she is any better, really?

Anne unzips her purse, slips out her phone. She fixes on the deep green trees, their outer leaves glinting with sun. Leaves blowing excitedly in the ocean breeze Anne can see but not feel or smell. She pictures the sterile white CTSCAN tunnel her mother was fed into for her own diagnosis of lung cancer.

Mother laid out at the mouth of the tunnel, looking frail, wearing her ladylike street clothes because the CTSCAN radiation was so strong, the nurse had cheerily explained, it could zap through anything. Anne had been allowed to stand with Mother as they'd prepped her, taping an IV to her inner arm. The nurse explaining that the injected 'dye' would cause Mother to feel a rush of heat down her spine, but that was 'normal.'

Nothing for Mother was ever normal again after that day, that test. Anne pokes the teeny phone icon, VOICE-MAIL. She re-presses Dr. Kumar's number.

Hears first what she heard all too clearly before: the doctor's aide informing her she must make an appointment tomorrow. Then with her breath held, with the first jagged grey rocks of the Atlantic shoreline thrust-ing themselves into sight, Anne hears the last words of the message.

...and Dr. Kumar wants you to—to know that the results she will discuss with you are preliminary. It will require an outpa-tient surgery procedure for complete diagnosis. Dr. Kumar will explain it all to you tomorrow but wants you to under-stand that these are preliminary findings with no final diag-nosis, not yet. Have a nice day, Ms. Malloy...

Anne half-jumps as the phone in her hand beeps, message complete. END, she presses, but maybe it's not; not yet. Hadn't Dr. Kumar warned before the in-office 'uterine lining scrape' that sometimes the samples obtained this way are too small? Sometimes a full D&C was 'indicated'? Anne quiets her specific further worries, just as she's quieted her phone. Which she slips back in her purse, before anyone can complain about its nearly inaudible noise.

She re-faces her window, knowing Conductor Bob may yet come back and make her move. And Doctor Kumar may yet tell her that whatever she finds in Anne's next test is cancerous. Then again maybe not, Anne dares to think, narrowing her eyes in golden late sun. Trees thinning out in the rockier sandier soil. *Maybe I'll get away this time. Maybe I'll get Watchful Wait-ing.*

A new catchphrase Anne has found online, or new to her. The diagnosis many doctors these days allow pa-tients who want to 'wait and see' before having their breasts or other bodily parts chopped off.

Hasn't Anne perfected watchful waiting, if nothing else, all her life? In ghostly window reflection, in his blue uniform, Conductor Bob strides into view. Anne freezes, invisibly. But he passes right by her seat without pause. As if he doesn't see her, or sees her but has forgotten her. Anne allows herself a brief half smile, to her reflection.

No one watching—maybe no Omniscient Narrator God watching, either—and that feels good. So what if it's only her own self, watching? At least Anne still has a window seat from which to watch. There is—Anne feels as lavish white-shingled beach houses flash into view— much to be thankful for, this moment. Even within her rickety Quiet Car of a life. A narrow life, to anyone looking in. But Anne feels quite expansively happy in her way, her heart opening up. The first stretch of Atlantic appears, darkly sparkling.

Along this pristine curved cove of Connecticut beach, a few hardy walkers stride the sands in the late May sun. Anne scans past the couples and the dog owners. The single solitary walker—swinging her arms, letting wind whip her short white hair—looks happiest. No chatting, quarreling. No leash to slow her down. Just walking and watching, waiting out the day's light.

Anne breathes in as if she can smell the sea air outside. She wishes she could open her sealed Amtrak window. She should take the T-train to the beach at Marblehead. Why hasn't she done that more often, in her years in Boston? Loving ocean air as she does?

Next stop Groton. Groton, Connecticut—

Behind her, Anne hears a stirring. In Anne's reflection, the neatly dressed young lady who'd found her purse steps into view. There you go, this Ghost Girl had said to Anne. *There she goes,* Anne thinks. Not turning her own head, due to the hot spark of tears. Her make-believe daughter steps forward toward the front of the car, the EXIT. Taking her place by the doors early, as Anne herself will do soon.

Anne un-latches her plastic tray, just to have something to hold onto. The train is still ratcheting forward relentlessly, not yet slowing for Groton. Anne pictures in the subtly darkening seaside sky the black Boston tunnel yet to come. She pictures too, again, the shiny-white CTSCAN tunnel.

The nurse raising Mother's stiffened arms, advising pale Mother, 'Hold on.' To the rounded overarching mouth of the CTSCAN tunnel, the nurse meant. *Hold on,* Anne had thought as she'd been hustled out of the chamber so the radioactive zapping could begin. *Hold on, Mom, or you'll be sucked into the tunnel of death.*

The Northeast Regional train ratchets more slowly, jerkily. Anne holds onto her plastic tray. Once the Groton stop comes, minutes away, she hopes to catch a glimpse of her Ghost Girl daughter, de-training. Not to be seen again. Maybe in another life, Anne starts to think, squinting at the final stretches of shoreline. But no. Anne grips her tray harder, correcting herself firmly, the way she's corrected her students all these years.

No, she tells herself as the train passes sunset-lit waves. There is no other life.

STUDENT SHOOTER

1. You Know Who

YOU KNOW WHO, he signed the pre-April Fools note that I shredded and flushed in the dank deserted West Concord Police Station bathroom; the note I'd so unwisely or maybe in the end wisely carried with me.

On me, it might have been written if I'd died. A note found *on the body.*

#428-03-0333, he signed his play for Playwriting 101: his student ID number, because he hated his name (he mumbled in my Office Hours in his young-smoker voice).

TO YOU KNOW WHO, he addressed the April Fools note which the police did find and seal in a plastic 'evidence' bag; the note which was referred to but not quoted in the Concord and Boston papers. The note to You Know Who which no one (I hope to hell no one) knows is me.

2. All in My Head

At first, on April 1st, 2006, I thought I was imagining the distant shots—no, 'pop's. They sounded only faintly above the droning campus mowing machine. Our tall wainscoted classroom window in Wheatley—known as Old Wheatley—was open to the loamy, fresh-cut grass of the long-delayed New England spring, the air certifiably warm. One of the two or three perfect spring days allotted us before all air went Massachusetts muggy. Something festive, then, in the day itself. So, the initial distant shots seemed to me possibly the pops of a few defiant daylit April Fool fireworks.

Fireworks that might well be (as so much in my life of late had been, including my maternal and/or sexual feelings for him) all in my head.

"Go on, Dawn," I murmured as Dawn Finnay hesitated in her reading, seeming to hear the same *pops* as me. Dawn blinked up from her One Act.

We were seated in our usual U. We'd dragged our old-fashioned desks into the sloppy earnest U-shape, reminding me of my Theater Major meetings back in college, when I was a high school Thespian dork darkly blossoming into a college theater star-of-sorts.

"OK, and then 'cause this part isn't really written yet, I'm gonna skip ahead to her and her boyfriend Dallas, who's, like, she finds out, this druggie—"

I shifted in my own creaky desk, my thicker-waisted but still-girlsize body fitting as easily as theirs into the wood seat. And I re-crossed my legs slowly, the way I'd found myself crossing them when he was in his desk at my side. The way I'd first started crossing them back at those Theater meetings when I'd discovered my too-skinny body and too-bony face and too-thick black brows and dramatically long black hair all could pass as 'striking' when I wore a black leotard, when my face was bathed in stage light, my acne whited out.

"'DALLAS: Drugs? What drugs, Diana? You act like I'm an addict.'"

"Whoa, whoa," the usually laconic Cal cut in. "'What

drugs' is right. You gotta, like, specify. Is the guy doing rocks, is he doing smack, doing meth—?"

I nodded along to this proud predictable list from cool Cal.

"Oh *c'mon,* Cal, this Dallas dude's way too lame to shoot up," chimed in spiky-haired Stevie, whom I'd mistakenly pegged as the class's Loose Cannon.

Maybe a couple more *pops* outside, maybe closer.

"...Yes, Cal and Steve," I cut in, "I see your point—both your points—"

"She sees 'both our points,'" Cal deadpanned to Stevie, who giggled. Then shot one real oh-my-God-does-he-dig-me glance at indifferent smirking Cal.

She sees both our penises, the chain-reaction smirks around the circle suggested Cal meant. Meaning: they knew about me? But there's nothing to know about me, I admonished my paranoid self. No *pops* just then; only mower and sun and sunlit leaves fluttering away those peaceful moments.

"OK," I told 21-year-old Dawn Finnay. "Go on, Dawn."

3. PROCEDURES AND SUGGESTIONS FOR DEALING WITH TROUBLED STUDENTS

TO: English/TheaterArts/Creative Writing Colleagues
DATE: Jan. 30, 2006
FROM: Dean Middlebrook

I'm attaching a brochure from the Counseling Center at University Health Services (located on the second floor of the Quinn Building). I strongly recommend that you contact that Center (x 7-5690) if you have concerns about a particular student or a particular event...

(And if the particular student or event that concerns you is at least in part your own fault, own doing? This I wondered as I pondered the brochure, read it really for the first time, in stormy mid-March)

> If you are having a conference late in the day, you may also want to ascertain whether a colleague will be on the floor during the meeting. None of this advice is intended to be alarmist, but if you find yourself in a circumstance that makes you uneasy you should not feel that you must face it alone...

(This last from kindly, lonely Professor Middlebrook did bring a spark of tears to my eyes; just in the sense that any habitually alone person is touched by the reaching-out, however distant and official, of another—which oddly and innocently enough was how it all started, with me and him; simply with the sense that this lonesome screwed-up kid was reaching out to lonesome screwed-up me and that maybe in some not-inappropriate way, I might reach back)..

4. After Office Hours

Here, then, is how NOT to deal with Troubled Students. Or it's clear to me now, looking back on that initial 'late in the day' meeting.

Setting: my cavelike Visiting Professor office, its single window framing the mid-February day. No snow, even, to deck the sharp-twigged branches.

Through my unvisited Office Hour (3-4PM, M/W) I'd been slow-sucking from the Valentines bouquet of Tootsie Pops that my long-distance friend Gary had advised me to buy. Gary was off in his own world on Off-Broadway.

I was nursing a Grape when the daughter of Lois the Poet giggled by my open door. "Oh Yo-Yo—" I called out like the Hansel and Gretel witch. And I lured Yolanda—briefly but brightly—into my den with a Pop of her own.

She gave big slurpy sucks, bouncing on her heels. "That's braggy!" Yo-Yo pointed her chocolate nub at my bulletin board. Flyers and reviews from my success at Bennington Theater Festival, years before. Only flyers from my most recent foray, at the Boston Playwrights' Theater. A fading clipping interviewing Emerging Playwright Amanda Hunt.

"You're right, Miss Yo-Yo." I stood and grandly swept my half-sucked Pop like a magician's wand over the bulletin board, as if to make it all vanish.

Lois the Poet called out from her office. Yo-Yo scurried away after planting a sticky sweet Tootsie kiss on my cheek, which I couldn't bring myself to wipe off. Wistfully, I fingered the crusty child-kiss trace. What Jeanie wanted too, Gary's voice in my head warned whenever my baby-lust swelled up.

Gary's late sister Jeanie: buddy to his boyfriends; cheery third grade teacher; motherly yet childless. Her toxic rounds of infertility drugs failed and a year later, when she'd decided to adopt, Jeanie was diagnosed with uterine cancer. No coincidence, Gary had fumed through the year of her dying. He urged Jeanie to sue her overzealous Infertility clinic. But no, Jeanie scolded us in her firmest schoolteacher manner. She'd signed the clinic's consent forms. She knew the risks. She'd taken the gamble; she'd done what my increasingly tactless grandchildless mother wants me to do at age 44, risky or not.

Like death, like birth, I scribbled. *Death from Birth, Death By Birth...*

My office was darkening. I shut my door. At my desk, I bent to my lowest drawer and pulled out as if it were pornography the Adoption Opportunities booklet from Wide Horizens. I opened the mimeographed pages at random to a heartbreakingly hopeful-looking girl from Laos, identified in her typed-up statistics as suffering from 'serious neurological delays.'

That was when, with a one-two punch, he knocked.

"Professor, um, Hunt?"

I slapped shut the booklet, wiped my sticky cheek. He'd already opened my door. Wayne Wilson. As ordinary-seeming as his name. The quietest boy—no; young man—from my Playwriting 101 class.

"Got my One thing," Wayne mumbled in his permanently hoarse young-smoker voice. He stepped in, dressed in his usual faded army fatigue pants. Almost as slight as me; his trim body undersized for his large head. Many actors I've met—I'd later tell him, at a bar— are built that way. Faces that look oversized in person, but extra-expressive onstage.

Wayne's offstage face, however, was extra-unexpressive. Pale, pale-eyed, blank. "Want you to—take a look. At my One Act whatever."

He tossed his manuscript frisbee-style onto my desk. It knocked the Adoption booklet askew, sent it flapping and flopping to the floor. Wayne bent fast, scooping up the limp mimeographed booklet.

"Huh." He stared frankly at the title, ADOPTION OPTIONS. "You gonna pick one-uh these Loser kids? Don't do it, Miz Hunt."

"I—I haven't decided what I'm doing. And could you please give that back?" I reached out for the booklet he was insolently flipping through.

"Wish they let the *kids* pick the *parents.*" He flapped shut the book.

"Are you—adopted, yourself?" I took hold of the booklet, hid it on my lap.

"How'd ya guess?" Wayne stretched out a bright fake gap-toothed smile. "Yep, see, I was in State Protective Services, back in Kentucky. But I got real real lucky. I got 'taken.'" He mimed finger quote-marks, his motions nimble and sharp. "'Cept it didn't 'take.'"

He dropped both his hands, dramatically.

"The—adoption didn't 'take'?"

Stiffly, Wayne shrugged his sturdy shoulders. "Yep, an' once I won me my so-called Needs Scholarship here, my so-called parents, they're like: So long; don'tcalluswe'llcallyou." He mimed a fly-swat goodbye wave.

"My goodness," I managed, my mom's old-fashioned phrase. "Sounds like a tough situation. Would you—like to sit down? And talk? You—you say you brought your One Act for me to read, while we're on Break?"

"Yuh-huh." He snatched up one of my Tootsie Pops. "So read this—" He tapped the hard-headed Pop on his manuscript. "An' just *forget* 'bout this—"

Like a drummer, Wayne bent low. He tapped his Tootsie Pop hard on the booklet resting on my lap. So hard I startled, feeling the tap in my crotch. Inappropriate touch? I wondered as Wayne lifted that booklet off my lap. Clenching my Adoption Options booklet under one arm, he spun round in his combat boots and marched out my open office door.

5. Like Death

Dawn's soft droning voice obediently resumed. Lulling us like the April air. Dawn Finnay—a mild-mannered Communications major from Maine—didn't 'act out' the lines she read. But she enunciated each word carefully like the Newscastress she hopelessly hoped to become. Dawn hunched forward so her freshly shampooed strawberry blonde hair hid her freckled face.

"'DALLAS: You've never looked so good, girl...'"

I smoothed my own bushy hair. The semi-permanent dye I'd had my hair 'treated' with earlier in the semester was wearing off. My true witchy white streaks bleeding through.

"'DIANA: As if I'd believe a word you say, you lying bastard!'"

Stilted dialogue, I penned on my Xeroxed copy of Dawn's One Act. Then I softened the 'stilted' with a *'Somewhat,'* penned in above as if written first.

Was it such a bad fate, if Wayne really had dropped my class, to go back to what I was before? A still-trim still-unmarried woman of 44; a 'somewhat' successful playwright teaching at a 'somewhat respectable' small college.

I might've blown that life, had I not done the right thing (right?) in my last Office Hour with Wayne. I turned Diana's page. And a third too-clear-to-ignore volley of *pops* sounded. Not inside the building yet, but directly outside. Fired, it was later explained, into the air. The gun re-loaded twice. Spent bullet casings were found all around campus for days afterward.

"DALLAS seized hold of DIANA," Dawn read as if not hearing, this time.

Pop-pop: downstairs sound; indoors sound. We all stopped—stopped doodling; stopped daydreaming; stopped not-listening to Dawn. The unmuffled, jarring, clearly *wrong* sounds: mini-explosions contained within walls.

"'—don't fight me, Diana, you beautiful bitch,'" Dawn plodded on, then she stopped too. We all looked at each other. A silence like the silence preceding tepid applause after a failed play; that silence like death, I used to think.

Dawn Finnay blinked her dazed hazel eyes. More *pops* echoed in the stairwell, closer. Dawn stammered to me, "You want—I should—go on?"

6. Not Bad

It was not bad. The play, I mean; Wayne Wilson's One Act draft.

Not bad by student standards; by my drastically lowered longtime-teacher standards. Not bad in a creepy noirish way that suited my mood. It starred a 'dead-pale' 'small and slim' adoptive Mom with 'white-black hair' and 'sexy legs,' surely based on me. After I read it, I studied my white-streaked hair. And I cancelled my long-dreaded 'preliminary conference' with an Infertility expert at Boston IVF. Instead, defiantly light-hearted, I drove into Boston that first day of Break and got my white streaks treated at a Newbury Street salon.

Later, I would field surprised-sounding compliments on how well I looked, what a restful Break I must have had. When really it had been the opposite. Restless: me pacing away my valuable writing time; typing extra-helpful revision suggestions for Wayne. Unlike many students, he at least listened.

7. Workshop Circle

As if the gods had planned Wayne Wilson's Special Effects, a hard March rainstorm pelted our classroom windows the second week back from Break as Wayne read aloud NON-MOM.

Good change here, I kept penning, smoothing my new darker shinier hair, feeling Wayne sneak hopeful glances at me. He'd thanked me for my suggestions at my Office Hours; he'd joked about signing his play with his student ID number; then he'd actually made my changes. But he'd kept the description of witchy pale sexy-legged 'Non-Mom'. Student eyes kept flickering toward me as Wayne read his still-melodramatic finale.

"NON-MOM: 'Because maybe I only thought I wanted a fucking son. Because maybe I wanted a—fucking, son.'"

The class tittered at Wayne's deft comma-pause delivery. My face heated up as Wayne described the predatory Non-Mom approaching then kissing her grown adoptive son. Then the son pulling away, pulling out the 'pop-gun' his Dad had given him. He raises the 'gun'.

And Wayne Wilson—in his less gory, somewhat improved version—cut short the scene there. To a raindrop-pattering silence.

"Gross," the usually polite Dawn broke out. "God. I'm sorry but that Mommy-son kissing-or-whatever just seems, like—"

"Gratuitously gross," provided nerdy English major James of the forgettable last name, who had a crush on Dawn Finnay. Wayne was looking down, not scribbling any notes.

"Hey, I gotta say at least this one wasn't boring—'

"Kinda scary too, kinda Goth—but the ending sucks."

I drew breath to agree that the play in its stylized creepiness was somewhat promising. But Wayne jerked his head up. He stood, neatly and swiftly. This kid could go onstage, I thought as he drew his own dramatic breath.

"Right, OK, I get it." Wayne lifted the 8-page manuscript lying on his desk, gripping each end of it so tightly the paper crumpled. Abruptly, in two strong startling motions, Wayne Wilson ripped his One Act in half. Thick rips.

We gaped in shocked silence at defiantly deadpan Wayne. Rain pelted the windowpane. "OK, class—I need to talk this one out with Wayne..."

"So we can go early?" asked Dawn in a chastened softer-than-ever voice.

"So yes, you go early today," I told Dawn, motioning to the whole uneasy shifty-eyed class. Eagerly obedient, avoiding looking at Wayne, they gathered their backpacks and shuffled as one out into the hall. Wayne and I heard their herd-steps thump toward the stairwell. Then we heard, from the old echoey stairwell, a sudden burst of chatter, of tension-releasing laughter.

So it felt, in that darkened rainy-day classroom, like it was Wayne and me against them, the rest. It took me back to my outcast highschool days, listening as the understandable unkind laughter in the stairwell died down.

First, quietly, I recited my teacherly lines about how he couldn't cut short a discussion, how we'd have to re-do his Workshop later. "Look, what you just wrote needs lots of work, but it's—interesting, unpredictable..." I saw, felt, a light emerge in his pale shamed eyes. "And you read it with real flair..."

"Yeah, sure, Miz Hunt..." Wayne began backing out of the classroom, clutching his script. But I couldn't let him get away, my best audience in years.

"Wait Wayne—" I pulled myself up. "Listen, there's a Staged Reading that the Advanced Acting class is giving next week, of a One Act of my own...I'd like you to take part." I took a step toward him, meeting his dubious but rapt gaze. "You could play either the innocent boy or the dangerous boy; most actors could do only one role. But you, you could go either way..."

8. In the Third Floor Classroom

Maybe it wasn't altogether surprising to any of us in the half-circle—already alerted by those contained stairwell explosions—when the classroom door banged open to reveal him: Wayne. Wayne in the blank t-shirt and faded fatigues that seemed to be his only outfit; Wayne wearing his palest face; Wayne holding at his side, pointed down, a small metal handgun.

Somewhat gun? I dropped my pen. It rolled across Dawn's 'somewhat stilted' dialogue; it fell onto the classroom floor. Its click the only immediate sound. *Somewhat gun.* Toy-sized but heavy-looking. Hanging in Wayne's hand, pointed, for now, at the floor.

"Wayne," I croaked, holding out hope that this was

some April Fools joke. But I saw no light of mischief in Wayne Wilson's flatter-than-ever eyes, his blanker-than-ever face. Just a tremor in his jawline. Like an actor paralyzed onstage. "Wayne," I prompted, his equally paralyzed co-star. "What are you doing with—that? You need to get—get back of here—"

Get back in the hall or Get out of here: one or the other I'd meant to say.

"What, Miz Hunt? Get—get back to where in hell—?"

"Anywhere—the hall in hell! Just—get back!" My own voice came out as overanimated and squeaky-fast as his was flat and slow. From the hallway below us, there were voices drifting up the stairwell, saying, *Did you hear that? What was all that?*

"Can't get 'back,'" Wayne told us as if puzzling out the riddle of time itself.

A *beep-beep* sounded, a pulse-point of hope. My head whipped round: Stevie Katz was switching on his cellphone, bless him.

"No calls, Fag-boy." Wayne aimed his gun, but low, at Stevie. Stevie's knees. Then Wayne demanded in his slowed, maybe drugged voice, Kentucky Boy polite, "You *are* a fag, right?"

Stevie widened his pop-eyes, managing even at such a moment a Can-You-Believe-This-Guy face. But he set his cell down on his desktop.

"Don't you say one word, Fag-Boy. An' don't you dial one number—"

"Help," Dawn Finnay squawked, her parched-sounding voice barely carrying across our U-shaped half circle. Seven students and me.

"Is that even a real gun?" James half-raised a shaky hand to ask, and he added, ever the student, "Didn't he mention, in his play—a 'pop gun'?"

"Like the one that killed that girl at the Red Sox *game* —" Dawn jumped to her feet. Her freckled face even pinker than Stevie's. "That Emerson College student—Veronica-something! I knew someone who knew kids who KNEW her! She DIED with a—a BB thing-y in her EYE-"

"No she did not die, that girl," Wayne in his must-be-drugged voice stated.

"Shut the fuck up," Cal told Wayne, standing. Boldly, he stepped over to Dawn.

"But that girl DID die; the bullet or pellet or whatever, it hit her BRAIN—"

"Shut up," Cal repeated, gently this time, to Dawn this time.

He planted his free hand on Dawn's hunched shoulder. Cynical Cal and guileless Dawn: all this would bring them together, if they—if we—lived.

Wayne slipped into our U of desks and scooped up Stevie's cellphone.

"No need for no po-lice," he explained, pocketing the cell. "I just wanna talk to Miz Amanda..." Wayne thrust his gun back up, shakier than James. Stepping toward me; pointing it at me, my thumping chest. "You said you would, y'know, adopt me—"

"Give me that gun—" I cut in, teacher loud. Bad line; badly delivered.

"Give me—a kiss," Wayne answered back flatly, the students all listening.

I shook my head, my throat tightened. But it wasn't me who screamed.

"She DID DIE—The girl DID DIE—" Dawn broke away from Cal's side. Wobbly in high-heeled sandals, she ran toward the open window. Her strawberry blonde hair shone wildly in the squared sunlight. "We gotta get OUT—Someone's gotta HELP us OUTA HERE—"

She was crying into indifferent leaf flutter, planting her knee on the sill.

"Stop, Dawn," I commanded like a crazed director.

The other students were all standing, Cal shoving them aside as he rushed toward Dawn.

"Yes, you must *stop*," Wayne repeated like a loud scared robot.

But Dawn was forcing the window higher. "HELP HELP—"

That's when Wayne fired. Not *pops*. Explosions. Three rapid explosive *cracks*. Dawn shrieked, loudest of us all. She toppled, Cal half-catching her. He lowered her to the floor, her sunlit blood shining. Its red flashing with the thump of my heart.

Wayne began backing toward the open door, clutching his gun in one hand and feeling his way behind him with the other. "Holy fuck, Holy fuck..."

8. Note in My Box

Days after Wayne's workshop discussion, days before Wayne performed so competently in my Staged Reading, I found in my faculty mailbox a manila envelope containing my battered ADOPTION OPTIONS booklet and, paper-clipped to it, a note signed YOU KNOW WHO.

> *To Miss Amanda Hunt:*
> *OK, I give this back to you*
> *Cause you gave lots to me*
> *Cause I'm gonna ACT cause of you*
> *Cause I'm gonna do LOTS, me think,*
> *Cause of YOU*
> *So OK, check out these LOSER KIDS*
> *But then in the end—*
> *Cause it's meant to be, Me think—*
> *Will you, won't you*
> *ADOPT ME?*
> *xxx from*
> *YOU KNOW WHO*

It wasn't like he was coming on to me (I told long-distant Gary by my cell, locked in my office); it was kind of sweet, him wanting to be my son. It was a poem, maybe? A joke? It was, if nothing else, the first piece of writing in a long while to make me tremble.

9. Please Please

Her blood pool widening, shining scarlet in the sun. Blood oozing from her shoulder as Cal knelt beside her. Cal cursing; Dawn moaning. Other students pushing toward them.

"Holy fuck." Wayne stopped backing toward the door. His eyes suddenly focusing; his cheeks feverishly coloring. He looked like he just now realized he was holding an actual firearm. Actual acrid metallic taste in the air. Actual blood on the floor.

And a girl—Dawn Marie Finnay—moaning louder and louder like a woman giving birth.

"Wayne," I rasped, my voice coming from far away, along with the siren I thought I heard. "Wayne—drop that gun. Before anyone gets here—"

"Holy fuck." Wayne shook his head, blinking. His gun aimed again at me, my chest. "Holy fuck, the fucking police—"

Our voices came at each other rapidly as a siren outside grew louder, larger.

"Wayne: please please don't make this worse—"

"Can't be no worse—"

"Just drop the damn gun! You don't want them to find you with that—"

"Find me; they gonna find me—"

"I'll protect you, OK? If you just drop the gun—"

"Yeah right," Wayne scoffed. "I ain't worth shit, not now—"

"No Wayne," I lied to him a final time, "No, wait Wayne—" But he was turning on his boot heel, barreling into the hallway. "Wayne—Please please—"

10. Staged Reading

He was not bad. In my play, I mean. Its informal Staged Reading.

At the student hang-out afterwards, Wayne told me in husky mumble what everyone had been saying in brighter less sincere voices. That my One Act was strong, eerie. I beamed and told our crowded bar booth why Wayne had a perfect-sized actor's face. Later, still high on the grainy red wine, I found myself sitting alone in that booth opposite Wayne. Only one other teacher left in sight: Lois the Poet, lingering by the jukebox, punching in Golden Oldies.

"First time in a long time I haven't felt like an 'Oldie' myself," I mumbled.

"Wha'd you say, Miz Hunt?" With brisk efficient on-stage movements, Wayne stood up. He stepped around to my side of the booth and slid in beside me. He bumped my shoulder, slid back an inch. But still close.

"You Know Who," I recited gently, wine-smiling at Wayne. He looked at the booth's tabletop. "That was you, right Wayne?" He stared dolefully at the tabletop rings left by his fellow castmates, multiple mugs of beer. "Listen," I told him in a rush. "I found that note to be tempting—no, I mean touching. I mean I've even been carrying it round with me..."

What am I saying? I was thinking in drunkenly muf-fled horror.

"I mean it, every word." Wayne looked up, his face boyish in the bar light. "You can—you oughta—adopt me, Miz A-man-da."

"But, but, that's impossible," I managed, trying for a light tone. "C'mon now, Wayne, we don't even know each other. Besides, you—you're 18 years old; isn't that too old for anyone to 'adopt' you?"

"No Ma'am." Wayne shook his head, convincingly firm.

"Real-ly?" I asked dubiously, drunkenly, trying to stop the unbidden mental image of Gary and me sitting in this booth where we'd had shared many a melancholy drink—only this time young Wayne would be sitting with us, my adopted son.

"Really, yeah—So you're *really* thinkin' about this, Miz Amanda?"

I lurched to my feet, stared dizzily down at Wayne. "I —I don't know what I'm thinking. Look, I can see you need a—big change in your life. Me too..." Jesus, what-all was I saying? Had I really told this boy he tempted me? "But first I need—another drink..."

Exactly what you don't need, my inner-teacher voice chided me. So I made my swaying way past Lois the Poet at the jukebox, then out the bar doors.

11. Mouth to Mouth

He shot himself in the mouth, off-stage. Out of, I mean, my sight.

I did not see the shot itself, as I explained over and over later, feeling each time that I was lying. I heard it, I kept saying—and I felt it, I kept to myself. The jolting close-range crack; the thud. Wayne's body —tall for once —sprawled across the third-floor hallway.

He's hit his head on the floor, I thought, running to him, not seeing blood till I stepped in it. Not grasping he'd shot himself till I bent and seized the pistol itself. Shockingly heavy for something so small; gripped by me by the wrong end. By its warm muzzle.

Men on the first floor were shouting, men connected to the siren. But Wayne's gurgly clogged-sounding breaths were all I could hear.

Mouth to mouth, was all I could think. I rolled Wayne on his back, his body limp. Men's foot-thumps sounded on the second floor. I straddled Wayne's sprawled-out body.

Puff puff, into victim's mouth, I remembered. Hold victim's nose; puff into victim's mouth; feel victim's chest to see if air gets through. *If windpipe is obstructed.* By a bullet? Wayne's blanched open-mouthed face faced up, blurred by my tears. I saw a blood gash streaking his throat. *Give me a kiss.*

I pinched his nose—hot and slimy with blood or tears or snot—and I planted my lips over his stiff-lipped mouth. Sour taste of smoke plus blood. All wrong: my *puff puffs* too feeble and his chest under my hand too still. *Puff-puff* again, a hideous sticky-meat taste in my mouth.

I pulled back to see, at the base of his throat, a new bubble of blood. Had I somehow blown blood through his torn—bullet-torn—throat?

"I did it wrong—" I screamed to the policemen charging up the last flight of stairs. "Did it wrong; did wrong —" I was shrieking like Dawn, pointing my blood-slimed finger at the bubble of blood that had now vanished, popped.

Wrong wrong, I cried out raggedly when I meant to say *Wayne, Wayne,* when the fattest policeman gripped me under my arms and hauled me up off the dying boy, the meaty taste of his blood in my mouth.

12. All a Big Mistake

What had I been thinking? I asked myself the Monday after my Staged Reading, when I trudged down the English Department Hall to my afternoon Office Hours. I spotted Wayne Wilson pacing outside my closed office. His hair unbrushed, unwashed.

"Hello Wayne—what's that?" I nodded at his over-stuffed canvas satchel.

"Just some stuff—just—Lemme tell you inside..."

I unlocked my door uneasily. Wayne entered, dragging the bag. Only later did I learn that Wayne had just that weekend been evicted from his studio apartment; that his parents had, in fact, cut off all support; that his loony plan to live with me was the only plan he had.

"I—I packed up some stuff. So's I can—make a big change, like you said..."

"Like I said?" I backed up a step from him, his un-showered sweat smell.

"You told me I need a 'big change,' like you said you need too—And you said that you kept my note and all—said it was 'tempting' and all—"

"Touching," I managed, "I meant to say it was—was very touching..."

"Touching—yeah, A-man-da. I wanna be very touching you—" He took hold of me, my shoulders. And Wayne Wilson pulled me close like no one had done in years. "We—" he mumbled into my hair, smoky-breathed, "We can *tell* everyone you *adopted* me, see—But really, really-really we'd be-"

His firm warm body now pressing mine. The almost forgotten motions of desire. I pushed back, my hipbones against his; another perfect fit.

"No—" I shoved him away, stumbling myself, bumping shut the door. "Wayne, listen—You need to talk to a, a counselor—I'll give you a name—"

"No," Wayne blurted out, straightening up. "No, god-*damn,* don't you go tellin' *them.* I swear, they'd throw me outa this school—"

"Wayne you've gotta calm down. This is all a big mistake..."

"Mis-take, Miz Amanda? You made some. If you tell 'em about me, them damn dumb 'coun-se-lors,' I'll tell 'em bout you, Miz Amanda! I'll tell 'em how in the bar you was sitting up next to me, tellin' me you was tempted by me—"

"Look, look—" I raised both my hands to ward him off. "Look, I—I'll leave the counselors out of this if you. If you go now and, and drop my class..."

Wayne Wilson slung his half-zipped bag over his shoulder, a yellowed white sock bouncing out. He banged my door open then shut. I sat at my desk with my heart hammering. If I'd called the counselor in that shellshocked moment, they might've found in the school records that Wayne had dropped every other class but mine. But I sat at my desk as my heartbeat slowed, telling myself no; it would only make more trouble for him, for me. My position on the faculty was fragile. My behavior at the bar had been questionable at best. Shouldn't I do as Wayne asked and hope he'd simply drop my class?

I stood. I whipped his incriminating sock off my floor and stuffed it in my otherwise empty trash.

13. Sworn Statement

TO YOU KNOW WHO
You coulda done what you SAID
When you looked in my eyes—
But you a NON-Mom
like my real, like my fake
You coulda taken me IN
I gonna take you, take all you, OUT
from
YOU KNOW WHO

The note found on the student shooter's body never made it to the press. But I was shown a Xerox copy of it (the bloodstains rendered merely a darker shade of grey) during my questioning. In case, the weary pudgy officer told me, I could provide any clues as to the 'motives' of this 'disturbed young man.'

The note, I agreed with the stumped officer, might be addressed to Wayne Wilson's adoptive mother, whom authorities were unable to contact. His adoptive father eventually flew in to West Concord for questioning but by then I had taken my unpaid Leave. My students, when questioned, recalled Wayne demanding I kiss him, claiming I'd said I would 'adopt' him. I had, I swore to the police, no idea where all that was 'coming from.'

14. April 13, 2007

"You don't want to read that," my mother tells me, lifting the folded front-page Providence Journal from my hands. Since I am obeying my mother these days, letting her nurse me like an invalid, I let her take the news.

News from Virginia, far away from my mother's retirement condo in Rhode Island. News of a Creative Writing student, better armed and trained than Wayne Wilson. More of a murderer. Setting a record. The part I'd been reading when Mom lifted the paper away had been about other students, how they'd heard shots and crouched round a computer in a professor's office to see, online, what the hell was happening. How the police made that particular group of students leave the teacher's office with their hands over their heads.

Because they didn't know, a girl told the paper, *if the killer might be among us.*

"It's time," my mother reminds me, leading me into her shadowed bedroom. I lie on my back on her queen-size bed. I hike up my sweatshirt. My fingers smell of silverware polish. Mother's hands—she was once a nurse —are clean.

It's been over a year now since our own school shooting, which never made it beyond the Boston area papers since only the shooter himself died. I rest my hand on my bared stomach as my mother prepares my injection. The highest dose the Fertility Clinic will allow. My stomach is rounder these days, but only from the starch-heavy pasta meals I make for Mother and me. She accompanies me to the clinic; she approves my insistence that they make the dose as high as it can go; Mom's nest egg will cover what insurance won't.

I dream now of giving birth, sometimes miniature Baby Waynes. Who die, as he did, between my legs. Sometimes I still wake with a metallic blood taste in mouth and I rinse over and over in Mom's minty old-lady mouthwash. Nowhere near strong enough.

"Are you ready?" Mother asks me, her former professional manner revived. Seventy-six years old but her ex-nurse's hands still steady.

She draws her bedroom shades. I brace my back, offering up my stripped swell of belly. The needle two times each day; the cold metal prick, then the pain. That pain plus what it might bring—be it a baby, be it cancer, be it both—are the things that keep me going.

Mother bends over me. Her needle sinks into my belly, the meat of me. I yelp like a dog, like Dawn. I gasp as Mother expertly withdraws the needle. The one thing that makes me feel—twice a day, for two flashpoints of pain—like I'm alive.

IF YOU PLAY
JONI MITCHELL

May, 2020

Long Beach doesn't look so long until you walk it. Which man whispered that in her ear, which summer? Joan Logan wobbles on Cape Ann Inn's sun-paled wood steps, descending toward the beach for an unwise unaccompanied afternoon walk. She's not letting small fears stop her now, in late spring of 2020. The old steps creak, gritty with fresh sand.

The men, now, must be mostly dead. Her summer men.

Or 'most of you' must be dead, Joan corrects herself. *And if you're not, you—we—may soon be.* She sinks barefoot into warm but no longer hot beach sand. Joan is visiting Long Beach in Gloucester, Massachusetts for the first time in years. Ensconced in a so-called Independent Living Retirement Community—its dreaded Care Center swept by the Covid virus—she secretly fled to this hotel, where her son, driving nearby on business, agreed to stop and see her.

She hadn't wanted him even entering the Concord condo where she'd been self-quarantined all April, though as she keeps telling him by long-distance phone, she's safe as long as she can stay out of the damn doomed Care Center. The mini hospital she hates to glimpse from her condo window. She feels safer here, at the beach. Her favorite place, if truth be told. When you get as old as her, you can tell the truth, at least to yourself. And you can tell, in your early 80s, your travels long behind you, that you will never love another place as much as this one.

Joan slogs through dry sand toward wet, picturing her former summer lovers. Men from decades ago, from the single wild period of her otherwise quiet life. Summer of 1967, '68, '69.

Slap, slap, slap: her flat feet meet damper sand. On this cool May day, off season, everything even more deserted than usual, Long Beach stretches before her nearly empty. It's 3:30. Surely she has time, before her son Harry 'drops by'—if he drops by—for a walk.

Hasn't she driven all this way, really, for one more walk, one rocky end of the crescent-shaped beach to the other? A masked Red Sox t-shirted woman, unbound bosom bouncing, jogs by in wet sand. She splatters Joan, shakes her balance. In Joan's day, women didn't jog, didn't run, unless—like Joan pounding down Long Beach that last worst August day—they were running to or from something bad.

But were her men (really there were only four) all bad?

Mostly dead, Joan repeats to her shaken self. Because even pre-pandemic, men live on average so much less long. Her husband Howard, a classic average guy to the end, died seven years ago. She straightens in the chill brackish breeze, the bright May sunshine. Shading her eyes, Joan faces down the heaving Atlantic, its choppy bluegreen dazzle.

Tide coming in. Bubbly cold surf slicks the sand beneath her feet. Joan wiggles her yellow-nailed toes. Someone calls something behind her. Her name? Her son? He'd make her turn back, afraid she might fall. She should be afraid too: one fall, and you land in the Covid-ridden Care Center. Yet she doesn't feel afraid, doesn't feel she needs a mask. Not here.

With stiff-necked effort, she glances back at the Cape Ann Inn: three stories; rows of rooms facing shared wraparound balconies, all empty now. Sliding glass doors Joan used to draw her shades to block, to darken her room.

Three wild summers planted amidst her 30s and the country's '60s. If, that is, the '60s were measured properly, from 1965 till 1975. Joan pivots her head slowly back, her neckbones popping, her gauzy grey-blonde hair blowing in her mouth. Longish hair for an old crow. *Always keep your hair long;* which one made her promise that? The man who called her Joni, who said she looked like—only in summer, with sun lightening her blondish brown hair—Joni Mitchell.

Wish I taped that damned show, Joan thinks crossly, rubbing her neck, recalling a PBS documentary on Joni Mitchell. PBS is Joan's companion most evenings, the least depressing television tranquilizer when she's too sleepy to read. She marches forward, tired already today. But she draws a determined breath, passing the giant piled rocks where starfish wash up; where Joan and her truck-crazed son discovered a flat-bottomed rectangle cut between two rocks.

Mommy it's a *parking* lot, Harry had gasped. He'd raised his solemn dark eyes to her as if she had created that 'lot', those rocks, herself.

A Mama's boy, his father Howard worried. Straight-browed Harry parking and re-parking his rusted metal trucks in that naturally occurring parking lot. Joan 'parking' Harry there with the Spanetti girl on certain long Long Beach afternoons.

"Watch yourself—" A breathless voice admonishes. Joan sways as another runner, an unmasked man gleaming like a seal in spandex, speeds by.

His hair blows back, brown going grey, like Harry's. Harry had told her he'd meet her for lunch up here. Then after she'd wasted her one Long Beach morning on her balcony, awaiting his call to set the time, he'd phoned at two to announce that he'd drop by later. I'll be there by 4:30, he'd informed her in his brusque Software Engineer voice. *But I can't stay long.*

Surely busy Harry won't come early. Surely if he does show up while she is walking, he'll have the sense, the heart, to wait. In a last backward look, Joan scans the Cape Ann lot for Harry's new car. What had he proudly told her he'd bought?

Nexus, Sexus; no, that's Henry Miller. Lexus.

Joan bows her head, walking briskly now, wishing as sun heats her scalp that she'd worn her floppy sunhat. Maybe her mask, too. To hide me, she adds to her lovers, from you.

Not that any of you are still here to see me. Not that you'd want to, anymore.

Slap, slap. Her bare feet march on wet sand, spoiling its glassy sheen. Up ahead, a white-legged old man approaches. If he was, somehow, one of those summer men, would she even stop? The guy lowers his pinkly bald head like he too fears being recognized. Would she recognize him, any of her hims?

That dent in his chin; the twin chiseled dent above his upper lip. His face ordinary-handsome one moment and the next—as sun lit those two dents while he and she first chatted in the surf—the next moment he was, damn him, striking and seductive. Irresistible; unforgettable. His face. Her first.

His face so quickly close to hers, lit gold.

"Whoo, it's comin' in fast an' cold—" The bald oldster calls weakly above the waves to Joan. She answers with a curt nod. A gush of tide swirls around her ankles. Joan stumbles, half expecting the geezer to helpfully grip her arm.

But he doesn't; nobody much touches her anymore. The old goat shuffles past fast, as if she'll waylay him. This ain't the Golden Girls, Joan tells him silently. Not that she often watches such fluff. Granny actresses flirting for laughs in reruns with once-sexy Grandad actors. Isn't aging hardest on the once-sexiest among us?

Chop, chop, chop.

Joan bumps into a bent-backed boy. Swaying, she peers down at him. He gazes up in annoyed alarm. A serious dark-haired boy—Harry? No, Harry is over 50 and driving toward her. Turning from her, the boy resumes his vigorous digging in firm wet sand, chopping at it with his plastic hoe. His abandoned mask lies beside him. Joan steps over it, her feet sinking into this thickest sand. Wet without going gooey. Harry's favorite cement-sand.

Chop, chop, chop. Plodding on, Joan feels her tightened lips twitch with a smile. She recalls a televised Monty

Python skit that made her laugh aloud, weeks ago.

Stock footage of aged prisoners hacking away at a prison garden with their hoes. A deadpan British voice-over announced, Newscaster style, that the prisons had developed a new system of dealing with their oldest inmates.

They chop them up and bury them!

Here on Long Beach, Joan lets out a bitter appreciative *Ha*. These days, especially, isn't it all too true? 17 oldster bodies stowed—hidden—in a shed in a nursing home in New York state, where no one noticed them gone amidst the Covid carnage.

But Covid hasn't caught her, not yet. Joan strides forward, toward her bridge. Hardest, yes, for the sexiest: the femme fatales, the dangerously handsome illicit lovers. All reduced to shuffling Seniors—or as she jokes to herself, when that word comes up, 'Sneers.'

Old ladies barely able to walk a beach. She's now—how far down?

Which house? That's how she and Harry used to measure their progress. Cape Ann Inn sits proudly at one end of Long Beach. The rest of the beach is lined by summer homes, built before all summer houses looked alike. Joan and little Harry used rank their favorites: the gothic two-story with spiky iron fencing and the widow's walk (Joan's); the shingled ranch with the mermaid statue (Harry's).

There she sits: not 50 feet from Joan passing by. A bare-breasted mermaid statue, painted half green and half flesh pink. Her curling blonde hair coyly covers her breasts where her nipples would be. *Mermy,* Harry called her, like 'Mommy.'

Was it because baby Harry had breastfed so passionately and so long that he was drawn to that statue? It lounges still on the patio, defiantly lifesize.

The Mermy House. The last place Joan wants to see.

She squares her shoulders, speeding her steps. Unwise to be out here, unsteady and unaccompanied. She should head back from here, the halfway point. Take time to tidy herself up before she sees—all too rarely does she get to—Harry.

But the bridge. She came here this weekend to visit the bridge. The Lyft leaves early tomorrow, speeding her to her train, then another Lyft back to her Concord condo. Joan keeps walking. As in the old days, she is beelining against her better judgement toward the bridge end of the beach. Her and her long-gone lovers' old meeting spot.

Better hurry. High tide is in fact coming in fast and cold, no stopping it.

Joan Jersild grew up a tomboy in green and shady Concord. JJ, her brothers dubbed her. How intrepidly she trailed after those big blond brothers. She learned to swim and ice skate with them at Walden Pond. Though she read and ciphered well, she dreaded school and her itchy wool skirts, loved summer.

Even back then, summer transformed her. The brown-haired grey-eyed girl with the too-wide mouth and too-big teeth and too-thick lips suddenly had rose-shadowed cheekbones and sunstruck gold streaks in her hair.

She shed her skirts for dungarees. She ran barefoot night and day, her soles as tough as her brothers'. She raced round the yard, up and down Walden Pond beach. She danced on the porch in the evenings when Mom played her radio. Secretly Joan liked her own flat-chested long-legged body, rangy and graceful in its way.

Then high school hit. Concord High, her summer face paled. Joan pressed books to her too-flat chest. Too skinny, too tall, too ashamed of her wide mouth to wear candy-red lipstick like the other girls.

Her grades got her into Wellesley. It was 1955, and her brothers' buddy Howard Logan—who had always rescued her from head-dunkings in Walden Pond; who liked her boyish body—quiet beetle-browed Howard got accepted at MIT.

He had, Mom decreed, a future. He was, she meant, Joan's future. So, Joan left Wellesley her sophomore year. Howard was shy like Joan about his own stocky solid hairy-chested body. At first, on their wedding night, they kept as many clothes on as they could. Even after they got used to being nude, Howard stayed shy.

In their dank basement apartment in Inman square, Joan spent evenings alone. Howard was working late at the engineering lab. Joan was supposedly 'keeping house'.

Really (or this was the part of her dazed newlywed life that felt most real) she was taking the trolley to Harvard Square, lingering on her errand runs to listen to 'beatnick' bands that gathered outside cafes with their guitars and bongo drums. Playing jazzy songs that made Joan stop and sway, her grocery bags growing heavy in her hands. Then came Harry, and Kennedy.

Joan was a young Mommy, a nursing Mommy. Really her first 'affair' was with Harry. Joan had plump breasts for the first time; Joan had a baby boy with Howard's dark eyes, only a warmer more chocolatey dark.

Big brown baby eyes locked with hers, gazing up at her in unspeakable gratitude when she'd bare her breast. He 'attached,' as the admiring nurses told her, so perfectly. He'd suck and tug at her nipples as she'd rock and rock, facing through the fuzz of the small black and white screen John F. Kennedy. His unsettling unblinking stare, his fabulously fitted suits and his chiseled sun-ruddied face, his Boston accent thick as her brothers'. His boyish lush hair perpetually windblown, as if he stood forever on a beach.

Rocking, nursing, watching JFK.

Folding flyers with other JFK-crazed housewives. Then crying along with them and her fussy snuffly toddler through the assassination, the riots. And once Harry was in nursery school; the war. More flyers folded; more tea and cookie peace meetings with other young wives of other earnest young engineers. What a relief, after the election crash, in the summer of '67, the summer Joan turned 32, when she finally talked frugal workaholic Howard into two whole weeks at the beach.

Long Beach in Gloucester, where Joan used to visit her cousins. Howard, who rarely took vacation days, would work during the week. Joan and little Harry would stay alone for most of their two weeks at Cape Ann Inn.

Industrious and methodical as his father, Harry rolled his metal construction trucks, loaded with sand, out to his parking lot in the rocks. Joan followed languidly, her long-legged strides slowed to Harry's plodding pace. She swayed to snatches of Joni Mitchell playing on some-one's, some man's, radio.

She pinned up her hair—longer and lighter since she rinsed it in lemon juice—and 'jumped waves' with Harry, gripping his hands. He held on tight; he clenched shut his eyes before each wave hit. Then he gasped in delight-ed surprise as the swell of the water lifted them together. *Hey Hey, LBJ!* She'd chant for Harry, leaving off the *How Many Kids Did You Kill Today?*

No one was listening anyway, Joan told herself as she toweled off in the shallow surf, half an eye on Harry gathering shells, and half on the tallish blondish man stepping up beside her, the one whose radio played the

Joni Mitchell songs she loved.

"A *backward* wave!" Harry splashed up to announce, pointing, entranced. They all laughed as a rogue wave swelled and crashed in the wrong direction.

"A backward wave," Joan repeated with a proud smile, glancing—as she'd do with Howard when Harry said something clever—at the man beside her.

He grinned, his bluegreen eyes glinting. He was just a tan wry man on the beach. But when he turned his face to hers, taking her in; when the sun lit the dent in his chin and the angel's finger crease above his upper lip, he filled her sight.

Oh God he's gorgeous, Joan Jersild Logan was thinking when she said to him, as if she hadn't said it in years, her name.

The next tidepooled stretch of beach Joan crosses fastest, eager to get past it. Somewhere along here, one block of houses up from the Mermy house, is where she'd left him, Harry. Just for a minute. But it was a day when time ran askew; when Harry wouldn't—because he knew something was up?—budge.

Is time running askew again now; is she losing track of it? It can't be beyond 4PM yet, can it? The bridge is so close, isn't it? Wind and sun whip round Joan's head. The first man suggested meeting at the wood bridge near his rented summer shack. The last man always met her in the Cape Ann Inn lobby with the Inn's parrot Joey cawing his own name. Quickly, Joan splashes along the tidepooled sand where Harry had planted himself so unyieldingly.

Tide rushing in hard now, sucking at her, but she'll beat it, she'll make it.

Oh, those visits to the bridge.

A simple wood bridge: repainted and reinforced now with metal handrails, but as far as Joan can see from the last stretch of beach, the same bridge. It leads to the farthest rockiest end of Long Beach. The 'Stone Quarry,' young Harry dubbed it. They always brought his tennis shoes so he could walk 'like a real scientist' over the mounds of ocean-smoothed stones.

Harry fell badly only once, that last week of their last real summer visit. He toppled on the rocks and scraped his foot so deeply he had to wear it braced with an Ace Bandage. But Harry insisted on hobbling along the beach beside her those last August days, keeping an eye on his distracted lust-befuddled Mother.

So it was that he and Joan found themselves outside his sick sitter's house at the far end of the beach that final Friday. The day before Joan's lover was set to leave Cape Ann with his family. One more tryst, they'd planned, to end their summer storm of sex.

Joan had nodded coolly enough when her lover with his unblinking JFK-esque gaze spelled this out. Of course, as he spoke in his low never-raised voice, he was touching her. He was always touching her when they found a moment alone in his cramped toy-cluttered room or hers, or behind the Inn's dumpster (Joan never did get its sour smell out of her best bra). After two summer vacations of secret sex, Joan had grown practiced at hiding, and Joe clearly had—in every way—even more experience.

Then the last day, their plan fell through when Harry's usual sitter, the Spanetti girl, claimed a fever. She doesn't have a fever but I do, Joan thought as she walked and Harry hobbled away from the Spanetti cottage. Her lover was awaiting her in the Inn lobby; Joan had to reach him to tell him the plan had changed. Harry turned not toward the Inn as Joan urged (because Joan urged it) but toward the bridge.

Joan steps with care around imbedded rock slabs leading to the bridge. Foamy cold water surges to her knees, wetting the hem of her terrycloth pullover. What had been her first excuse the first summer? What had she told her sitter she was doing down at the far end of the beach?

Joanie, the first man called her the first day, as in Joni. Their private joke that drizzly afternoon. Just as Rainy Night House was their private song.

Joan Logan breathes deeply the bracing Atlantic air. Then she splashes up to the bridge itself, the air around it stiller, swampier.

On hot days it—or the tidewater pond stagnating on one side of the bridge—stinks. That first hot day, waiting for the Joni Mitchell man that first time, swatting gnats and mosquitos and breathing the rank air, Joan had asked herself what she was doing. How it could possibly be worth the risk.

Yet she paced the splintery bridge in the muzzy prestorm air, breathless with shame and thrill. She spotted him coming far down Long Beach; she stood at the foot of the bridge like a soldier blocking his way.

Joan can see her young—well, thirty-two-year-old—self now, standing staightbacked for once, proudly tall and slim and tan.

Ocean's not really blue, this first man with the charming dented chin told her. They stood on the bridge looking over the water as if it were their own. On sunny days, he explained, the ocean simply reflects the sky, its blue. He rested his cool fingertips on the sweaty tensed small of her back.

Ocean blue is, he added as he fingertip-turned her toward him, a grand illusion.

Joan half staggers to the foot of the old bridge. She grips the new metal handrail. Then she pats with her tremulous hand the wood rail, still there. She feels it under its slick skin of newish paint: the old wood, sunbaked.

He called her Joni and she—rather dramatically, in retrospect—didn't want to know his name. See, it was 1969, she would say to Harry if she ever had to explain. People were doing way worse on the news. Free Love—and it really was, really did seem, free. No AIDS, anyhow; no obvious looming price to pay.

My own Joni, he joked. He lit candles, asked if she'd have some wine. If you play Joni Mitchell, she replied. Then she was the one playing Joni, picturing herself as Joni as his *Ladies of the Canyon* LP played, as she pulled off her clothes to its slow dreamy beat. Shacked up in his Sea Shack on the bridge's swampy side, all afternoon.

Years later, watching the Joni Mitchell special she should've taped, Joan Logan would stop sipping her evening wine to listen to one of Joni Mitchell's lovers describe—in tones of jolting intimacy, for PBS—how he saw young Joni (Joan, he called her) singing in a bar, songs like he'd never heard before. Then he and she were back in his or her hotel room, with candles lit, he said, and *Joan so beautiful and.*

A pause. The documentary maker permitted a real and human pause as this gaunt once-handsome man swallowed. He finished simply. He told the camera, told Joan: I will never forget that first night.

She will never forget that first night. Well, not night but late afternoon. Harry and his sitter left behind at Cape Ann Inn with take-out seafood and Joan gone so long on some lame excuse. Taking photos, maybe *(Joan and her photos)* or seeing a woman who might sell her guitar *(Joan and her singing)*.

All those psuedo-artistic pursuits that came to nothing. Just as her summer men came to nothing, except—what? Joan presses her palm harder on the painted wood rail, feeling the aged warmth of that wood.

Beauty, of a kind. An artwork—performance art—for one audience of two.

His dented chin catching candlelight as he threw back his head; her hair glinting in the same flickering light as he smoothed it, again and again, over his hairless chest. A male angel chest, she whispered to him.

One wet candlelit afternoon.

Joan shuffles up, reaches the peak of the curved wooden bridge. She tosses one dense pebble into the sluggish tidal swamp water, watches its slight circles spread. Then she turns windward. Her gaze narrows but she is too far from Cape Ann Inn to make out the parking lot, the cars. How long will it take to walk back? Would Harry actually leave, if she isn't there?

Drop-by, he'd said. Not staying long. She may miss his Drop-by. Miss it for a walk on the beach that she'd foolishly estimated would take no more than thirty minutes, because that's what it took years ago. Joan thumps barefoot back down the bridge.

Sinking back into the dank sand, she tenses her now-aching leg muscles. Without a backwards glance at the bridge she'd worked so hard to reach, she plunges forward again. How had she imagined—the August 1971 day with Harry—that the Inn was close enough for her to keep him in her sight?

She doesn't have a damn fever, but I sure do.

So Joan had told herself after she'd led limping Harry away from the Spanetti girls' house. Joan's own face burned, her plans run aground. All day she'd awaited 4PM and the sitter and her planned dash down the beach to the Inn, the lobby, him. And now Harry was crouched in a tidepool, stubbornly digging.

She'd had, since the relatively simple Joni Mitchell tryst, three other men: a distracted Dad with a red beard and sunburnt skin and rough hands, the same week as the gentler Joni man. Then the next summer when she and Harry stayed in Gloucester, a thirtyish surfer.

This last man—the summer Harry was nearly eight—he caught her eye by the parrot cage the first day of her stay. His strong collarbone, she noticed, and his rich tan and his pale lazily carnal eyes. Joe, his name was. She couldn't help but know since he stepped over to the parrot cage and repeated it to Joey, the bird, but really to her. *Joe, I'm Joe too.* Yet she prefers to think of him always as her last man.

They smoked his pot together the single afternoon his family was out and her Harry Spanetti'ed. Then after languorous sex in his and his wife's motel bed, they swam together, high together. Sunlight formed wavering diamond patterns on the water's surface.

A net, Joan told herself. A luminous net, and she was caught in it, floating with him. She licked salt from the hollow of his collarbone, wrapped her underwater legs around him. Her last summer man; her best in bed, and she lost him, lost more than him, that day.

No, you didn't lose your son, not really. Not all at once.

So Joan Logan tells her windblown self, panting hoarsely. She trudges along the broad glistening sands. She lets her sore feet sink into the warmer water and oozy fine sand-bottom of a tide pool. Harry sank his own feet, that disappointing day, into a pool this size. He bent in that pool, poking its sands with a stick. Even if he had budged, it would have taken too long to lead him on his bad foot down the beach to the Inn. By then he'd be—Joe; his family always nipping at his heels— gone. Joe wasn't a man to wait around.

Wait here for Mommy.

"Some Mommy," Joan mutters, standing and swaying too long—how long?—in the soothing lukewarm tidepool. Her son only seven then; too young to lose sight of. But she'd told her foolish self she never would lose sight of Harry: his bent bare-backed body.

Harry, at eight going on nine, was way too aware for Joan to try anything the next summer. Not that she wanted to by then. Her appetite for all that had been burned out, willed away. She knew after the scare of that last August day that she needed something else, needed work like Howard had. So she went back to school, to Junior College; so she chipped away at a Music degree, teaching Chorus at North Shore Community College, a long weekly drive she savored.

Along with unspoken crushes on her more soulful surfer-boy students.

Till one summer week, when Joan was past forty, she ran into one of those big-shouldered obliviously beautiful boys hefting his board on Long Beach sands. Joan had been striding along in her swimsuit beside her own lanky teenage son.

Um, Miz Logan?

The boy student had startled her, falling in step beside her as he'd sometimes done in the halls of NSCC. Looking her over. In the glare of the Long Beach sun, tall Harry halted his own barefoot steps so they all halted, awkwardly. Harry glared.

We have to go, Joan told her student rudely. She sped her strides, catching up with her son, annoyed at her own flushed face. She was past all that, wasn't she?

Harry wouldn't look at her. He kept his dark-haired head bowed as he walked. Howard's close-cropped hair and square-jawed face; her own wide mouth and her tall brothers' body. Harry watched his pale bare feet. He had stayed inside so much this trip with his Sci Fi paperbacks. Joan had persuaded him this day to walk the beach.

Foolishly, to fill the silence, Joan asked if Harry wanted to check for his old 'parking lot'. A bony-shouldered shrug. Harry stood back watching with his pale black-haired arms folded; Joan searched among the slabs and finally admitted that the sands had shifted. That it—Harry's miniature parking lot—was gone for good.

Then Howard gone too, Joan reminds herself as she trudges out of her tide pool. Wind in her face and late slanted sun knifing bright into her narrowed eyes. She wobbles. But she slogs along, not turning her head, not wanting to see the damn Mermaid House again. Chill wind echoes in her ears, intensifying their usual dull ache. Were achy ears a sign of Covid-19?

She wishes she had practical Howard here to ask. He'd know how to look it up. She wishes she had Howard's solid hairy arm to hold onto. Wishes she were walking the beach with him—not that they'd walked it often when he was alive. But maybe if Howard had lived into his 80's like her, she and Howard would've walked beaches together at last, would've shared the hard-earned comradery of longtime parents.

Wasn't that what she and Howard had been best at: discussing Harry and his quirks, his intelligence, his acne, his accomplishments? Harry was their one shared passion. If Howard were at her side, he'd feel as anxious as she felt to get back to the Inn in time to greet Harry, make sure oblivious Harry didn't simply take off.

Just the way, Joan tells Howard in her head, Harry took off on the day I never told you about, never told anyone. The day I lost our son.

You can wait here, can't you? For a few minutes? For Mommy?

Her voice so breathless that another Mommy with another tidepooling son glanced over. If she'd been in her right mind, Joan would have asked her, Mom to Mom, Can you watch my son for a minute?

But Joan turned her flushed face abruptly away from the Mom's merely curious gaze. Harry nodded in the brusque way of his Dad, as if Joan's voice was a distraction from important tasks. Harry didn't look up from what he was poking with a stick.

I'll just be a minute, OK?

Joan touched Harry's shoulder. He was poking an open clamshell, the quivery pink clam inside. Like, Joan thought in a crazed flash, an aborted baby. Maybe I'm carrying his baby, she told herself. Ridiculous, when she used a diaphragm every time. But somehow that irrational thought—a baby connecting her and her lover of two weeks—gave Joan permission to turn on her heel, leave her Harry.

Late late late. Those words thumped with Joan's heartbeat, then and now.

What Joan remembers with aching clarity—as she strides closer to the Inn, as the parking lot comes into focus through sunspots dancing in her eyes—is her urgent heartbeat thudding her chest. In those days before joggers clogged the surf, Joan ran down the beach easily, stealing glimpses over her shoulder of Harry, smaller and smaller.

The parking lot looms bigger now. And, yes, Joan can make out several new, or new to her, cars. One dark blue and shiny. What she remembers Harry's to be when she saw him last, last Chirstmas. A whole weekend; their longest visit in too-long.

"Harry—" she croaks into the wind, much too far off for him to hear.

Vanishing point.

Joan kept gazing back, panting and momentarily slowing her run, to make out Harry's small bent form. The other boy still crouched there too. Joan even told herself as she ran on that maybe it would be good for shy Harry to have her gone briefly. To connect—would he, for once?—with another boy, without her.

Were the two boys bending side by side now? And which (Joan squinted, staring backward while jogging forward) was which? If she was far enough away that she couldn't tell which boy was hers, shouldn't she turn back? But she was (she faced front again, panting hard) so close.

From the side of her sight as she ran faster, she glimpsed the deepest gleaming green. The green that only showed in the arched underside of waves about to crash. The chill exhilarating green she'd dived into with her lover, headfirst.

She forged ahead along the hot summer sand. The next time she turned her head to peer back through her long blowing hair, Harry was gone. No, not gone, Joan told her lightheaded self. Just too far away to see.

Joan Logan is losing her wind, her focus. She is only one block of beach houses away from Cape Ann Inn and the navy blue Lexus (or he called it Midnight Blue?) she knows to be Harry's. How could she have left her cellphone behind? How could she not have known she was too old to attempt this walk so quickly? But wasn't it always this way, to one degree or another? The exhilaration of the walk out would fade; the exhaustion of the walk back would set in.

"I'll be right back—" Joan shouted over her shoulder, in the shadow of Cape Ann Inn. Into the sunstruck August afternoon. A few heads among the scattered weekday beach-blanket crowd rose. A few nearby kids splashing in the surf stopped, made sure this too-loud shout hadn't come from their Mom.

A pointless shout, absorbed by the ocean air.

Of course, Harry, so far down the beach that she couldn't see him, couldn't hear. Of course not, Joan told her overheated thirty-four-year-old self. And she ploughed into the shaded dry sand that led up to the Inn.

Like a sign he appeared: the other him. Joe stepped out onto the wood balcony at the lobby entrance. He turned his head, casually scanning the sands. She waved wildly, swinging her hands like a castaway.

He lit a cigarette as if that was why he'd stepped out. Good; she wouldn't have to waste time running up into the lobby. She wouldn't shut a door between her and Harry—just as, at home, she'd run inside briefly when he was playing on the lawn but she'd leave the door open between them. So she thought, dazedly, as she slogged through the last heaviest sand to stand—sweaty, scraggly-haired—below him.

He wasn't a man to kneel. Another lover, more thoughtful, might have knelt so his wind-bedraggled mistress could whisper the message she'd carried to him all the way down the long beach. But he stayed standing.

Gazing at him from below, God help her, Joan savored the strong line of his collarbone. She wanted to grab hold of it, hoist herself up by that bone.

"We—I—my sitter's sick. But—but later, round ten, after H-Harry's asleep, in the lobby, if you can—can get away..."

One nod, so slight he must have meant it to be unnoticeable. Then he turned. He tossed down his barely smoked cigarette like a dart. It smoldered for a second in the sand beside her. He was striding back into the lobby, as if someone else was waiting there.

Like little Harry was waiting. Joan staggered back from the smoky butt. Harry: waiting like a good boy for her, right where she'd left him?

Joan hadn't caught her breath from her first run when she was running again, her feet sinking in dry, then smacking damp sand. *Slap slap.* She ran raggedly hard, her salt-sticky hair flying into her half-open mouth, her throat raw from the breaths tearing through her. But her body, her fit thirty-four-year-old body, kept running.

She fixed on distant figures, waiting for those small bobbing shapes to coalesce into two boys, one of them Harry. As Joan neared the halfway point on the sunny beach, the scattered figures ahead of her turned too big. One of them had to be Harry. But the nearer she ran—her gut clenched and her eyes burning with sweat—the clearer it became that these figures, these teenage boys, were not her boy.

Her bare feet slap-slap-slapped. *Not, not, not.*

Ocean wind blows Joan Logan's thinned greyed hair furiously sideways. A cloud passes over the sun, wind ringing in her aching ears. Rain is predicted tomorrow. Joan had felt this was her last daylit chance to walk the beach. But Harry had warned her he can't stay long. His not-so-distant car seems to simmer in the late sun.

Pale Harry always hated to be out in the sun too long. So he must be waiting inside in the lobby. *Must be, must be.* Joan stumbles through the drier sand. She starts the long slog up past the last few houses toward the Inn. The glass of the lobby door flashes; a bony-shouldered darkly dressed man steps out into the light. His square-jawed face half-masked.

Harry, Joan wants to cry though he's still a little too far away to hear. But can't he *see?*

*"Har-*ry—?" Joan Logan nevertheless calls, or caws, into the immense gritty indifference of the wind.

"Harry, Harry—?"

Dread rose as Joan's voice rose, calling his name like a crazy woman. She pounded up the beach. Tears and sweat burned her eyes so she could barely see the normal Mommies and the watched-over children that she streaked past. *Smack smack;* her sore feet against the damp sand, her hands swinging useless at her sides.

She *was* crazy, to have run down this long beach, away from her boy.

She stumbled into drier sand, past the house with the Mermaid statue, fixing her intent wavery gaze on the tidepools where she'd left him. Only boy-sized barefoot prints marked that stretch of sand now. Circular pacing figure-eight prints that led nowhere. The other boy gone and hers too.

A new Mommy in a pink skirted swimsuit bent sideways walking her chubby-legged toddler. She glanced in mild surprise at sweaty crazy Joan.

"My boy—my boy—dark hair—navy blue swim-trunks —and limping on his right foot and, and—" Joan gasped for breath, pointing in all directions at once.

A redheaded leopard-freckled lifeguard with white zinc on his nose ambled toward Joan, fingering his whistle.

How could you? everyone was asking Joan without saying it as Joan stammered out some version of what she'd done.

Then *smack smack smack.* Everyone's bare feet were marching round what the all-at-once soldierly lifeguard called the 'radius'. They—the other mother, the lifeguard and Joan—called plaintively, Harry Harry.

Following the lifeguard's boyish-voiced but sure-sounding commands, Joan headed toward the bridge end of the beach. She threw her parched voice into the wind and punishing crash of big breakers. The relentlessly approaching High Tide.

She stared into the dizzying blindingly white surf, braced for a boy's broken-backed body floating in the black seaweed. Harry; oh Harry.

Her eyes raked the familiar suddenly sinister sun-faded beach houses. Anyone might hold Harry, weeping and terrified, kidnapped and killed. Desperately Joan fixed her swimmy gaze on the wood bridge ahead. But Harry was not there.

Not not not, wave crashes echoed.

At least, at last, those waves washed from Joan's paralyzed brain any thought of any man. She would only realize past midnight that she'd both made and broken a last date with her last illicit man. All that was over.

Her whole life—it seemed to her as she stumbled toward the bridge alone and wailing her son's name—was over. Then *(slap slap* behind her; the barefoot running steps of the breathless young lifeguard) not.

The other mother had found him. Harry had been 'curled up,' as the lifeguard described it to Joan in a subtly reproachful voice, against the mermaid statue's base. His cut foot was bloodied. Joan pictured Harry in tears, in motherless panic.

But when she finally reached him at the Mermaid house, he gave her a cool blank stare. He stiffened when she hugged him. Harry ignored Joan and the others, bowing his dark-haired head, acting as if it all was no big deal. He'd just gotten, he told Joan curtly, sick of waiting. He'd just picked his bandage off from boredom.

Sorry sorry, Joan said it so many times the word was like a meaningless chant. To blank-faced Harry, to the lifeguard and—not quite meeting her righteous blue gaze —to the other mother. Harry's cut had opened up all over again.

Still, Harry with his limp bloody foot would not hold Joan's hand as they made their slow hobbled way back down the beach, back to their room. Once inside, cleaned up and re-bandaged, Harry pulled away again. He curled up sullen and silent on one double bed. Joan lay exhausted and empty-headed on the other.

In the years that followed, Joan Logan would tell herself: don't be silly. It didn't happen that one day. But from this distance of 30-plus years, it's clear to her what that August day, those summer men, cost her. The single clear fact inside Joan's mind as she stumbles her last sandy steps toward the Inn. The single fact in her mind that long-gone August night as she drifted into a fitful sleep.

It had happened, the worst. She had lost him.

"Harry," Joan Logan gasps at the foot of the sandy wood steps. She sucks gulps of air, glad no one is jostling behind her. She wishes she had the time and strength to crank on the Inn's faucet and rinse off her sand-caked feet. Catch her breath. But isn't that Harry, her lanky dark-haired Harry, standing in her brothers' long-boned body just behind the sliding glass door to the lobby, above her?

Harry does not step out onto the balcony again, does not spot her down here. In fact, her outlined son behind the door is turning away as if about to wander across the lobby, out the Inn's front door. Into his Midnight Blue car and away.

"Harry—" Joan calls louder, her old-lady croak drowned by the sea breeze now at her back. She tightens her grip, painfully, on the painted wood rail. She tenses her legs, already so sore from her walk. But her legs won't work right. She starts up the steps too fast and her knees buckle. Her bones disconnect—or that's how it feels as she falls.

She loses hold of the wood handrail, a splinter sliding precisely into her palm. She topples sideways in the wind. Her body thumps wood; her hipbone cracks—she feels it as plainly as the splinter—and she lies sprawled over the lowest wood step. The Care Center flashes in her head. A bed in the Care Center, a ventilator, No Visitors. All that flashes. A shock of pain spreads from her hip to her twisted spine.

It twists her mouth too, numbs her tongue.

Help or *Harry,* she starts to say. *Heh Heh* like a strangled gasping laugh. A little girl from an upper balcony screams; the sliding door to the lobby cracks open at last.

"Mom, it's my mom," comes Harry's voice—only not his clipped manly voice of recent years. Calling her 'Mother' on the phone. This was his hoarser looser boy voice, though muffled by his mask. Harry rushes down to Joan, wood steps shuddering, as he hasn't rushed in years. His strong capable hands—Howard's hands—grip her arm, half lifting her.

Joan can only moan, as her broken hip shifts. A cry of pure pain.

Don't move her, a woman's voice is commanding. Call 9-1-1!

"Mom, what did you do?" Harry demands of her, his mask-muffled voice edged with exasperation and concern. He tugs down his mask with his left hand. But he keeps his right hand—bless him—on her arm.

He is kneeling awkwardly beside Joan, her fallen body leaning against his sturdy bent legs. Joan seizes his knee, his squarish kneecap warm through his pants. She holds on, braced against the burn of pain electrifying her own old bones.

"Heh heh—" is all she can answer, can gasp.

But she meets Harry's lit-up gaze, his dark eyes brightened under his straight greying brow. He is flushed with alarm, his whole man-sized body tensed. His body so near, at last, to her own.

I've broken my hip, Joan tells herself. I've taken my last walk on Long Beach. She lowers her muddled head toward her son's thigh, his lap, her heartbeat making her body throb. Maybe, she thinks as she sinks against him, he'll stay here for a little while.

—END—

THANKS

Thank you to DeWitt Henry and to Kurt Lovelace; THANK YOU to my Girl Groups: Ann Harleman & Gail Donovan (x2) & Debra Spark; THANK YOU to all who read & published these stories, especially Lee Hope & all at SOLSTICE magazine; THANK YOU to my family and friends: Kate & Bill; Jessica Treadway & Lise Haines & Suzanne Strempek Shea; most of all: THANK YOU to my inspirations, my guys, John Hodgkinson & Will Hodgkinson.

ACKNOWLEDGMENTS

Story Publications: These stories appeared, sometimes in a different form, in the following magazines; grateful acknowledgment to all who worked on these publications:

WOVEN TALE PRESS MAGAZINE
('The Mask of the Red Death')
SOLSTICE ("The Drama Room")
WORDS & IMAGES ('Bloody Show')
HAYDEN'S FERRY REVIEW ('When You Watch Me')
POST ROAD ("Tonya & Nancy: The Rock Opera")
FANZINE ('Candidate's Daughter Tells All!')
MASSACHUSETTS REVIEW ('Hamman's Castle...')
MASSACHUSETTS REVIEW
('Pandemic Porn'- published as 'Sick Play')
SOLSTICE ("The Ones Who Are Gone")
SOLSTICE ('The Quiet Car')
SEATTLE REVIEW ('Student Shooter')
NEW ENGLAND REVIEW ('If You Play Joni Mitchell')
'Bloody Show' appeared in a different form in
We Got Him (New Rivers Press, 2011)

Elizabeth Searle

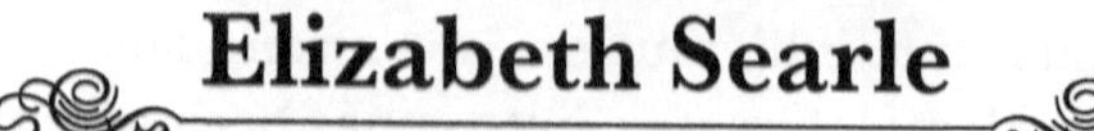

Elizabeth writes fiction and scripts. She is the author of five critically acclaimed books of fiction and is a playwright of a widely performed rock opera, and she is co-writer of the feature film I'LL SHOW YOU MINE (2023) by *Duplass Brothers Productions*. The film was released in select theaters and is available via Amazon Prime, Peacock and more on home screens. Elizabeth won the *Iowa Short Fiction Prize* for her collection MY BODY TO YOU (James Salter, judge). Her novel A FOUR-SIDED BED was a Boston Globe paperback bestseller and a finalist for an ALA award and is in development as a feature film. Elizabeth's most recent novel WE GOT HIM was a finalist for the *Midwest Book Award* and released as an AudioBook.

Also, her novella CELEBRITIES IN DISGRACE was described by the *New York Times* as a 'miniature masterpiece' and made into a short film. Another short, FOUR-SIDED, was screened at over 20 festivals. Elizabeth has published over 30 stories in magazines such as *Ploughshares*, *AGNI*, *New England Review*, *Kenyon Review* and more, and in over a dozen anthologies. Both Elizabeth's theater work, TONYA & NANCY: THE ROCK OPERA, and her 2023 feature film, have drawn national media attention. Elizabeth teaches fiction and scriptwriting at Stonecoast MFA. She lives near Boston with her family.

Also by Elizabeth Searle

FICTION

WE GOT HIM
New Rivers Press, 2016
American Fiction Series paperback original
(published in AudioBook version in 2018)

GIRL HELD IN HOME
New Rivers Press, 2011
American Fiction Series paperback original
eBook editions on Kindle and more
from *New Rivers Press*: Winter, 2011/2012

CELEBRITIES IN DISGRACE
Graywolf Press, 2001
eBook editions (Kindle, BookNook etc)
from *PFP/AJAR Contemporaries Press*, 2011

A FOUR-SIDED BED
Graywolf Press, 1998
Re-issued in new paperback and eBook editions
by *PFP/AJAR Contemporaries Press*, 2011

MY BODY TO YOU
University of Iowa Press, 1993 hardback original
Winner of the 1992 **Iowa Short Fiction Prize**
(James Salter, judge)
New paperback and Kindle eBook edition
from *University of Iowa Press, 2011*

ANTHOLOGIES

Co-Editor

IDOL TALK: WOMEN WRITERS ON THE TEENAGE
INFATUATIONS THAT CHANGED THEIR LIVES
Elizabeth Searle and Tamra Wilson, co-editors
McFarland Press; 2018

SOAP OPERA CONFIDENTIAL: WRITERS AND
SOAP INSIDERS ON WHY WE'LL TUNE IN
TOMORROW AS THE WORLD TURNS RESTLESSLY
BY THE GUIDING LIGHT OF OUR LIVES
Elizabeth Searle and Suzanne Strempek Shea, co-editors
McFarland Press; 2017

www.ingramcontent.com/pod-product-compliance
Lightning Source LLC
Chambersburg PA
CBHW021157010826
48971CB00014B/2719